Brian

with all good wishes
and thanks for your help.

Vaughan
18.2.97

CW00724316

# A REASONABLE MAN

# A REASONABLE MAN

*A Modern Hero of Our Times*

Vaughan James

The Book Guild Ltd
Sussex, England

The Book Guild Ltd.
25 High Street,
Lewes, Sussex

First published 1997
© Vaughan James, 1997
Set in Baskerville
Typesetting by Raven Typesetters, Chester
Printed in Great Britain by
Antony Rowe Ltd, Chippenham, Wiltshire

A catalogue record for this book is
available from the British Library

ISBN 1 85776 173 1

*If you live among wolves,*
*howl like a wolf.*
(*Russian proverb*)

*For Stephanie*

# MOSCOW 1990–1991

# 1

To get to Mochítsky's dacha you took the Tula road south out of Moscow for about 15 kilometres from the city limits, ignoring the cluster of high-rise apartment blocks in the fields to your left unimaginatively named Southtown, on past a miserable group of huts on one side of the road and, unaccountably, a thatched well on the other, all shamefacedly marked by a mud-stained, barely legible sign that said Polevóye Seló, and down a steep hill curving gradually to the right until you came to a narrow track veering off to the left through the trees around the skirt of the hill. As Mochítsky would gleefully tell the bemused guests to whom these directions were addressed, if you got to the bridge at the bottom of the hill, you'd gone too far, but you'd have to go on at least another three kilometres before you found anywhere to turn. Inexperienced drivers, not yet used to possessing their own cars, he would advise to follow this procedure anyway, coming back across the bridge and moving slowly up the hill until they came to the turning they had missed on the way down. His hospitality did not extend to setting up any sort of sign to indicate where the dacha lay.

Mochítsky's sense of humour was not universally appreciated. He could not in anyone's opinion have been considered a jolly man, but there were occasions when an incongruous burst of irreverence would involuntarily shatter his normally rather cautious demeanour. A high-pitched giggle, totally out of character, would presage some more or less outrageous comment on what he instinctively saw as the comic aspect of a situation or personality. In a number of instances such irregular behaviour had clearly annoyed various of his superiors, and his career had suffered as a consequence. He had probably climbed as far up the greasy pole of party promotion as he was ever likely to reach, and even his hold on his present position felt sometimes less than secure.

On the other hand, in the estimation of many of his colleagues, under the apparently innocent guise of such misplaced flashes of humour he had got away with expressions of criticism, implied if not explicitly stated, which would have cost most of them a good deal more. His mere presence would add a little excitement to otherwise interminably boring political deliberations, since his unpredictability lent a certain tension to the atmosphere. By the same token, he experienced a certain success socially. Almost in spite of himself, he could be very good company. For many women he had an attraction they found it difficult to resist; for men his company was enjoyable but he was not necessarily liked.

In fact, the dacha did not really belong to him, but to his wife, Márfa Timoféyevna, who even during the most savage onslaughts of the mordant winter frosts preferred to spend her time away from the din and stink of the city, leaving her husband alone in their soulless, official apartment on Kutúzovsky Prospékt or, more often, in the cosy flat of his mistress off the Mokhováya, as real Muscovites persisted in calling the ancient street even when it had some outlandishly grandiose Soviet label. Mochítsky really used the Kutúzovsky apartment only when entertaining for official purposes or when his student daughter Zoya was at home during vacations. This arrangement was an open secret, never discussed but tacitly agreed. Márfa Timoféyevna was childless and never gave any sign of awareness of Zoya's existence, nor was it ever suggested that she should.

When Mochítsky elected to entertain at the dacha, his wife provided traditional Russian food of a quality that tourists gagging tetchily on their insipid, supposedly Western-style pap in dingy hotel dining rooms would never have dreamed

4

of. Her soups and salads, in particular, offered impossible combinations of delicately nuanced flavours and unexpected piquancy that eluded identification or description. Their ingredients were not to be found in cans or packets: they came straight from the fields and hedgerows to the pot or the chopping board, enlivened by the bunches of dried herbs and mushrooms that dangled from the ceiling of the kitchen, into which only those specifically invited would ever dare to enter. If the menu lacked the refrigerated, shrink-wrapped exotica of the city delicatessen, it had the tasty crispness and pungent succulence of produce plucked fresh from the trees or out of the soil. Here in the countryside just a few kilometres from the capital she was little affected by the shortages that poor distribution inflicted on the city housewives, nor had the gastronomic tyranny of the supermarket censored taste and smell or ironed out the changes of the seasons.

On special occasions, or as the whim seized her, Márfa Timoféyevna would prepare exotic Georgian dishes, for which she had acquired a taste during visits to the Caucasus with her engineer father before her marriage. The fashion for spicy, aromatic Georgian cooking was still very much alive in Russian intellectual circles, though less so in the opaque half-world of academic politics that Mochítsky inhabited, where Italian and French cuisine was considered more socially chic. Mochítsky would divert foreign guests with tales of wild feasts in Tbilisi, and he would introduce them to the custom of appointing a *tamadá* or toastmaster, who would call upon various of those present to propose the health of the hostess, the guests, and so on. The fact that such toasts should be offered in accordance with strict protocol if grave and sometimes violent offence were not to be given was soon lost on a company sailing on a wave of vodka, and the meal would sometimes degenerate into a concatenation of drunken speeches avowing peace and friendship in garbled Russian, punctuated by shrieks of maniac laughter and by bouts of vomiting over the veranda rail and lurching into the bushes to 'water the horse'.

Márfa Timoféyevna never sat with the guests at table and was seen only as she shuffled wordlessly to and from the kitchen like a faithful old family servant in a nineteenth-century play. To those rash enough to enquire, Mochítsky would explain that she was not interested in the sort of topics they would discuss, though somewhere deeper in his awareness he suspected that her motives for refusing to join the company were rather more profound than that and less than flattering to him or to them. Once again, he never took issue with her on the subject, and no explanation was ever volunteered.

To party dignitaries and privileged members of the *nomenklatúra* on the fringes of whose circles Mochítsky operated, the word *dacha* signified a new and well-appointed villa, equipped with state-of-the-art mechanical and electronic domestic appliances and a double garage with remote-controlled doors, in visibly well-guarded grounds. It was a treasured perquisite of membership of the upper echelons, an envied symbol of status. The Mochítsky – or, more properly, the Sokolóv – dacha, had belonged to Márfa Timoféyevna's family for several generations, indeed, it had been built by her great-grandfather, and apart from minimal adjustments in the plumbing and cooking facilities, it had remained largely unchanged throughout its history. Even for Mochítsky it still exuded an atmosphere of home that his bleak city apartment could never hope to rival.

In its architecture, if that is not too grand a word, the dacha had more in common with the peasant houses hugging the foot of the hill along the banks of the stream, hardly more than a trickle in summer but a torrent in winter and especially in the spring thaw. A single-storeyed structure, it was built almost entirely of wood, which may at one time have been painted in several colours but was now the uniform, gnarled grey of much-weathered timber. Around the windows there were still vestiges of intricately carved, traditional Russian folk-patterns, but much of this had rotted and fallen away, to be replaced in some parts by simple slats and in others not at all. The felt roof, unencumbered by telephone wires or television aerial, had originally been edged with decoratively carved designs, but over the years these too had in many places fallen away. There was not a straight line or level plane in the entire structure. The interior doors had not for many years been capable of closing, and the floors sloped at quite alarming angles, so that the furniture was propped in position with flat stones tugged from the hillside and in some places by books. To casually inquisitive eyes these were not easy to identify, but they seemed of no great age.

The wide veranda ran along the whole of the front of the house, which faced south, looking down into the valley, and along the western side, to catch the setting sun. Along the front elevation it described a series of gentle waves: a hump in the centre descended on each side into a distinct trough, rising again to its original level at each end. This was echoed in the curves of the veranda rail. On the west side, the veranda sloped gently from back to front and was reached via a series of rickety wooden steps which comprised the sole means of access to the interior.

The dacha clung to the contour of the hill, the rear wall resting squarely on the rocky slope and the front of the house raised about a metre and supported by a rough stone wall which extended in two wedges at the sides and constituted the only part of the entire structure that was not made of wood. The space under the front of the veranda served Mochítsky as a wine cellar, penetrated only by raising several boards in the veranda floor, an operation that added yet another hazard for the uninitiated, especially when the contents of the cellar had already been raided more than once during a convivial or, conversely, a difficult meal.

The wines were mostly Georgian – white Tsinandáli and red Mukudzáni – which Mochítsky had wisely laid down in some quantity before they had disappeared almost entirely from the shops, supplemented by some tolerable whites from Moldavia and the Crimea. For the undiscriminating, he would produce virtually undrinkable Russian *samtrest* cooperative reds, and when he felt it was expected of him he would even open flatulent bottles of Soviet champagne, but he drew the line at the so-called *portwéin*, a sticky, red fluid, halfway between cough linctus and furniture polish, which was all that the city stores usually had on offer. For those who demanded it, he kept a small stock of whisky and French brandy, but the bulk of his liquor store consisted of vodka – the basic, all-purpose Stolíchnaya, a bottle or so of Zhítnya rye vodka, a variety of fruit-flavoured Polish vodkas and, though he never touched it himself, some infamous Polish Żubrówka, turned a bilious green by the insertion of a stalk of bison grass, the only vodka guaranteed to produce not only loss of memory (and consequent agonies of anxiety), but also a vicious and persistent hangover that defied all remedies known to man. But the pride of the cellar was the old, matured Russian vodka – *stárka* – the colour of liquid gold and almost as hard to come by. Only very special guests were served with this precious fluid, and then only in tiny glasses, to be sipped rather than swallowed in one salvo in the fashion customary for lesser vodkas.

Being entertained by Mochítsky at the dacha was never simply a social occasion; always there was some devious motivation on the part of the host. To the Soviet guest, the whole ambience was quintessentially Russian, conducive to relaxed conversation and sometimes to less than discreet confidences; to the foreign visitor it had a quaintness and rural charm that dispelled all notions of distrust and caution. In both cases, it could be manipulated to Mochítsky's advantage.

Something of the sort was at the back of his mind on that autumn morning in 1990 as he sprawled in the back of his chauffeur-driven car impatiently thrusting its way through the Moscow traffic toward the Tula road. Today's lunch was to be more a reconnaissance than part of a specific campaign, and hopeful though he was of its eventual outcome, he allowed his thoughts to roam freely rather than directing them to the elaboration of a definite ploy. He was not happy. Everyone had known that after Brézhnev's death (the joke in Moscow was that he had in fact been dead for years but no one had dared tell him), there would have to be changes. His immediate successors had not lived long enough to do much, but under this man Gorbachóv it was all getting out of hand. Not content with cutting back on the corruption and putting an end to the nepotism (or transferring it to different beneficiaries), he seemed hell-bent on turning everything upside down. He was certainly no Stalin, and Mochítsky doubted if anyone would actually be shot, but God knows where it was all going to end. No one felt safe any more, and this included Mochítsky himself. At the present rate, even the party itself was under threat. It might not be perfect – and Mochítsky had plenty of first-hand evidence of that – but what, after all, was the alternative? And how, which was the crux of the matter, was he going to cover his back if the worst came to the worst?

Mochítsky rehearsed in his mind all the familiar arguments. He was a reasonable man. He had never wittingly done anyone actual harm. If the system was all there was, then you had to play it by its own rules. That was only common sense, wasn't it? Either you did, and survived, or you didn't, and went under. So what choice did he have? It was true that he had what by Moscow standards was a spacious apartment, which in fact he rarely used, and he had his official car and driver, while most people had to make do with the grossly inadequate public transport service. But he held a responsible position in society, and the ordinary people expected their leaders to live in some style, didn't they? They'd soon have something to say if government ministers, for example, started fighting their way onto crowded buses in order to get to their offices in the morning. How could ministers be expected to do their jobs properly if they had to live like that? Of course, he was fortunate in that his job took him abroad quite often, so that he could buy his clothes in London or New York, and at home he had plenty of foreign currency to spend in the Beryóza shops, which wouldn't accept rubles. But after all, he was officially responsible for supervision of cultural and academic exchanges with other countries, so he had to keep up appearances, didn't he? He could hardly appear on the platform at a United Nations meeting, for example, in the sort of government-issue suits that everyone in the West made fun of . . . And as for the little sum he had tucked away in Switzerland, it was only fair to his family that he should be able to look after them financially if the need arose. In any case, it was chicken feed (he liked that term and repeated it aloud, in English, to his chauffeur's mystification) compared with what the really big boys had salted away . . .

In fact, the more Mochítsky thought about it, the more he convinced himself that his lifestyle was beyond reproach, and in a just world he had nothing to fear, whatever happened.

But he was still not happy. If the party lost power, he could see only one body that might be able to keep a grip on the country – the army – and that was not a consoling thought, since he had very little influence in the military sphere. For the old politicians he had occasionally done the odd favour: after all, cultural exchanges covered a pretty wide range of activities by all sides, and no one any longer pretended otherwise. As a major in the KGB he might still have a certain amount of clout, but the army had always been rather less than cordial to intruders into their affairs. Mochítsky had never paid more than lip-service to ideological principles. The party was his employer, and he depended for everything he possessed on the party apparatus. So if the party went, Mochítsky went with it.

But surely it was out of the question that the party should lose power now, after 70-odd years in total command? Surely Gorbachóv himself never intended that such a thing should happen? The whole idea was preposterous. And yet . . .

He shifted in his seat as doubts began again to invade his thoughts. What if the unthinkable really did come to pass? Where would he be then? Perhaps he had not been as clever as he had believed he was? Perhaps he should have been thinking bigger? A man in his position should surely have taken out more 'insurance' than in fact he had. There must still be something spectacular that he could accomplish . . .

Mochítsky sighed. Well, his guests today were a young and

10

thrusting politician and an old but widely respected army general. He did not regard them as friends: friends were people with whom one became identified in other people's eyes, and he had seen more than one good man come a cropper that way despite his obvious innocence. So he preferred to have no friends; he was a loner by intent. Today's guests might give him an idea of which way the wind was blowing, so that he could plan which way to jump. (On some subjects he had trained himself to think in English, almost as though he feared that even his inner thoughts would be overheard if he formulated them in Russian. He smiled now at his own command of English idioms: it was amazing how close Russian and English could sometimes be.)

Mochítsky was a 'natural' linguist, whose facility in languages was certainly reinforced by his irrepressible love of talking. In particular he had a remarkably good ear and instinctively captured and reproduced patterns and nuances of intonation, the linguistic feature which he realised early in his studies was easily the most distinctive single aspect of typical speech. As a student he had been known for his ability to 'do accents' and would indulge when the spirit moved him in savage mimicry, capturing not only the accent and timbre of his victim's voice but the facial expressions, gestures and other accompanying body language. Much in demand at student gatherings, both prearranged and impromptu, he would reduce his companions to helplessly giggling heaps. But inevitably this led him eventually into serious trouble. Cries of 'Do Khrushchóv' or 'Do Brézhnev' were detected by the wrong ears and a severe reprimand resulted. Aping one's fellow students or even certain of the more tolerant teachers was one thing; ridiculing political masters was quite another.

Refraining from deliberate exercise of his talents was difficult but not impossible. Much less easy was controlling his automatic, quite unwitting behaviour when conversing for even the shortest time with someone who had a speech peculiarity such as a strong regional or foreign accent, a speech impediment such as the inability to roll an 'r' (a phenomenon just as common but infinitely more serious in

11

Russian than in English: *sam Lenin* suffered from this defect), or exaggerated grimaces or gestures. Quite without realising it, he would begin to adopt the same accent, the same posture: an invaluable asset in learning a language, perhaps, but in a social or, worse, an official context, this unconscious copying could all too easily be misunderstood and cause offence. Combined with sudden barbs of Mochítsky's somewhat zany brand of humour, it could be devastating. The line between mimicry and mockery is impossible to draw ...

Realising with a start that the car was already halfway down the hill, Mochítsky leaned forward and asked the driver to pull up. 'You pick me up at four o'clock,' he said. 'I'll go the rest of the way on foot.'

Had he been required to explain his motives for this impulsive change of plan, Mochítsky would have been at first unable and eventually unwilling to do so. It no longer came easily to him to admit to any trace of sentiment. Perhaps it was his heart-searching on the route out of Moscow, with its incidental review of his past life, that had unconsciously evoked a resonance of the emotions he experienced the first time he came this way. They had both still been students at the Foreign Language Institute when Márfa invited him to visit the family dacha, and they had clung in mock and sometimes real terror to the back of a waltzing country bus as far as Polevóye Seló before walking the rest of the way. At the place where he now alighted from his car, she had taken him by the hand and led him without warning along a scarcely visible path until they scrambled half on hands and knees, puffing and giggling, to the top of the hill. As they crossed the brow they were suddenly confronted with a tightly packed grove of silver birches, their slender, silvery blue trunks incandescent and shimmering in the slanting rays of the morning sun, forming an intangible but seemingly impenetrable barrier of light. He slumped to his knees with a gasp of heart-stopping wonder as Márfa clapped her hands in delight at the strength of his reaction. At length he recovered his aplomb and gravely bowed his head to the ground in mock obeisance, until she raised him to his unsteady feet... Even today he

12

grinned wryly at the memory of past innocence; no matter how far he and Márfa lost sympathy, he still found it within himself to rejoice that his genuine reaction that day had given her so much pleasure. Life had all been so simple then.

From the brow of the hill, beyond the birch grove, Mochítsky looked down on the roof of the dacha, flanked on two sides by a thicket of shrubs and soft-fruit bushes, where raspberries and gooseberries, redcurrants and white currants, loganberries and many more whose names he had never learned merged in a tousled mass from which Márfa Timoféyevna culled a seemingly endless supply for the juices and jams, sauces and preserves that stocked her crowded larder. In front of the house and slightly to one side was a cluster of pines, beneath which Mochítsky's car took refuge from the sun or the rain, and which to the great annoyance of his driver deposited on its gleaming surface globules of virtually indelible sticky resin, together with the equally unwelcome contributions of jays and wood pigeons, and of the countless lesser birds. As he paused to gaze down on all this, Mochítsky saw the black, shining roof of the General's elongated limousine as it bumped its protesting way along the track from the Tula road. Good, he was just in time.

As the General's ZIL drew up in front of the dacha, Mochítsky appeared at the top of the steps to welcome his 'distinguished guests' to his 'humble abode'. (How he hated the clichés that seemed nevertheless to tumble automatically from his lips. That was the result, he realised, of the interminable hours of turgid speechifying to which he had been mercilessly exposed on his climb up the party ladder.) General Perdéyev, short and rotund, encased in a stiff army greatcoat which reached almost to the ground, so that his feet were invisible as he walked, giving him the appearance of gliding over the surface, muttered some suitable rejoinder, and this was elaborated fulsomely by his companion, Khúyin, a product of the Moscow School of Journalism (Faculty of Marxism-Leninism), looking somehow absurdly overdressed in studiedly casual clothes. They made an odd couple, and Perdéyev had not been too gracious in agreeing that Khúyin should be his passenger, but it was part of Mochítsky's design that they should arrive together, rather than with him. You could not be too careful whom you were seen consorting with.

Like good Russians, they greeted each other before entering the house, not inviting bad luck by shaking hands across the threshold. Having paid their respects with scarcely concealed curiosity to Márfa Timoféyevna, the guests were installed in solid wooden chairs on the veranda and each was presented with a small glass of vodka, a tumbler full of home-made currant wine and some hot, crumbly biscuits. The serious eating and drinking would come later.

Mochítsky soon joined them, and though their exchanges were at first stilted and staccato – they were not close acquaintances – the fact that they had all agreed to ren-dezvous in this comparatively isolated spot bound them conspiratorially together and, becoming conscious of this, they gradually began to converse more freely. Mochítsky employed all his social skills to that end, so that by the time they took their seats at the table, a rather rickety structure balanced awkwardly on the waves of the veranda, the atmos-phere was a great deal more relaxed.

This process was completed as the meal progressed, and soon the topic on everyone's mind began without any prompting from Mochítsky to monopolise the talk. Acting unobtrusively as a sort of chairman, Mochítsky subtly mani-pulated the dialogue from time to time without himself making too great a contribution.

General Perdéyev, it seemed, was totally mystified by what he called Gorbachóv's 'antics' and personally affronted that everything for which he and his men had fought and in large numbers died was now being ridiculed and reviled. His analysis was neither subtle nor profound, but he echoed the sort of genuine, honest dismay that Mochítsky had been hearing with increasing frequency in Moscow. His reminis-cences of the hardship and privations of wartime and post-war years were .somewhat rambling, and facts merged inextricably with hearsay, but the tenor of his discourse was plain enough. There might be lots of things that needed attention, but by and large the mass of the population had never been so well off. (Had he known the famous 'never had it so good' he would certainly have adopted it.) It was a pity these youngsters hadn't themselves had a taste of what things were like in the forties and fifties: they wouldn't be so quick to criticise everything now. The party had made mistakes, of course, and Stalin had certainly gone too far, 'but without the party, where would they be today? That's what I'd like to know.'

Khúyin, a delegate to what Perdéyev dubbed 'this newfangled congress thing', confessed that to him the Congress seemed like little more than a talking shop. There were some excellent people in it, but whatever they said made very little difference. Some of them simply liked the sound of their own voices: Yevtushénko, for example, made speeches that sounded like poetry readings, but no one understood what on earth he was getting at. Gorbachóv made a great fuss about *glásnost'*, but in fact he took little or no notice of what anyone else had to say.

Warming to his theme, Khúyin launched into a more reasoned argument than the General had been able to muster.

'The structure of the Soviet state,' he began, as though addressing an auditorium of first-year students, 'is monolithic. This is not nowadays a fashionable term, but it remains nevertheless apt. This means that every element is closely interrelated with every other. They form a complete and elegant system, and any change in any element will have a direct effect on the whole. It cannot be tinkered with. You can, of course, improve various aspects, and I am not saying that this isn't necessary or, in some respects, even urgent. But that simply implies improving the existing structure, not changing it. There is nothing wrong with the system as such.'

Khúyin looked at his companions as though anticipating comments, but they only nodded and said nothing. Whether this signified agreement or simply that they had heard him was not clear. He continued his argument.

15

'Now Gorbachóv,' he said, 'seemed to me to begin by simply wanting to put an end to some of the obvious abuses of the system, but then he started tinkering with the system itself, so now it's all getting out of hand.'

More nods, and a grunt from the General: 'My very own words.'

'He's opened Pandora's box, and if he doesn't put the lid back on pretty soon, it'll all blow up in our faces.' (The image seemed a little questionable, but the import was clear.) 'Gorbachóv doesn't seem to realise what he's done. He's lost control. The logic is quite obvious: either we keep the system and make it work, or we abandon it and go back to the old alternative, capitalism. It's a simple choice.'

There was a pause as all three pondered what had been said, avoiding each other's eyes.

'Well,' Khúyin threw the challenge to Mochítsky. 'Am I not right?'

Mochítsky blinked. He was not used to having such direct questions flung at him, but he was adroit enough to avoid answering this one.

'Capitalism,' he said mischievously. 'Ye-e-es, I've seen the joys of capitalism. I know all about the wonderful market economy in England and the USA. Freedom, for the bosses, means freedom to throw people out of work, to cut their wages and benefits, to repossess their homes. And freedom, for the workers, means freedom to live in cardboard boxes, freedom to beg for a living, freedom to die for want of the money to pay for medical treatment. Oh yes, I've seen capitalism in action.'

Khúyin stared at him in open-eyed incredulity, his head tilted to one side, but Perdéyev took the bait at one gulp. This was too much for him; having been rumbling with anger throughout Khúyin's monologue, his face progressing through a deep red to an ominous purple, he now exploded, startling them all, including apparently himself, by the vehemence of his outburst, as he blurted out the bluntest formulation of what was in all their minds.

'Gorbachóv has got to be stopped! If he can't be per-

16

suaded to see sense, then, there's only one alternative...'

'More *stárka*, General?' Mochítsky leapt in to break the reverberating hush that followed this outburst.

Perdéyev grunted, belched loudly and stretched out his legs on the rungs of the veranda rail. '*N-da!*' he rumbled. '*Da!*' But it was not clear whether he had in mind the vodka or the unspoken alternative.

They lapsed again into silence.

'The trouble is,' Mochítsky said mildly, 'Gorbachóv doesn't seem to be open to persuasion...' His voice tailed off, and in this minor key he left the topic hanging in the air.

The General drained his glass and rose uncertainly to his feet, 'Well then,' he said in what seemed intended to be a brisk and decisive tone, but which in fact emerged a little blurred. 'Can't sit here gossiping all the afternoon, you know. Better get on with it.' He called a brief farewell to his hostess, clambered down the steps and waved to his driver. The limousine came gliding soundlessly from the shelter of the trees.

'Splendid lunch, Mochítsky,' he said, motioning to a curiously muted Khúyin to get into the car. 'Enjoyed talking to you. Must have another little chat soon.' Then he eased himself carefully into the back seat and was gone.

'Yes indeed,' Mochítsky said silkily after him. 'Yes, indeed we must.' He smiled smugly. That had all gone very nicely. Very nicely indeed.

He did not hear what Márfa Timoféyevna muttered to herself in the kitchen. 'There's one freedom you forgot to mention: the freedom to hold that sort of conversation. And you can thank Mikhaíl Gorbachóv for that.'

# 2

Valentín Perdéyev was a soldier of the old school and would
have been perfectly happy to hear himself described as such.
Known affectionately to his irreverent juniors as 'the old
fart', he was well past the age at which he ought properly to
have been pensioned off. When scarcely out of his teens he
had distinguished himself as a rash and dashing officer in the
Kursk offensive on the southern front, where he had caught
the eye of Zhúkov and subsequently fought alongside him all
the way to Berlin. He had risen steadily up the promotion
ladder until his mentor fell victim to vaulting ambition and
to Nemesis in the unlikely shape of Nikíta Khrushchóv, after
which he had been pushed subtly sideways into a job in
logistics and apparently forgotten. But he had displayed an
unsuspected talent in his new duties, and though officially on
the retired list he was still semi-employed. Having been
charged with somehow disposing of obsolete weapons of
World War Two vintage, he had developed an acceptable outlet by feeding them to Fidel Castro, whose Cuban troops,
despite increasing murmurs of discontent at home, were
testifying to their leader's solidarity with the Third World by
fighting a forgotten war in the land from which many of their
ancestors had been snatched into slavery – the newly independent Angola.

This situation suited the General very well. The work was
hardly demanding but allowed him to continue to wear uniform, to retain his treasured car and chauffeur, and to move

18

in military circles, the only milieu in which he felt in any sense at home.

Perdéyev belonged to what cynical observers liked to refer to as the 'mother-was' brigade. This comprised men – and some women – of impeccably proletarian origin, whose autobiographies opened with a permutation of the formula: My mother was ... a factory hand in Tambóv/ a milkmaid on a collective farm/ a cleaner at a rural party headquarters... The father was rarely mentioned, though he might have been: killed in an industrial accident/ an alcoholic who had disappeared before the child was born/ an innocent victim of a Stalinist purge (no one was ever guilty). There was sometimes also a sister called Akulína, who was raped in chapter three. In the classical Russian tradition, the strongest personality and dominant influence in the child's life was always the mother.

And indeed Perdéyev's mother (he knew nothing of his father) had been illiterate in early life but had taught herself to read from Marxist-Leninist tracts – the latterday religious texts – and had been determined that her son should take full advantage of the opportunities for a better life in the new society that was taking shape after the 1917 revolution. Perdéyev was in a real sense a child of the revolution, a creation of the party, for whom the concept of the new man, inspired by the noble ideals of Soviet patriotism, which transcended tribal and nationalistic rivalries and the machinations of political and religious factions, had a very real meaning.

A Russian by blood and a veteran of the war in the Ukraine and in Byélorussia, he belonged to the stratum of society that ignored such outdated geographical boundaries, putting its faith in a unifying Soviet nationality and a Soviet culture, and pledging allegiance not to Russia or the Ukraine or to any other of the republics, but to the Soviet Union.

He knew little of the free-enterprise society, the market economy, or private commercial empires except that they were simply aspects of capitalism, which he and his fellows had been conditioned to abhor. In his opposition to

Gorbachóv he was merely reasserting his faith in a system that had provided for him everything he had found valuable and worthwhile. It was not a negative reaction so much as a positive reaffirmation of his dedication. Glib, perjorative labels like 'reactionary', 'conservative' or 'hardliner' were really quite meaningless when applied to such a man as Perdéyev, who despite the horrors he had lived through remained at heart an innocent.

It was the disingenuousness of Perdéyev, as well as his admittedly tenuous connection with Cuba, the only Soviet-style socialist country that seemed intent on remaining so, that had prompted Mochítsky instinctively to sidle up to him as part of an insurance plan only just beginning to take shape. For his part, Perdéyev sensed that in some indefinable way he was being manipulated, but was as yet not alarmed because he did not see what Mochítsky had to gain from him. No doubt it would all become clearer in time.

Their next 'little chat' took place once again at the table, but this time at a tête-à-tête lunch in Moscow at the House of Friendship, the former town house of the Morózov merchant family, a *jolie-laide* building of extraordinary vulgarity, where Mochítsky and other party predators used to receive foreign visitors from non-socialist countries and which had an excellent, subsidised restaurant.

As he entered the building, Mochítsky saw with a shudder that in the outer hall one of his staff was hosting a reception for a group of English teachers of Russian. The party seemed to be going well; the speeches were just beginning... He hurried through to the dining room, where the head waitress greeted him obsequiously and showed him to his private table in an alcove, away from the sight and sound of most of the diners.

'General Perdéyev will be joining me', he said, 'and there'll be another guest later. Please show them to my table. And we'll have the usual drinks.'

Though it was more than her life was worth to acknowledge it, the waitress had a pretty shrewd idea of the nature of Mochítsky's little luncheon parties. She knew the location of the switch that enabled him to record the most interesting moments in the conversation as an aid to the memory – his own and those of his subsequently rueful guests. A carafe of *stárka* and a bottle of chilled Tsinandáli quickly appeared. Mochítsky sipped his wine as he waited.

As a burst of laughter from the English party testified that the vodka was having its inevitable effect. Mochítsky reflected on the role of vodka in Russian affairs. Two general secretaries had tried to cut down on the consumption of vodka – Khrushchóv, after his heart attack, and now Gorbachóv – and both had failed. Khrushchóv's restriction of orders to a hundred grams had become a standing joke, causing poor waiters to be run off their feet as diners ordered first a hundred, then another hundred, then another. And now Gorbachóv had been forced to make his first humiliating climbdown and abandon his campaign. Why did they do it? Was it for a purely practical reason, or was there still a streak of revolutionary puritanism left in them, even after all this time? Drunkenness remained a grave social problem. Alcohol was still the 'scourge of the people'. But hadn't these fellows read their Dostoyévsky? Didn't they know that self-flagellation was the Russian's national pastime?

Mochítsky was unaccustomed to – and not very good at – such philosophical reflections and was somewhat relieved to find the General approaching the table. He rose to greet him. They shook hands and the General took a seat.

'Interesting meeting?' Mochítsky enquired in a sociable way. He knew that on Wednesday mornings the General made his weekly report at the old Ministry of Defence in the Stalinesque skyscraper on Smolensk square. His intonation implied that he did not really expect to receive a reply and would not care what it was if he did. Even so, Perdéyev looked at him with astonishment. It was quite unlike him to make such a direct enquiry about official proceedings. But rather to his own surprise, he gave a pertinent answer.

'As a matter of fact,' he said, 'it was. Going to be a bit of a change from the old routine. Sending stuff direct to Cuba from now on. Might even have to visit the place myself. Ever been there? You've been knocking around the world a bit in the last few years.'

'Yes indeed,' said Mochítsky enthusiastically. 'Marvellous place! Sunshine, flowers, music, seafood, gorgeous girls, and rum with everything.'

He came close to simpering at his own flippancy, but the General was not impressed. His eyebrows rose.

'Hmm,' he grunted. 'Not really my kind of thing, you know.'

To cover his discomfiture at this mild rebuke, Mochítsky busied himself with pouring the wine, to the annoyance of the hovering waitress, whom he irritably waved away.

'Seriously, though,' he said, 'it's a really splendid island. Very poor, of course. the US embargo makes certain of that. They've never forgiven them for that business with the missiles in sixty-two, though in fact most Cubans didn't know much about it, and still don't. And as for the Girón affair...'

Perdéyev began to show interest. Some years earlier he had made a study of the abortive Bay of Pigs raid as part of a training course. What an extraordinary business it had been! As a military exercise it had been so incompetent that it was difficult to believe it had not been sabotaged right from the planning stage. Wrong place, wrong time, wrong equipment ... a logistic nonsense. And wrong intelligence: banking on popular support, which it had no chance of receiving, since thousands of potential dissidents had been put in preventive detention. Such a flop, in fact, that when it was all over, the detainees had been let out again as no longer constituting a threat.

'You wouldn't hear much of this free-market nonsense there,' Mochítsky broke into his thoughts, 'even though they are right on the US doorstep.'

Perdéyev mumbled some inaudible comment, but his mind was still on the Bay of Pigs. It would be interesting to see where it had all happened.

'So you think it might be worth a visit?' he asked. 'Not a

22

young man any more, you know. Bit of a journey, that. Not sure I could manage it.'

'Well, yes, it is a long way, and it's not so easy to get there at all.' Mochítsky reflected for a moment. 'But as a matter of fact,' he said, 'I might be able to help you, if you like. I'm thinking of working on a couple of projects with the Cubans myself, so I'll probably have to go there quite soon.' (And the sooner the better, he continued to himself, if things here go on like this ...) Mochítsky was a great believer in making policy on the hoof. To a charge of opportunism, he would probably have answered 'Well, why not?' Keeping an eye on the main chance was simply common sense. If you saw an opportunity, you took it. It sure as hell wouldn't come round again in a hurry.

He was saved from the necessity to extemporise further by the arrival of Khúyin, a little premature, who stood before them smiling. 'May I join you?' He looked interrogatively at the General, then at Mochítsky.

'Our pleasure,' said the latter, waving to the waitress to attend to his latest guest.

'Bring me a beer,' Khúyin ordered brusquely. 'Imported. No vodka for me today,' he said to his host. 'I want to stay awake this afternoon.' He ordered fish, to be followed by ice cream. The beer arrived and he sipped it with exaggerated restraint. 'I hope I'm not interrupting?'

'Not at all,' from Mochítsky. The General simply grunted. There was, however, a noticeable hiatus in the conversation, until Mochítsky, as usual, threw up a hasty bridge.

'So what's the news from the talking shop?' he asked, with a hint of sarcasm in his voice. 'Anything of interest to report?'

Khúyin paused, with a smug expression on his face. It was now the spring of 1991; several months had passed since the lunch at Márfa Timoféyevna's dacha and Perdéyev's outburst against Gorbachóv, and the situation in the former Soviet Union had changed radically. From apparently involuntarily causing the disintegration of the union, Gorbachóv could now be seen to be desperately but ineffectually trying to hold what was left of it together. It was now Borís Yéltsin, soon to be President of the breakaway Russian Republic, who seemed intent on destroying an increasingly marginalised Central Government and with it the General Secretary of the Communist Party and Executive President, his sworn enemy, Gorbachóv. It was on this theme that Khúyin began to hold forth.

'Borís Yéltsin,' he began, 'has recovered from his car accident last November, and now he's after Gorbachóv with a vengeance – literally, I mean. Gorbachóv thought he'd got rid of him for good, and Yéltsin's still smarting at how he "destroyed him with words". So God knows what's going to happen next. The man will never let go. He's a real muzhík.'

'*V.o.o.!*' chorused Mochítsky and Perdéyev in unison. 'Exactly!'

This was not a flattering assessment to make of any man, implying, as it did, that he lacks sophistication and is prone to excess – to violence, to drunkenness and to sentimentality – but it was certainly a popular view, at least in some circles in the capital. Yéltsin had already been something of a legend as a party boss, and everyone joked about the way he used to storm into shops and offices, abusing the staff for their incompetence, demanding to speak to the manager and announcing imperiously, when asked who the hell he thought he was: 'I am Yéltsin!' When well out of earshot he was often referred to as 'Tsar Borís'.

'They are pretending to work together on this new economic plan,' Khúyin continued. 'But it can't possibly come to anything. Yéltsin is posing as saviour of Russia. Gorbachóv is finished.'

Khúyin's judgement provoked no joy in his companions, both of whom remained silent. Despite his previous antipathy to Gorbachóv, for Mochítsky this was not good news. He was identified with the Central Government, and if that went, there would quite simply be no place for him in whatever new system eventually emerged. His worst fears would become reality.

'My money's on Yéltsin,' he heard Khúyin say, apparently

quite happy at the prospect he had painted for his shocked companions. Mochítsky, on the other hand, needed time to compose himself. He took refuge in his usual flippancy.

'Well, it's all happening, comrades,' he said with a giggle. 'Exit Shevardnádze left; enter Yéltsin right. Never a dull moment.'

'I must say, I was rather sorry to see Shevardnádze go.' Perdéyev took him up as though glad of a distraction. 'Did quite a good job, I thought. Mind you, speaks horrible Russian. Couldn't understand half he said. That awful accent. But that was nothing new, I suppose.'

But Khúyin was not to be deflected and for the rest of the meal he elaborated on his theme, hinting at all manner of behind-the-scenes machinations to which he claimed in some unspecified way to be party. As the meal drew to an end, Khúyin's monologue began to dry up. But now he wanted something in return. 'Well,' he said, 'that was my news. What about yours?' He was looking now at the General, who seemed in no hurry to answer.

'Actually,' Mochítsky took over, 'when you joined us we were talking about Cuba.'

'Ah! *Cuba, que linda es Cuba,*' Khúyin half spoke, half sang the line.

'Didn't know you spoke Spanish,' Perdéyev said in surprise.

'I don't. But I used to have a Cuban girlfriend. A dancer in that group you brought over, Mochítsky. Remember Lola? God, how those girls moved! Talk about rhythm.'

'Oh yes?' The number and nature of Khúyin's girlfriends was common knowledge. 'He'll fuck anything that moves' was how one of Mochítsky's assistants had inelegantly put it. Rhythmically or otherwise, Mochítsky supposed. Useful to know, that. Might come in handy one of these days.

'Are you still in touch?' he asked. 'Where is she now?'

'Not really,' Khúyin replied. 'She's back in Cuba, of course. Havana, or some place called Cienfuegos. There's rather a good theatre there, I believe.'

'The Tomás Terry, you mean? Where Caruso was booed off the stage, back in the thirties? Yes, it's a splendid place.'

General Perdéyev was out of his element. He coughed and looked pointedly at his watch. Mochítsky, too, wanted to bring things to a close. 'I expect you'll want to get back to your debate,' he grinned at Khúyin. 'Affairs of state to be attended to.' They all rose and he shook their hands in parting.

Signing the bill, Mochítsky felt a great need to relax and think about the significance of all that he had heard. He stepped into the spring sunshine and sauntered in the direction of the Mokhováya.

With the General he was clearly in business. Precisely what kind of business, he was not yet sure, but he did see the broad outline of a plan beginning to take shape. At all events, he was pretty certain of getting the old boy's cooperation, willing or otherwise, if he needed it. Perdéyev had already said enough to have him locked up for the rest of his life. Amazing. Once he got going on the *stárka,* it was like turning on a tap. You'd have thought someone with his experience would have more sense. But with his whole world crashing about his ears, maybe he was past caring.

Khúyin was a different kettle of fish. A slimy character, that one. Mochítsky was not quite sure where he would fit into the scheme of things, but he had a feeling he might. He seemed pretty well informed about what was going on behind the scenes in the Congress sphere, which might be very useful. He was one of those people it was very difficult to pin down. Did he in fact have the connections he claimed, or was this just talk? If he could really tip Mochítsky off when anything important was coming up, he would be well worth cultivating further. Getting a handle on him shouldn't be much of a problem. He had already run off a bit at the mouth. Then there was the question of girlfriends . . .

To the surprise of a group of tourists through which he was automatically threading his way, he burst into the song that Khúyin had quoted, which was acquiring a whole new significance for him:

*Cuba, que linda es Cuba . . .*

It was quite true: Cuba was beginning to look more attractive every day.

# 3

Like all capitals, but possibly more than most, Moscow was uncomfortably overcrowded, its indigenous population swollen by traditionally rural dwellers, especially the younger generations, decoyed from the land by the lure of city life. There were the functionaries and managers, clerks and office workers of the governmental bureaucracies of the Russian Federative Republic and of the union, with all their ministries and affiliated bodies. There were the students at the universities, the institutes, the research establishments, the schools, the conservatoires, and all manner of institutions dealing with education or its lunatic fringe. There were the millions of Soviet tourists from Central Asia and the Caucasus, from Siberia and the Urals, from the Black Sea and the White Sea, from the Carpathians and the Baltic coast, speaking a hundred different languages and dressed in a thousand different fashions, who passed through each year or somehow contrived to stay; and there were the foreign tourists from all corners of the earth. It is said that in London's Piccadilly Circus you will sooner or later see everyone you have ever met; in Moscow they would be lost in the crowd.

No city could adequately house so many. Residence permits intended to provide some degree of control could be only partly effective. Flats meant for two were inhabited by ten. Thousands slept on other people's floors, often paying outrageous sums but unable to appeal to the local authorities, who would have driven them out of the city. Whole families moved into single student rooms, or set up house in railway stations.

To repel the horde, every building had a vigilant doorman to keep out all but authorised persons, and every hotel floor had a sharp-eyed sentinel at her desk by the lift who checked all visitors in and sometimes chased them out. But inevitably these systems of protection were used and seen as means of oppression, of checking on everyone's movements, of keeping out the politically undesirable, and of spying on the guests, and opportunities for corruption were too great to be resisted.

Foreign visitors, who spoke no Russian, knew little of the Soviet system and were frequently less than well disposed toward it, were carefully sequestered by Intourist in special hotels, with space, food and a degree of comfort possibly inferior to what they enjoyed at home but certainly greater than was known by most other people in Moscow. 'Unfair', cried the Muscovites, forgetting the precious hard currency the tourists contributed. 'Ghettoes!' cried the tourists, titillating each other with tales of electronic bugging and little men in headphones, buried in basements, monitoring the secret sounds of bathrooms and bedsprings, or with stories of long-legged blonde spies who – alas! – never actually crawled unbidden between their sheets in the small hours.

Vast new estates of identical high-rise apartment blocks grew up on the periphery, reached only by interminable journeys on crowded trains and ancient buses, awaited for what felt like hours in sub-zero temperatures. There was a constant, scarcely subdued rumble of complaint: not enough flats, not enough trains, not enough buses, not enough ... not enough ... Only rarely was the reverse of the problem baldly stated: there were quite simply too many people.

In all this pullulating throng, the native-born Muscovites were a tiny minority and they watched with dismay as their city was swamped and despoiled. Like Napoleon III in Paris, Khrushchóv drove wide new avenues through the approaches to the city centre, sweeping away the ancient churches and historic buildings in their path. Old Moscow street names, famous throughout history, were replaced by bizarre titles like *Karl Marx Prospékt*, and houses which had for centuries given Moscow its distinctive appearance were pulled to the ground, making way for concrete blocks that differed in no single detail from those in any other town in any country from the Atlantic to the Urals. Was this de Gaulle's vision of a single Europe? Passions flared, but there were certainly two sides to the debate. Would you prefer – the question was put – to bring up your children in picturesque squalor or in uniformly ugly comparative luxury? And it was noticeable that the cries of conservationist outrage came not so much from the inhabitants of the old houses, but from doubtless well-intentioned outsiders who had probably never entered and certainly never lived in such dwellings.

It was the redevelopment of the Arbát, one of Moscow's oldest and most historic areas, which for many symbolised the spiritual independence and continuity of the city, that really focused the dissent. Though the 'New Arbát', which preserved a tiny church set like a jewel amongst the glass walls of the new high-rise blocks standing like a row of open books, had a certain grandeur of its own, old and new Muscovites protested in unison at policies which disregarded so much of what was valuable from the city's past, and, incredibly, their voices were heard. Redevelopment went on, but with greater regard for the ancient character of Moscow. The traditional Moscow houses were modernised, with their façades preserved. It was in one such house off the old Mokhováya that Raísa Lázarevna lived.

As he approached the house, Mochítsky cast a critical eye on the architecture of the street as a whole. He was beginning without realising it to look at things as though he were seeing them for the first, or perhaps the last, time. His sub-conscious, it seemed, was preparing him for a radical and probably traumatic change. So far, however, he had not made any conscious plans, though he felt the inevitability of approaching drama and sensed that a decision could not much longer be delayed. This would depend to some degree on Raísa Lázarevna and, he supposed, on Zoya, though she had already made clear her lack of sympathy with his reaction to recent events and was distancing herself with increasing rapidity from him. A final break, he thought, would not cause either of them much pain.

Almost uniquely in the new Moscow, the houses on each side of the street were only two storeys high and gave directly onto the pavement, with no semblance of a garden or barrier of any sort between them and the stream of traffic. This, admittedly, was hardly excessive; even so, it was noisy and smelly, and as the wheels of the heavy lorries rumbled over the many potholes, the windows of the houses shook and seemed sometimes about to shatter. Occasionally, as Mochítsky well knew, one could feel the whole house tremble.

The façades of the houses were, in Mochítsky's estimation, hardly things of beauty or worth much effort in conserving. When the controversy over their preservation had raged, he had not really understood what all the fuss was about, though he had wisely refrained from saying so. Raya and, in particular, Zoya had been vociferously in support of conservation.

Originally wooden, the walls of the houses were now made of stone, dressed with cement shaped to resemble large horizontal slabs and painted a dull ochre, which caused a constant battle with the weather that could never be won. It is sometimes forgotten that the summer in Moscow can be as hot as the winter is cold: neither extreme favours exterior decoration of this sort. But the battle raged, as it did in Leningrad and a dozen other northern cities. Mochítsky had read that in Havana, too, a similar problem occurred, exacerbated there by the humidity, but at least the Spaniards could be forgiven for trying to imitate the architecture of their own hot but dry homeland. Here in Moscow there was no better reason than just the aping of fashions in France or Italy. He doubted if there was in fact very much intrinsically Russian about the houses; but then, did a capital ever really represent the rest of the country? 'I really don't know,' he said aloud, to the surprise of a woman passing.

The ledges between the wall slabs were traps for dust and

grime, which swirled in the tiny whirlwinds provoked by the passing traffic and momentarily blinded passers-by. The window sills, head-high, would also gather little piles of dust in their corners, and this would somehow penetrate into the cavity in the primitive secondary glazing, where it gathered in similar triangular heaps before infiltrating the interior, to coat the strands of cotton dangling from the net curtains that covered most of them. Originally, perhaps, white, the curtains had turned a patchy grey which made them look old and grubby even when freshly washed. The windows were all of casement design but were never opened. Instead, a small hinged section or *fórtochka* at the top of one of them might be eased back just a tiny crack. In winter, the secondary-glazing cavity would be half-filled with snow, which melted and froze a dozen times until it became a solid sheet of ice, thus further reducing the already dim light seeping through the net curtain. On the inside sill there would always be a miserable-looking potted plant, gasping for light and for the air which, if admitted, would instantly have poisoned it. All the woodwork was painted a sort of battleship grey, which in Moscow filled the role played in Britain by the depressing war-surplus chocolate brown (there were other more earthy descriptions) of the forties and fifties. The chief attribute of the paint, which seemed to be in endless supply, was that on application it immediately flaked.

Each house was divided by storeys into two flats, and the most noticeable feature of each was the smell, difficult to define and impossible to eradicate. It was the sort of smell that could produce different reactions, depending on whether or not one had some idea of its source – rather as coffee grounds can smell like onions or rancid sweat. Beauty was in the nose of the beholder. Even when the old shell had been gutted and totally rebuilt, the smell persisted, emanating, it would seem, from the fabric of the building itself. It might be overlaid with others resulting from human habitation, but despite the obvious variation in these later admixtures, it was never overcome. It was as though it devoured any interloping odour and reasserted its own rights of possession. It was not at all like the other smells for which Moscow is so memorable: the gagging gas emanating from wet padded jackets and felt boots; the stench of vodka and garlic locked in intestinal combat; the stink of a thousand strap-hanging armpits; the glorious olfactory anthem of all three combined, giving a whole new dimension to the concept of the great unwashed.

As Mochítsky continued along the sloping street, the air about him hung with the blue fumes of cheap low-octane petrol from which there was no escape in any Soviet town and which added its own acrid tang to the malodorous cocktail.

He turned into the grimy entrance between two houses and let himself into the side door of Raya's apartment, pausing as he entered for his eyes to adjust to the dim light that filtered through the single casement. He switched on a modern art deco lamp balanced unsteadily on a pile of magazines on the hall table, and looked around him. The hall was short and narrow, almost square, with black wire pegs on the wall to the right, on the street side, for coats, net shopping bags and umbrellas. On the left, it opened up into a longer but equally narrow bathroom containing a toilet, a small handbasin and a shower, but without a window. As he opened the door, the smell of damp clothing and peeling plaster made him gag. The large off-white wall tiles were unevenly applied, with ridges of slippery grey grouting protruding between them, and rivulets of condensed steam trickled to the linoleum-covered floor. A huge spider scurried off behind the shower curtain, disturbed by the opening door. God knows where those damned things come from, he thought, or where they go to, for that matter. He shook his head with incredulity, recalling Zoya's reaction when she had once seen him corner such a creature and prepare to crush it. 'Don't kill it!' she had shrieked, tugging at his arm. 'This is his world, too!' As he began to close the door he saw that the shower rail, festooned as usual with drying female underclothes, bore items of two different sizes and styles. 'Blast!' he muttered. 'That means Zoya is home. What is she doing in

Moscow? And how long is she going to stay?'

He moved on through the inner door and into the living room. In effect, this was the only other room, apart from the kitchen, which formed a sort of mirror image of the bathroom so that they took up a strip along the entire side of the flat. The far end had been loosely curtained off, and the area beyond it was agreed to be Zoya's territory, affording her a modicum of privacy, though when she was in residence Mochítsky would retire to his Kutúzovsky apartment. This, he supposed, was what he would have to do now. Unless, of course, she had just come to Moscow to take part in one of those ridiculous demonstrations that she had suddenly become so keen on. 'Democracy, that's what it's about,' she had snapped when he quizzed her. 'Real democracy, not just talking about it.' Democracy, indeed! What she and her noisy fellows understood by democracy was probably a private car and a washing machine. 'You are sick!' she had said scornfully when he suggested this. 'And you are mad!' had been his hardly intellectually convincing reply. 'Well,' she had retorted, 'if to be sick is sane, I glory in my insanity.' He had found no answer. That had been Raya's doing, he thought with perverse pride, recognising the words of Chátsky.

In his new mood of gloomy introspection, Mochítsky looked around the room. The walls and ceiling were covered in a soft, powdery plaster, held more or less in place by a coat of lemon-coloured distemper. This already had a somewhat sweet but stale smell all of its own. A Bohemian glass chandelier dangled at a slight angle from the centre of the ceiling, and along the left-hand wall, behind which lay the bathroom and kitchen, were a closet and several glass-fronted bookshelves filled with paperback editions of nineteenth- and twentieth-century literature, with a preponderance of poetry and works for the theatre, especially ballet, as well as various wooden dolls and items of kitsch misguidedly donated by visitors from other countries. A ponderous television set, with a V-shaped aerial and a telephone perched on top of it, stood on a stool in the corner by the window, and in the centre of the room was a reproduction dining table with a heavy glass bowl of imitation fruit, and with four matching chairs around it. Along the right-hand wall were two divans, which doubled as beds, above which hung strips of coarse-weave cloth embroidered with traditional designs in bright colours, echoing the rugs on the uneven parquet floor. In Zoya's area, he knew, the walls were covered with travel posters of Western cities and photographs of international film stars whose names Mochítsky did not know and whose faces seemed remarkably similar. In a row above the window of the main room was a series of small, stylishly framed water-colours of Budapest.

Mochítsky recalled his Western visitors' surprise that in Russian households the concept of a separate bedroom was almost unknown. Conversely, he remembered his own re-action when first being shown such a room in an English house. What an incredible waste, he had thought, to have whole rooms that are used only at night. Something of this attitude still lingered, though the anecdotes that arose from the Russian system were, of course, legion. He had once over-heard a colleague describing to an English guest, in the later stages of a banquet, how it affected his sex life. He shared a two-roomed flat with his wife, her mother and their two small sons. The mother-in-law had one room to herself, leaving the couple and their children to sleep in the other. 'I have three problems,' his colleague had said. 'The first is to get my sons to go to sleep, the second is to get my wife to stay awake, and the third is to maintain any interest myself. I don't very often solve them all at once.' But when asked about his wife's atti-tude to all this, he had said that she seemed not to mind very much. She'd already had three abortions...

The denouement, Mochítsky knew, had been even stranger. The boys had grown up and left home, and mother-in-law had died. There was now an empty room. What should they do with it? Making it a separate bedroom was unthink-able – literally so, the idea had never been entertained. Should they have a room each? But why? They were in no sense estranged. Should they turn it into a study? But did they really need a study? They had debated and argued, and

34

when Mochítsky had last heard, some two years after the old lady's death, the room was still unused.

As his gaze moved slowly around the room, Mochítsky saw that whereas there were various evidences of Raya's presence – a notebook and pen on the table, a pair of shoes under one of the divans, a woman's woollen jumper on the back of one of the chairs – there was absolutely nothing of his to be seen. Even the pile of literary journals through which he had been skimming the previous evening had been tidied away, with the few other possessions he had left lying about, into the depths of the closet. Those journals had almost caused a quarrel with Raya. '*Glásnost'!*' he had scoffed. 'As far as I can see, all it means is sexually explicit description and a lot of foul language.' But she had echoed Zoya's tone: 'You just don't understand.' 'Well, I still don't,' he said now, aloud, recalling their argument.

From looking at this room, he concluded, I might simply not exist. His thoughts turned to the Kutúzovsky apartment; most of his possessions were there, but he had never even tried to stamp his own personality on it, never tried to make it look like someone's home. Many of his acquaintances seemed somehow to endow wherever they lived with a quality that was peculiarly their own. No matter how many times they changed their flats, they always managed to make them feel the same, so that when one entered for the first time, the place would seem already familiar. It was more than simply using the same furniture; it was a question of the atmosphere they created. Mochítsky, on the other hand, would never engender the remotest feeling of belonging; the Kutúzovsky apartment was simply a shell in which he dumped things and in which he occasionally slept. This room was unmistakably Raya's, redolent of her personality, whether she was actually present or not. Mochítsky it somehow ignored.

A feeling of depression began gradually to possess him, leading to a mounting sense of desperation, as acute as it was unexpected, churning his stomach and restricting his breathing, so that he almost fainted and with an audible gasp clutched the arms of his chair for support. This was Raya's apartment: he had helped her financially and made the arrangements with the cooperative, but it was in her name and he had no legal claim on it. Moreover, at least when Zoya was near, he was no longer welcome there. The Kutúzovsky apartment was ministry property; he lived there by permission of the party authorities and could be ousted without a moment's notice. The dacha belonged to Márfa Timoféyevna, who made little attempt to disguise her low opinion of him. He had scarcely passed a single night there in the last ten years. So who was he? Where did he belong?

As his panic gradually subsided, leaving him bruised and still lightly panting for breath, he began again to take stock. The Kutúzovsky flat was his for the present only; no long- or even medium-term plans could be made for it. The dacha had never been more than a useful adjunct; it was Márfa Timoféyevna's domain. That left Raya's apartment. Until recently, his relationship with Raya had been warm and close, but if she had now to choose between him and Zoya, he knew what her choice would be.

Raísa Lázarevna was a Hungarian Jewess, born of an artistic family which had escaped in the early 1940s to Palestine, taking the three-year-old Raya with them. Though her father's name had been Lazar, technically she had no patronymic, and it was only after her marriage to a Russian that she had adopted the Slav style of name, though it immediately betrayed her Jewish origin, which was not always an advantage. In her professional life, in fact, she still used her original name and was known simply as Raya Takács. She had lived in Tel Aviv until her twenties, following the family's tradition of involvement in the arts. From her painter father (the watercolours of Budapest were done by him) she had inherited a feeling for colour and texture, and from her mother a love of the theatre and, in particular, of the dance. A passionate romance with a visiting Russian dancer had led her to a precipitate and, it transpired, brief marriage, which had nevertheless lasted long enough for her to settle in Moscow and acquire a Soviet passport. A brief career as a dancer at the Bolshói had led via stage design to involvement in administration and, because of her knowledge of several languages, in the international relations section, bringing her into Mochítsky's orbit and, eventually, into his bed. That was 20 years ago – God, how time flies! – a much longer time than many marriages lasted. Whereas he had profited from visits abroad to indulge in trivial liaisons, Raya, as far as he knew, had not, though precisely what she did during her occasional absences from Moscow she had never found it necessary to divulge, nor had he mustered the temerity to enquire. For despite her apparent role of faithful wife in everything but name, she somehow contrived at some levels to keep her distance, to preserve her own space. Like so much in Mochítsky's private life, this was not open to negotiation. There was no explicit agreement of any sort, and no discussion. That was simply how it was; take it or leave it. For many years he had taken it; perhaps the time was now coming for him to leave it.

Well, he thought, in typical reassertion of his cynical self, it's not such a big deal anyway. Surely I can do better than this.

# 4

Nagórno-Karabákh, wherever that is, with Azéris fighting Armenians (*Well, they would, wouldn't they!*); Russian soldiers killing Georgians on the streets of Tbilísi (*Just like old times!*); Moldavians wanting to join Romania (*They must be joking!*) – all peripheral stuff and nothing to panic about. Factories on strike. Neo-fascists in the *Pámyat'* organisation holding anti-Semitic rallies. Pot-bellied priests caressing black beards and licking obscenely red lips like poisonous berries in a bush. Nothing in the shops but everything on the black-market stalls around the corner. Rubles not worth the paper they are printed on. Shopping by barter. Congress chattering like a tree full of rooks. Blame it all on the party.

Gorbachóv thrashing about, but the lid won't go back on Pandora's box. Touring Western capitals with his begging bowl, lionised abroad and loathed at home. And now people being shot in Latvia, and Kravchúk wants to take the Ukraine out of the union. The end of the beginning of the end. I can smell the smoke. Stop the world, I want to get off . . .

Mochítsky recalled Khúyin's dictum at lunch at the dacha: 'You can't tinker with the system.' But tinker they did, and now the world as Mochítsky knew it was coming to an end. For the first time, he began to think seriously about Cuba. Dismantling the Soviet system formally would take a little time, even if it was already falling to pieces. With luck, he'd have three or four months to set something up.

Mochítsky's statement to Perdéyev that he might be working on projects with the Cubans had been pure fantasy – or had it been a flash of inspiration? In any case, there was no reason why he should not actually initiate such projects, which could take him legitimately to Havana and give him time to work something out. From the state of almost frozen despair which had clutched him for the past few days, he began now to assume a more rational and dynamic attitude to the problem of 'insurance' and to apply his devious mind to finding a solution.

First, he required a little fact-finding. Summoning the senior members of his staff to an extraordinary meeting, he asked Túsya Tambóvskaya, head of the Latin American section (which also took in Cuba) to list what cultural exchanges had taken place in her area in the past three years, and with his customary skill he steered the discussion towards the topic that interested him most. No initiatives had been taken by the Soviet side within that period; there had been just the one visit by a Cuban group, the tour by the ballet troupe in which Khúyin's girlfriend had 'moved'. That was all.

Mochítsky spoke at some length about the unsatisfactory state of the exchange programme in general and about the implied neglect of 'one of our most loyal and valued allies'. He feigned indignation and displeasure with the unfortunate Tambóvskaya, even though she was in no way to blame – if, indeed, the question of blame even arose. Mochítsky was perfectly aware of this but wanted to make use of her discomfiture to evoke a feeling of urgency in dealing with his next proposals. Something had to be done to rectify the situation, he told them, and quickly. He would therefore take personal charge of the programme he now had in mind and required the cooperation of the entire staff in setting it in train without delay.

Mochítsky instructed his section heads to draw up a list of all arrangements currently in hand for exhibitions of Soviet art treasures within the territory of the Soviet Union and with other countries of the old socialist bloc. In view of the uncertain relationships with various of the republics and countries concerned, it might be advisable to divert some exhibits to cities in Latin America instead. This would save a great deal of time and kill several birds with one stone. He did not enumerate the birds in question. Included in the programme would be a visit to Cuba by a troupe from the Bolshói ballet, with performances in Havana and Cienfuegos. Mochítsky would take personal responsibility for negotiations with the Cuban authorities, both in Moscow and in Havana, enlisting, of course, the expertise and experience of Túsya Tambóvskaya. The chastened head of section was clearly gratified at this unexpected mark of restored confidence and made clear her determination to make a special effort to prove her worth.

Shouldn't have any trouble from that silly old bat, Mochítsky assured himself. A little touch of applied psychology is all you need.

In a little under two weeks, Mochítsky had the information he needed. A collection of religious ikons had been assembled, consisting largely of items which had only recently been brought out of the ingenious hiding places where they had been concealed since Stalin's persecution of the church, and which had therefore remained unseen throughout much of the Soviet era and were known to only a few people, of advanced age.

The collection, which contained some outstanding examples of the school of Andréi Rublyóv, possibly even of the master himself, and of others dating from the sixteenth century, had been intended for exhibition in Kíev, Mochítsky was told, but in view of uncertainties in Russo–Ukrainian relations, with arguments over claims to hitherto 'Soviet' items, he might think it wiser not to continue with the Kíev venue at the moment? Insurance arrangements amounting to hundreds of thousands of dollars had already been made. The ikons were all crated up ready for dispatch and were stored in the vaults in the basement of the House of Friendship. Because of the enormous value of the ikons, no public announcement of the proposed exhibition had as yet been made.

Mochítsky restrained himself with some difficulty from

rubbing his hands with glee – he could hardly have invented a better idea – but instead he expressed a hesitant doubt about the suitability of the subject for Latin America (which he now used as code for Cuba), allowing himself gradually to be persuaded and eventually giving a reluctant go-ahead. But even better was to come.

A collection of paintings 'recovered' by the advancing Red Army in the later stages of the Great Patriotic War had been intended for exhibition in Bucharest. It comprised some 30 items and included also two Picasso drawings which had been considered by the Soviet authorities too shocking to be shown and had therefore never been on public exhibition. This, too, was ready crated for transportation, and all the necessary insurance arrangements had been made. Would this also be a suitable candidate for a change of venue?

Even Mochítsky was unable this time to conceal his enthusiasm, though he did try to present it as pleasure in the efficiency and cooperation of his staff. He gave instructions that the appropriate authorities should be told that the exhibitions would go ahead in new, unspecified venues. In the case of any sign of hesitation by those authorities, it was to be implied that negotiations were well under way to transfer the exhibitions at a later date to New York, for the ikons, and Chicago, for the paintings. These negotiations, too, would be handled by Mochítsky himself. Having arranged another meeting to review the question of transporting the two precious exhibits, he wound up the discussion, sending his staff away with the impression of a situation retrieved and a feeling of optimism and goodwill.

For the second meeting, he called in only Túsya Tambóvskaya, whom he secretly treasured as the best-trained fool in the business, and one other senior member of staff. He instructed Tambóvskaya to have the paintings brought from the Leningrad Hermitage to Moscow and, in the interests of security, to have both sets of exhibits repacked in plain crates giving no indication of their contents. The other member of his staff was to prepare detailed documentation setting out all that was known of the provenance of each of the ikons and each of the paintings. This was to be highly confidential, for Mochítsky's eyes only.

For Mochítsky, now, the game was really beginning, and there were several more important meetings to be held, two of which would certainly require all his skill and a willingness also to show the iron fist. But first, more fact-finding.

At lunch with Perdéyev at the House of Friendship he had been somewhat deflected from what had seemed a promising conversation about the dispatch of arms to Cuba. With his usual acumen, Mochítsky had planted an idea that he and Perdéyev might have a common interest, but had not since followed it up. Indeed, until today he had not really felt the need to do so, but now things were different. He needed now to discover what stage the proposed arms shipments had reached, as well as what sort of arms they were likely to be; but equally, he needed to discover all this without actually being seen to be asking. An oblique approach, and possibly a bit of pressure lower down the ladder, was called for.

Then he would have to have a serious business talk with the First Secretary at the Cuban embassy, who was his opposite number and contact man for security matters. This might be a difficult session, and again he felt the need for a better briefing before he tackled him. This, at least, he could obtain through his own KGB channels, but again he did not wish to invite curiosity by being seen to ask. Perhaps an hour with the files would solve that one.

As a first step, Mochítsky decided to approach the General obliquely at a semi-social level. He therefore asked his secretary to telephone Perdéyev on his behalf, saying that he was beginning to plan a visit to Cuba and wondering if the General might be doing the same. Mochítsky's visit would be in connection with the projects he had mentioned to the General; was Perdéyev in a similar position? In short, the secretary was to pump the General's secretary, if not the old boy himself, and find out whatever she could. Mochítsky might then follow up whatever she discovered at a later date. It all seemed a bit tentative, but *tíshe yédesh'* – gently does it. In the meantime, he could put together a little dossier to jog Perdéyev's memory if he didn't want to play.

With every move he made, Mochítsky was increasingly aware that he was burning his boats, but every time he began to question the wisdom of this, he came back to the same dilemma: What is the alternative? What else can I do? The writing, surely, was on the wall, and his days of influence and comfort really were numbered. The degeneration of Soviet society into an entrepreneurial rat race was increasingly visible; the party would no longer be a power in the land, at least, not as the party he knew. It might and probably would come back in one form or another – who else but the Communists had any idea of management? – but how long could he wait? And what would happen to him in the meantime? Mochítsky never found it difficult to justify his actions or to find plausible excuses for doing what at one level he knew was wrong, and this was no exception. It never even occurred to him to accept the 'new order' and work to make it successful, and he lacked Perdéyev's principled commitment to the old system, which might have prompted him to make a stand in its defence.

Looking around him, Mochítsky could see that many of his former colleagues would slough off their skins like snakes and become new men, at least on the surface. There were certainly fortunes to be made by those who had the drive and ingenuity, not inhibited by too many scruples. He had for a while wondered whether he could become one of their number, but his heart had sunk at the sheer effort it would have entailed and the uncertainty of the outcome.

Mochítsky had several times come close to self-pity; it really was too bad that at the age of 51 he would have to start absolutely over again, and not simply from scratch but from a number of paces behind the starting line. But he would shrug his shoulders, as though physically shaking off such gloomy thoughts, and begin instead to plan for the future, for one big coup that would settle all his problems. One regret was that it would mean leaving the Soviet Union, or the Commonwealth, or whatever it was now going to be called; but on the other hand, it was all changing so quickly, and so unattractively, that he was in any case not sure that he would want to go on living there. So Cuba it was to be, at least at first. Afterwards, who knows? From Havana, on a good day, you can almost see Florida...

# 5

The dispatch of Soviet arms to Cuba had begun rather sooner than Mochítsky had anticipated. With his usual simplistic logic, Perdéyev had merely switched the consignments originally intended for Angola to their new destinations. A considerable quantity of automatic rifles and ammunition had been unloaded in Havana and stored in the sixteenth-century El Morro fortress built by the Spanish after the depredations of French and English pirates, and more were already in transit. More sophisticated consignments of ground-to-air missiles and launchers were bound for Santiago de Cuba, the original capital, at the other end of the island. Helicopters and spare parts would be landed at a port yet to be designated. Shortage of storage facilities and worries about security accounted for this dispersal, as did the location of military camps and airfields. Mochítsky noted with interest that a number of the items mentioned dated from decidedly later than World War Two. Presumably they were prototype versions and were included under the heading 'surplus to requirements', meaning unreliable or ineffectual. The Afghanistan adventure had taught some hard lessons.

Such were the basic facts gleaned by Mochítsky's secretary. Sketchy though it was, this information enabled him to speak with such apparent confidence in his conversation with the Cuban First Secretary that the latter believed him to be rather better informed than he actually was. And this, in turn, led the First Secretary himself to speak more frankly than he might otherwise have done, so that eventually Mochítsky had, in fact, a more or less complete knowledge of the arrangements Perdéyev had made. Moreover, certain other intriguing facts also emerged. It transpired that the Soviet decision to send the arms to Cuba had been made virtually unilaterally: after all, if Cuban troops were to be withdrawn from Angola – a fact perhaps implied but never, to Mochítsky's knowledge, officially announced – they would not need the weapons, would they? So what was now taking place, and seemed likely under its own momentum to continue, amounted to little more than arms dumping. And not only were the arms unwanted: it must surely be obvious that Cuba was so impoverished by the US trade embargo that there was simply no way in which they could be paid for. The First Secretary spoke excitedly of an island awash with deadly weapons that no one wanted, poorly guarded and in danger of falling into the wrong hands, while at the same time thousands of battle-hardened soldiers were coming home to the prospect of shortages and unemployment instead of a more appropriate welcome for returning heroes. He seemed not to notice the avid interest of his companion in this scenario, or the absence of any element of dismay in the reactions that it aroused. But anyway, the First Secretary ended his peroration, it was not really his responsibility. The Military and Commercial Attachés would have to sort the problem out.

Lavish entertainment of the Military Attaché, involving quantities of hard liquor and the good offices of a dumpy but energetic blonde, consumed a great deal of time but produced nothing of any value. The Cuban proved to be much more interested in getting his hands on American arms than in anything the Soviets had to offer. From Mochítsky's point of view, he was useless. But in Fernando Pérez, the Cuban Commercial Attaché, Mochítsky found an unexpectedly sympathetic ear.

Pérez began by commiserating with Mochítsky about the dramatic collapse of the Soviet Union, which by now they both saw as imminent, with the uncertain future that this spelled for him. The two men had never before had direct dealings with each other, though the complementary nature of their interests had necessitated a certain oblique contact on several occasions. Their discussions were lubricated by the fact that Pérez was well informed about Mochítsky's official duties and status in the party, and similarly by the homework that Mochítsky had done on Pérez before their meeting. Pérez was clearly able to empathise with Mochítsky and to understand his present worries, but what surprised Mochítsky was that despite the apparent stability of the Cuban political scene and the seemingly unchallenged authority of Fidel Castro, Pérez himself foresaw great difficulties when the Soviet–Cuban relationship was ruptured, as it clearly would be if the new regime in Moscow continued to distance itself from its Communist past. So dependent was Cuba on Soviet aid that if the days of the Soviet regime were numbered, then, so Pérez feared, were those of the Cuban regime. Castro would tough it out for as long as he could, of course, and he still enjoyed the affection if not perhaps any longer the unqualified confidence of most of the people, but sooner or later, under American pressure, the regime would collapse. In fact, Pérez was as worried about his own future as Mochítsky was about his. From this it was a short step for the two of them to elaborate an urgent programme of mutual aid.

The vision of Cuba as a dumping ground for unwanted Soviet weaponry, outlined by his colleague, was shared by Pérez, but he, like Mochítsky, saw this not as a problem but as a challenge and an opportunity. If Cuba did not want and could not pay for the arms, why not sell them on to whoever did? Why not turn the island into an entrepôt for supplying arms to, say, Venezuela or anyone else in South America with money to pay for them? The Americans wouldn't like it, of course, but for a short time at least, there would be some good business to be done. With a little judicious marketing, there would be no shortage of takers.

Meeting outside Moscow in the recreation area of Silver Woods, the two conspirators, for such they now acknowledged themselves to be, began to develop their embryonic

47

plans further as they strolled along the river bank beyond earshot of their own staffs.

Various intermediaries, they agreed, would have to be given a rake-off, but with a little greasing of palms and perhaps some discreet arm-twisting, it should be possible to set up a profitable system, at least for the short term, without too much trouble. Certain little adjustments to Perdéyev's present arrangements would have to be made. To provide a comprehensive service to the client – they were now using the jargon of the market place with remarkable facility – they would have to be able to supply whatever was required rather than simply putting on offer what they happened to have in stock at the time. Was Mochítsky, Pérez asked him, in a position to influence Perdéyev in the choice of weapons selected for dispatch to Cuba? Well, yes, Mochítsky rather thought he was...Then there was the question of who would handle the project on the spot, in Moscow, if Mochítsky thought it wise to leave the country. Did Mochítsky have anyone in mind? Well, yes, again he rather thought he did... On the other hand, if what Pérez euphemistically termed 'adjustments' were to be made in the existing arrangements at the Cuban end, who would be responsible for organising and supervising them? In other words, who would be interposed between Perdéyev and the actual dispatch of the Soviet arms to Cuba, and who would take charge of their reception and redirection when they arrived?

Mochítsky believed that Perdéyev would refuse to do anything that he considered contrary to his principles or against orders, but that he could certainly be used without realising it. Indeed, Mochítsky had plans to do precisely that, though he did not propose to disclose them to Pérez. He undertook to see that arrangements at the Soviet end were placed in reliable hands, and in return he required assistance in organising his own intended move to Cuba, including an open-ended residence permit, the indefinite use of a luxury villa, a car and driver, plus the use of a new pick-up van, adequate fuel and all the usual privileges accorded to Cuban party officials of comparable rank. Since Pérez was approaching the end of his tour of duty in Moscow and would soon be returning to Havana, he could handle the arrangements at the Cuban end, and when Mochítsky arrived, they would organise the sales procedures jointly. Pérez anticipated no problems in meeting these requirements, and though numerous details remained to be worked out, by the end of their afternoon walk the basic structure of the scheme was agreed.

Having been reluctant at first to accept that his source of ease and privilege was about to dry up, and consequently somewhat slow off the mark in seeking an alternative, Mochítsky was now a man in a hurry, and every idea seemed to spawn so many others that he was having great difficulty in keeping up with them. He began to like this game and to play it with increasing finesse, but he needed also a partner, someone informed, energetic, ambitious and not overburdened with scruples; someone hungry. who understood the new system and could not only play it but beat it. Most of his colleagues had some of these features, but not all. They were either fat cats who probably had enough hard currency stashed away to last them for the rest of their lives and therefore did not need to take any risks, or they were so paralysed with shock at the shattering of their familiar little worlds that they were incapable of coherent thought or decisive action. He needed someone younger, who still had a career to make and would be looking forwards, not back over his shoulder. And so he came again to Khúyin.

Since their lunch at the House of Friendship, Geórgy Khúyin ('Call me George') had embraced the spirit of the new entrepreneurial society with great vigour and enthusiasm. Clearly, his earlier forecast that Gorbachóv's 'tinkering' would destroy the old system completely had been vindicated, but he was losing no sleep mourning its passing and was intent now on taking maximum advantage of the opportunities on offer for lining his pockets. As with Mochítsky, his adherence to party ideology had been simply incidental to his chosen career and was now a thing of the past. He was now a member of the Russian Congress of People's Deputies, but such was his instinctive understanding of the working of Western-style democratic institutions that no matter what was said to the contrary, he saw no problem in combining this function with the launching of various business ventures profiting from the inside knowledge that his position afforded. Democracy was just a word; capitalism was the name of the game. So when Mochítsky broached the subject of arms sales, Khúyin was already ahead of him.

Making use of Perdéyev's little scheme would, he thought, not present any great difficulty. (Khúyin had adopted the universal fixer's 'no problem' formula as his slogan.) In his despair and dismay, the old boy had begun to hit the bottle more than ever and would be glad of all the 'help' he could get. But surely there were bigger fish to fry, or very soon would be? The cold war, as they had known it, was part of history, and with the break-up of the union, affairs in the old Soviet armed forces were in complete turmoil. What Perdéyev was peddling would be chicken feed (that phrase again!) compared with what would soon be coming onto the market – tanks, planes, warships, missiles, nuclear warheads... Mochítsky had turned pale and was swallowing hard, but Khúyin seemed not to have noticed.

'The stuff's lying around in half of Europe.' Khúyin was saying, 'and nobody knows what to do with it. We can pick it up for a song and name our price to the buyer. Iraq, Iran, Libya, Egypt, South Africa, Angola again – that business isn't over yet – you name it, there's always somebody who wants to fight somebody else. Maybe we could sell the stuff to both sides...'

'And South America?' Mochítsky asked almost timorously. He was getting well out of his league.

'South America, certainly,' Khúyin replied, with an expansive movement of his arms. 'Venezuela, Nicaragua, Colombia, Chile ... South America – no problem.'

With some tactful prompting, Khúyin came down to earth a little and began to talk in more practical terms. He and various unnamed 'associates' would set up in business in Moscow and probably St Petersburg...

50

'My God!' he interrupted himself. '*Saint* Petersburg! Petrograd would have been OK. Plain Petersburg I could just about take. But *Saint* Petersburg! *Bózhe moi!*'

He returned to his theme. They would set up a business. No problem. Strictly legitimate, of course. (This with a broad smile.) Mochítsky could leave it to him. And they'd look after Perdéyev, too. No problem. When would all this happen? 'Give me four weeks.'

'As soon as that?' Mochítsky involuntarily asked.

'Has to be,' replied Khúyin. 'First of August latest. Got to get it in before the balloon goes up.'

'The balloon? Do you mean the Yéltsin business?' Mochítsky was genuinely puzzled.

Khúyin laughed aloud, but there was no pleasure in his laugh. He looked at Mochítsky speculatively, as though trying to decide how far he could trust him. Apparently not very far.

'No, no,' he said. 'Not Yéltsin.' But he did not elaborate further. He had, however, given Mochítsky a clear enough tip to complete whatever his own plans were by that date, and Mochítsky was not slow to take it.

By the time he left Khúyin, it was understood that Mochítsky would be given a free hand in Cuba with the *matériel* already sent or scheduled for dispatch by the first of August, after which he would become a client of the Khúyin organisation, and this suited him very well. He knew nothing about the arms trade and had other irons in the fire. It was time to fan the flames.

From Túsya Tambóvskaya Mochítsky learned that the documentation on the provenance of the ikons was virtually complete. Verification was required for one or two items, but for this it would be desirable to bring into play the expertise of émigré Russians now living in London and New York. A similar situation obtained for the paintings, but this time consultation was needed with experts in Paris, too. The exhibits had been recrated according to Mochítsky's instructions and his orders were now awaited concerning transportation.

It was time, Mochítsky decided, to call on General Perdéyev's services. He made an official appointment as Director of Overseas Cultural Exchanges with the Controller of Armaments Export (Cuba). The meeting was to be semi-formal, though not to the extent of being recorded in minutes or other such documentation. No other person was to be present.

Briefly, Mochítsky explained, he had been entrusted with two medium-sized crates of items of the utmost importance to the state for urgent transportation to Cuba. It had been decided 'at the highest levels' (a formulaic expression that always brought an anxious frown compounded of awe at being within the orbit, however obliquely, of the august personages in the Kremlin and terror at what that might augur) that 'for security reasons' (another magic formula that unfailingly brought the hearer to attention and inhibited any querying of whatever followed) these items would best be included in the regular shipment of armaments, in containers giving no details of their contents and indistinguishable apart from a stencilled code from all the other elements in the consignment. Such was the degree of secrecy requested that no formal documentation would be issued. General Perdéyev enjoyed the absolute confidence of his superiors and Mochítsky had full authority to make all the necessary arrangements with him on a man-to-man basis.

Although Mochítsky did not anticipate any resistance on the part of Perdéyev, he had nevertheless begun their dialogue with a veiled threat by reminding the General of their interesting and stimulating conversations on current political developments, the tenor of which he had not, of course, relayed to any other person. Whether Perdéyev took the hint or not was never clarified. At all events, he did not for a moment demur and promised his complete cooperation. The next shipment was due to leave Odessa in ten days' time; would the items concerned be ready by then? It was quickly agreed that Perdéyev's staff would collect the crates overnight from the House of Friendship and fly them to Odessa for loading on the naval vessel bound for Cuba. It was

52

vital that this were done as unobtrusively as possible. The General understood that on arrival in Cuba the crates would be handed over to the civil authorities for forwarding to their unspecified destination. There his responsibility (and interest) would end.

On 25 July 1991 Mochítsky left Sheremétevo on the 7.35 Aeroflot flight to Prague. Having only hand luggage, he quickly passed through customs at Ruzyně and took a seat near the door of the snack bar, where for an hour he drank coffee and, ostensibly engrossed in a copy of *Pravda*, carefully scrutinised the faces of everyone crossing the not very crowded concourse. Eventually he made his way to the Lufthansa desk.

At 11, Mr I. M. Písemsky boarded a Lufthansa plane, and by two in the afternoon he had presented himself at the Bayer-Hofmann bank in Zürich. He was courteously ushered to a small office at the rear of the building, where he was interviewed briefly by a senior manager, after which he was escorted along brightly lit corridors, followed by the soundlessly revolving eyes of security cameras, through several electronically operated doors, to a small, windowless, underground room furnished with a plain metal table and one chair. His escort left him briefly, returning with a double-locked and numbered metal safety-deposit box, which he placed reverently on the table. After opening the first lock, he withdrew through the solid steel door, which locked automatically behind him. With his own key, Mochítsky opened the second lock, then checked the contents of the box and took out a number of $10,000 bills. Relocking the box, he pressed a button in the door, which immediately opened to admit his escort, who completed the locking procedure. He again withdrew briefly, taking the box with him, before returning to escort Písemsky back to the manager's office. There Písemsky handed over the $10,000 bills and received in exchange an attaché case filled with bills of smaller denominations. He signed a receipt, shook hands gravely with the manager and was shown out through a side door into a small square, where a taxi stood waiting.

From Zürich, Písemsky took an Air France flight to Paris, where he spent two nights of unaccustomed luxury at the Hotel Crillon, with a day of shopping, a gloriously gourmet dinner followed by a torment of indigestion, and a morning closeted with an aged art historian who had emigrated from Leningrad many years earlier. From Paris he flew by BA to London Heathrow and stayed two nights at the Hilton in Park Lane, with one day shopping and a second visiting several art galleries in the morning and in consultation at Sotheby's auctioneers in the afternoon. Five days after he had left Moscow, he took the 09.25 Venezuelan Airways flight VA711 from Gatwick to Caracas, arriving in a temperature of 35 degrees Celsius. At Caracas International airport he spent a sweltering three hours drinking endless cups of coffee and peering incredulously at a raunchy array of pornographic magazines and paperbacks, only slightly less shocking than the books describing rather prematurely the last, bloody days of Fidel Castro. At 18.45 he at last boarded flight VA976, and two hours later he arrived in a state of near prostration in Havana. Here he was greeted in rapid-fire Spanish by a beaming driver, who whisked him, at a speed he felt must have exceeded that of the plane, to the old town. He eventually collapsed into bed in the Plaza hotel, in a room backing onto the central courtyard, where he was denied a moment's sleep by the irregular hum of the ancient air-conditioning plant and a dribbling lavatory cistern. Whether he would in any case have slept, he very much doubted.

Lying alone in the semi-darkness, trying not to hear the concerted noise and irregular snatches of song from the area below, Mochítsky-Písemsky reviewed his last few hectic days in Moscow and the extraordinary behaviour of Raísa Lázarevna. 'Amazing!' he said to himself. 'Absolutely amazing! All that time I spent with her, and I had no idea . . .'

With what he had thought was consummate skill, Mochítsky had made his preparations for quitting Moscow. New name and passport, with all the necessary papers, all prepared by himself in his own department; a return air ticket to Prague on a flight he had taken many times before in the line of duty; no extra shopping; no rounds of good-byes. Nothing out of the ordinary in his routine behaviour. He would simply leave the apartment one morning and never return.

But when he had let himself into the Mokhováya flat the evening before his departure, there had been no sign of Raya: no vestige of her presence; no clothing in the closet, no personal belongings, no watercolours on the wall. Just a note in her handwriting in an envelope propped against the fruit bowl on the table:

> *Gone home to Tel Aviv. The flat is now Zoya's.*
> *Take care in Cuba.*        *Raya*

and that was all.

How the devil had she known? And what was this: *home to Tel Aviv?* As far as he knew, she hadn't set eyes on the place for 20 years. 'Amazing,' he said to the darkness. 'Absolutely amazing!' But at least there had been no face-to-face hypocrisy, no shouted recriminations. It was a clean break; not quite as he had intended, but complete, final. But why had she done it? Perhaps she was afraid to face the interrogation to which she would have been subjected when his disappearance was eventually realised. He had felt the odd pang of conscience about that when planning his escape – was that the right word? – but had been consoled by the welcome thought that it provided one more reason for not saying anything to her. The less she knew, the less she could tell them, and they would surely have to believe her. After all, what had she to gain by concealing anything from them? It was really for her own sake that he had decided to leave without warning her. It had been the kindest way to do it... And as for Zoya and the flat – she was welcome to it.

Písemsky tossed and turned in his narrow bed and punched his pillow savagely. Why was it that so many hotel pillows felt as if they were cement bags or stuffed with bottle tops? He punched a hole for his head and lay on his back, staring at the ceiling. It made no difference. He turned onto his side: what the devil do you do with the underneath arm when you are lying on your side? He must have slept in that posture a million times, but try as he might he could not find a comfortable position in which to stow the wretched thing. This was ridiculous. He turned onto his back again.

And still his thoughts would not give him peace. Think about nothing, he told himself. Empty your mind. Easy enough for some people, he giggled, including some in pretty high positions. But not for him.

If Raya had known about his plans, how many other people had? And why hadn't they done anything to prevent him from carrying them out? Or perhaps they had. Oh God! He sat up in bed. '*Oi, vey!*' as Raya would have said in fun. Damn Raya. So far, so good. He had his passport and some money, and that wretched journey was over. With luck, he'd make a bit of a killing on the arms deal while he waited for the big one. But what about those crates? Would they ever arrive? Had the General kept his word?

It was then, as he stared into the darkness, that he realised the enormity of what he had done. Well, he had crossed his Rubicon, and there was no going back now.

Towards dawn sleep came to claim him, but even his dreams were troubled by the strangely sinister echo of Khúyin's parting words: 'Don't worry about Perdéyev. We'll look after him. No problem . . .'

# CUBA

# 6

At 7.45 in the morning Písemsky's bedside telephone rang, shocking him out of the stupor of sleep that had taken pity on him barely two hours before. He groaned, thrusting out an arm that failed to locate the receiver but succeeded in knocking the whole apparatus from the table to the floor, accompanied by a glass of water. He leaned out of bed to rescue it, shook the water from the receiver and held it finally to his ear, his head sinking into the hole punched in the pillow.

'*Da!*'

'*Buenos días, compañero! ¿Com'está?*'

With a further groan, Písemsky recognised the horribly ebullient tones of Fernándo Pérez. 'Oh, hello.'

'How was your journey, *compañero*?'

'Awful. And what's all this *compañero* stuff?'

In Pérez, Písemsky had met someone whose English was just as good as his, and they had enjoyed throwing their mastery at each other, but today he found great difficulty in speaking any language at all.

Pérez laughed. 'Welcome to Cuba, comrade.'

Sensing that Písemsky was in no mood for small talk he got straight down to business.

'Do you know the Floridíta bar, where Hemingway used to drink? It's just around the corner from your hotel.'

'I expect I can find it.'

'Good. Meet me there at 11. We can have an early lunch and I'll tell you all the news.'

Písemsky replaced the receiver and closed his eyes; it is curious, he thought, no matter how badly you have slept, you do not necessarily want to leap out of bed. Even when you pray for the dawn, you usually meet it with your eyes closed. He dozed for an hour – a mistake, he realised, since this state of semi-sleep inevitably brings fantasies worse than nightmares, because somehow more real. For a moment he believed that his dreadful imaginings had actually happened. 'My God,' he said aloud, 'I'm just a bag of nerves. And what's more, I keep talking to myself. I'd better snap out of this.'

He had a shower in water that alternately froze and scalded him, dressed in new summer clothing bought three days ago (was that all?) in London, and waited ten minutes for a lift, though he could have walked down the stairs in two or three. It was the principle of the thing... In the dining room he helped himself to raspberry yogurt; he would have given a lot of money at that moment for a glass of astringent Russian *kefír*, with its magic curative properties after any sort of night out. He tried also the coffee, which was not at all bad, but when a gaggle of French tourists crowded in, gesticulating and talking incessantly, especially when their mouths were crammed with food, he deserted his table (which was immediately fought over by rival couples) and threaded his way through the crowded lobby to the reception desk, where he tried unsuccessfully to obtain a street map of Havana. With a resigned shrug he strolled through the main exit into the welcoming sunshine for his first view of the city by daylight. Despite his eulogy of Cuba for the benefit of Perdéyev, his experience of the island had been limited to two hectic days some years earlier, and all that remained was a feeling of warmth and a mental blur.

Before him lay a large, open square, with lawns and flowering shrubs in the centre and broad streets on all four sides. The traffic was light, comprising mostly bicycles, motorcycles with sidecars – a combination he had not seen for years – a few taxis and buses, and the odd decrepit lorry. He was instantly reminded of Tirana, except that the traffic in

Albania was even sparser and the buses and lorries were Chinese rather than Soviet. His strongest remaining memory of Tirana was the sound of shuffling feet. Here, too, there were many pedestrians, each undoubtedly bound for some destination but displaying remarkably little eagerness to reach it. The benches in the central pathways were occupied by groups of young people given to much giggling and occasionally bursting into song. Several children came up to him demanding *Chiclets* chewing gum, or, to his surprise, soap. In neither case could he oblige, but they did not seem to mind. A grin earned a grin in return. The general atmosphere was relaxed and somehow happy, bringing a smile to Písemsky's tired face as he crossed a narrow side road to the left and stopped before the windows of the Intur shop, the Cuban equivalent of the Soviet Beryóza, where all sales were conducted in foreign currency, which in Cuba means US dollars. The goods on display were almost exactly what he would have expected to find in a Beryóza, except that instead of flaxen-haired Ukrainian or Czechoslovak *pánenki* there were numbers of black, rag, *Tomasíta* dolls, with elongated arms and legs which flopped in all directions when he picked one up. Since golliwogs were no longer socially acceptable or politically correct anywhere in Europe, he was for a moment surprised, but since most of the faces around him were various shades of black, why not black dolls, too?

Písemsky turned and gazed across the square at the García Lórca theatre, to which he must soon pay a business call concerning the projected visit by the Bolshói ballet troupe. But that could wait a day or two until he had found his bearings. He turned down the side street to a little square and then to the corner of Obíspo Street, where a blue sign indicated El Floridíta restaurant and bar. As he approached it, the sound of guitar music emerged; he was soon to learn that this was as difficult to escape as the perpetual muzak in public places in America and England, but infinitely less awful, not least because it was live and therefore the musicians took occasional breaks. He entered the bar and chose a seat with his back to the wall and a view of the door, recalling unsmilingly how a visiting American had teased him about his Billy the Kid complex. Several couples were seated at adjacent tables, and at the bar were a group of Canadian tourists, with loud shirts and Bermuda shorts, and crowned with baseball caps. They had obviously already drunk quantities of rum, drowned in a variety of cocktails, of which their favourite seemed to be *Cuba libre*, more prosaically known as rum and coke. Písemsky ordered a daiquiri in honour of that old poseur Hemingway, and waited.

Studying the trio of musicians, Písemsky was struck by the way in which they illustrated the racial mix of the Cuban people. The man on the left, playing a guitar, was of medium height, slightly balding, with the Mediterranean features of the Spaniard and a Zapata moustache, but very dark skin. He ogled the girls as he sang, occasionally rolling his eyes and raising his bushy brows in mock invitation. In the centre, with the maracas, was an extremely tall man with classical African features: ebony black skin, curly hair, gleaming white eyes and teeth, thick lips, long arms, slightly jutting buttocks and very long legs. His eyes were fixed on the ceiling, and he kicked his feet alternately in time with the beat, without bending at the knee. The third member of the group, also playing a guitar and singing, had the sort of Red Indian profile figured on a United States coin: hooked forehead echoed in hooked nose, high cheekbones, thin, cruel lips and firm chin. It was difficult not to think of him as wearing the proud, feathered head-dress of a paramount chief. Playing and singing in perfect harmony, the three seemed to symbolise the unity of modern Cuban society that the official handouts liked to boast about.

As Písemsky watched, the group completed its rendering of *La Paloma* for the Canadian tourists and came to take up a position at his table. At a nod from the first guitarist, they broke into the revolutionary song made famous by Pete Seeger and hummed all over the world by millions with no inkling of its origin or import:

*Guantánamera, Guajira Guantánamera, Guantáname-e-e-ra*
*Yo quiero cuando me muera*
*Sin patria pero sin amo . . .*

'When I die, without a country but without a master . . .'
Písemsky recalled the words with a rueful, scarcely audible
sigh; they could not have chosen a more ironically appropriate song. Joseíto Fernández had hardly meant those words
for the likes of him, yet he, too, was a man without a country
now. He had disowned his native land – or had it rather disowned him? – but he had yet to find a new allegiance. He was
a soul in transit, with no known destination. But he was his
own master. He still held his Soviet passport – Mayakóvsky's
'purple bomb' that had become a damp squib – but he was
holed up in no man's land, undecided which way to move,
fearful of what lay ahead but unwilling to retreat. Well, at
least the decision was his to make.

The trio jerked him out of his reverie with a final, sharply
strummed chord and looked around in triumph. Písemsky
joined politely in the noisy applause of the Canadians and
thrust three dollars into the hand of the maracas player, who
rewarded him with a toothy grin. As the musicians moved
away they were replaced by Fernando Pérez, wearing an
equally broad smile and dressed in casual trousers and a
gaudy Cuban Guayabera shirt that made him look more like
a taxi driver than a professional diplomat. He thrust out a
hand for Písemsky to shake, but as Písemsky responded he
flicked his fingers upward so that instead of grasping hands
they clutched each other's thumbs. As Písemsky was later to
learn, this was a sign of acceptance, of being 'one of us'.
Pérez waved to the barman: '*Dos mojítos, por favor*' and took a
seat opposite Písemsky. 'So how do you like Cuba?' he asked,
looking at him expectantly. For perhaps the first time in his
life, Písemsky was lost for words.

Pérez laughed. 'Perhaps I should give you time to open the
other eye before I ask you questions like that. It's a tough
journey, isn't it? Maybe one day we'll have direct flights. It
would make things a lot easier.'

Písemsky agreed. 'Yes, I am a bit tired,' he said. 'And hot,' he added.

'Ah! The famous Havana humidity. Well, I've got you a splendid villa in Varadero, right on the sea, just along the coast from here. But you're going to stay in Havana the first week, aren't you, to get to know the place and sort out how we're going to operate.'

They had agreed in Moscow that Mochítsky-Písemsky would travel as a holidaymaker, not attracting the attention of the authorities ('Yours or ours!') and that he would stay for about a week among the tourists in the modest circumstances of the Plaza, an old colonial-style hotel that had certainly seen better days but was perfectly adequate. He would keep a low profile, well away from the embassy circuit, just to be sure, though he felt confident that none of the present personnel had known him in Moscow. It would also give them a chance, they thought, to see if anyone was taking too close an interest in him. His knowledge of Spanish was limited, mostly passive or at 'survival' level, but he was confident that with a little expert tuition and lots of practice he would soon become reasonably fluent. Pérez had undertaken to find a suitable tutor. In the meantime, he could get by perfectly satisfactorily in English and Russian.

They sat and listened to the music, and after the second *mojito*, on top of the daiquiri, Písemsky began to look a little less drawn and became more communicative.

'I'd like to change my room,' he said, 'to one that's a little less noisy. Can you arrange that?'

'No problem,' said Pérez. (*Oh God not you too?*)

'I see you have Canadian tourists,' Písemsky said, 'but no Americans.'

'That's right. The Americans aren't allowed to travel to Cuba.'

'Don't they ever get mixed in with the Canadian groups?'

Pérez gave a slightly vulpine smile. 'We-e-ll, you know...'

'Ah,' said Písemsky. 'Interesting...' But he did not elaborate.

They moved into a room at the rear of the building for a private lunch.

Having dispensed with the small talk, Pérez got quickly down to business. He had not been idle during the brief period since his return to Cuba. The authorities had welcomed his initiative in offering to take over the unwanted arms consignments, asking only a ten per cent levy on all sales and nominal payment for storage. The question of security had been settled by recruiting a small force of highly professional soldiers recently repatriated from Angola, who were being paid initially in pesetas from a secret government loan, to be repaid when income had been generated. All connection with the government was to be highly confidential; it was probable that Fidel Castro was not aware of the arrangement, but Raúl, who was responsible for military affairs and was less squeamish about arms dealing provided that it was profitable, had given the go-ahead. The security force, to be referred to uninformatively as the task force, had been promised large bonuses in dollars as sales progressed. On the assumption that the confusion in the former USSR was such that it was not necessary, at least at this stage, to worry about payment, the matter had been left open. At this point, Písemsky gave a selective account of his arrangements with Khúyin to look after the Moscow end, and since this was already agreed, Pérez had little choice but to consent. It certainly solved several problems, though he could see that in the longer term it might give rise to others. Still, they were not at the moment making long-term plans, having tacitly agreed with each other that when the right time came they would simply cut and run.

Two consignments of small arms had arrived and had been stored in El Morro fort and the Fortaleza de la Cabana, a military barracks, here in Havana. Confirmation had been received that two more were already on the way, both to Santiágo de Cuba. The missiles and launchers would be transported by road to Trinidád de Cuba, where they would be stored under guard by the task force in the warehouse of the former residence of the Cantera family, rich Creole merchants now in Miami. The house had been constructed on a casbah model so that it was in effect fortified and should be comparatively easy to make safe. The helicopters and spare parts were to be lodged under guard at the Santiago military airport. The beauty of all these arrangements was that the 'merchandise' was all accommodated in places actually designed for such purposes, so that no additional or conspicuous building had been necessary.

Písemsky was impressed, and said so with some enthusiasm. Being himself on unfamiliar territory in more ways than one, he was immensely relieved to hear the businesslike fashion in which Pérez had gone about things. As a more devious – he would have said subtle – operator, he would not himself have begun to know where to start. Though tempted to fancy himself as a slick businessman he suddenly realised that he had in fact strayed into bandit territory. He was not at all sure how he had got there and did not feel entirely in control. He was more than ever grateful that he had other shots in his locker.

But did he? Everything depended now on the Odessa shipment, which Pérez had not mentioned and about which, it seemed, he had no news. This led to the topic of communications with Moscow, which would clearly be increasingly important as the scheme progressed. Pérez, he learned, had completed a series of tours overseas and would therefore be home-based for three years, with access to all the facilities of his ministry, including telecommunications. He would therefore be able to check very easily on the final, fifth consignment under the old dispensation and in view of Písemsky's obvious concern, which he had apparently failed to disguise, he left the table to make a telephone call to the ministry. They would ring him back as soon as any information had been received. This they duly did, confirming that the shipment had indeed left Odessa and was due to dock in Cienfuegos in about two weeks. Arguments between the Russians and the Ukrainians over ownership of the vessels of the old Soviet fleet had caused a hiatus in communications, for which they apologised. Perfect! A much relieved Písemsky was able to relax and enjoy an excellent meal.

There remained the question of marketing the merchandise, which again lay squarely within Pérez's sphere of competence. He had put out various feelers through acquaintances at embassies in Havana, who in turn would make discreet enquiries in rather less official spheres. It was too early yet to expect results, and a great deal of consultation and planning would be required. For obvious reasons, the necessary meetings would best be held away from the capital.

The villa at Varadero was one of a number built for party dignitaries on the strip of coast which was being exploited for the budding tourist trade. Several new luxury hotels were already functioning and receiving numerous groups of sun-seeking Canadians and increasing numbers of tourists from further afield, including some from Europe and, especially, from South America. It would therefore be an ideal spot for unobtrusive meetings and dual-purpose social gatherings. The peninsula on which Varadero stood jutted out, as Pérez graphically put it, like a rampant penis from the body of the island, and was within easy reach of Havana by boat, by sea-plane or, via Matanzas, by road.

As part of the service at the villa, there was a part-time cook-cum-housekeeper, as well as a car and a driver who doubled as security guard, and the pick-up he had requested would be available. An expert Spanish tutor would be on call whenever convenient. It was understood that Písemsky had his own source of funds and would not require financial support, other than payment of the staff.

'Splendid!' Písemsky exclaimed. 'It all sounds quite admirable. I'm most grateful.'

Pérez waved his hands airily. 'No problem . . .'

# 7

For two days Písemsky was left to his own devices and spent his time as any tourist would, wandering through the streets, visiting museums, eating and drinking. Only on the morning of the third day did he do a little private business before meeting Pérez and his colleagues.

A guided tour organised by the Plaza hotel enabled him to get a general overview of the town and to orientate himself for future reference. He spent a minimum amount of time in New Havana, paying mandatory respect to the memory of José Martí and admiring, in spite of himself, the Cuban sculptor Sicre's extraordinary obelisk erected in the bourgeois revolutionary leader's honour. He noted with wry amusement that the statue of Martí originally intended to crown the summit of the obelisk had proved too unstable and that it now nestled obscurely at its foot. There was perhaps a moral in that, but he did not think it wise to articulate it. He had seen too many of such monumental sculptures in Eastern Europe to work up much interest. Posters and smaller-scale sculptures reminded him equally of the socialist realist art that adorned all Soviet buildings, though the Cuban versions somehow had rather more vigour and style. In the paintings, in particular, the brilliant colours, especially an amazing variety of greens, seemed to have more in common with the French Impressionists or with the *douanier* Rousseau – who had indeed soldiered in Mexico – than most Soviet pictures offered. As with various other manifestations of Soviet-style socialist Cuban culture, there was enough in common to make him feel at home, but sufficient difference to take him constantly unawares.

But it was Old Havana that both captivated and horrified him. As he sauntered through the avenues and, especially, the old streets leading down to the bay, he was appalled at the state of disrepair of what had clearly been magnificent buildings. He had seen how the crumbling baroque and Gothic façades of Prague had become dangerous to pedestrians and traffic alike, until they were swathed in wooden scaffolding that had remained so long in place that it, in turn, had begun to tumble onto unsuspecting heads. But that had all changed now, and it had certainly never been anything like this. Balconies and cornices had split and fallen away, bushes sprouted from neglected roofs, and daylight was visible through gaps in the ceilings. Wrought-iron railings of the sort he had so admired in New Orleans (the French influence visibly overlaid the Spanish colonial basic design) had rusted and sprung loose; on one building the balcony rail had completely disappeared, and he watched an ancient crone pick her perilous way along the unprotected outside of the building from one first-floor room to another. An occasional attempt at repair had been made, serving only to emphasise the formidable task that systematic large-scale renovation would present. Dismay at the state of the city now was compounded by realisation, confirmed at every turn, of how splendid it must in its heyday have been and how impossible a task it would be to restore it to its former glory.

But there was another impression that struck Písemsky with almost equal force. As he visited the city museum, the museum of colonial art, the music museum, the museum of fine arts, the folk museum, he found such a treasury of porcelain, glass, furniture and painting that he was constantly in a state of near panic that such priceless collections should be so casually displayed. It is true, there were the usual numbers of affable but vigilant ladies at the door of each room, and the guides – when there were any – were enthusiastic and informed, but even they seemed unaware of the incalculable

69

value of the collections in their charge. He watched in horror as one guide rested her weight on the top of the swinging door of a seventeenth-century French boudoir chest of mahogany and walnut, inlaid with mother-of-pearl, in which precious and semi-precious stones were set, and miniature portraits of exquisite workmanship. Brought together from a number of houses of the Spanish and Creole aristocracy or their even wealthier bourgeois merchant successors, the Meissen and Sèvres porcelain, the Venetian, Lalique and Bohemian glassware, and the silverware alone would have attracted a multitude of European and American collectors if they had been offered for sale. Their total value must be astronomic; how could this be reconciled with the decrepit state of everything around?

One incongruous feature did in some measure bring the two faces of Havana together, and this Písemsky was to see even more clearly in other towns. In all the museums he had admired the elegant wood and cane colonial furniture, especially the upright chairs and rocking chairs, which combined beauty of form with the practicality of being cool and airy. He was intrigued to see as he peered, he hoped not too brazenly, through the open doors and glassless windows of the virtually slumlike dwellings which most people seemed to inhabit, that the very same style of furniture was in common use. For some reason this gave him enormous pleasure. Comparisons with Raya's Mokhováya flat he wisely decided to avoid. Damn Raya.

On the morning of the third day he arrived by appointment at the imposing front entrance of the García Lórca theatre. It, was, of course, firmly closed, and it was only after trying half a dozen side doors that he eventually found himself in the foyer, from which a wide, ornate marble staircase wound gracefully upward to the first floor, around which ran a plain marble balustrade. Stout mottled-marble pillars arranged in pairs and crowned with trios of angelic muses with wings spread wide supported a stained-glass dome, through which the morning sunshine painted coloured pictures on the gleaming marble surfaces. Here, again, was a reminder of past splendours. Down the stairs, with carefully studied steps as though making an entrance on stage, came the elderly lady he had come to see, Señora Yoscelinda Gómez, a former operatic soprano, now Director of Repertoire of the Corps de Ballet. As she approached Písemsky she held out a frail hand; it was with great difficulty that he refrained from kissing it, and from the twinkle in her eyes he was aware of this.

Písemsky's plan had been to apologise that because of internal changes within the former Soviet Union, the projected visit by a Bolshói ballet troupe would unfortunately have to be postponed. Any such conversation, however, would clearly have to wait until he had first been given a guided tour of the theatre and then drunk several cups of excellent coffee in her surprisingly tiny office. Forcing himself with unexpected ease to relax and be patient, he found Señora Gómez charming, informed and sympathetic, so that he actually enjoyed her company. She reminisced about tours she had made in Europe; she had sung in Covent Garden, Paris and Vienna, but not – alas! – Moscow or Leningrad: 'Saint Petersburg we must learn to call it now'. She asked him many questions about the contemporary cultural scene in Europe, which to her and his own pleasure he was able in general to answer, and at his request she showed him an album of photographs of herself in various roles. She had clearly been stunningly beautiful; indeed, in a way she still was. He murmured his appreciation.

At length, reluctantly, she came to the subject of their meeting, taking the wind right out of Písemsky's sails.

'I am really very sorry,' she said with patently genuine regret, before launching more formally into an obviously prepared statement, 'but the economic situation in Cuba is now so difficult, and the energy shortage is so severe, that we can no longer stage any performances in our theatres. As you have probably noticed, there are power cuts in Havana each evening, when certain sections of the town have no electricity. We try to be fair and rotate the cuts, but every area has them. All unnecessary use of power is forbidden, and that

71

includes all places of entertainment – cinemas, theatres and so on. We are extremely disappointed, but in the circumstances it would be better if the Bolshói visit were postponed. I know this will be terribly inconvenient for you, but there is nothing I can do.' She really looked as if she were about to weep.

Písemsky, who had never intended that there should be such a visit and had done nothing in Moscow to arrange it, was suitably understanding and consoled Señora Gómez in words so gentle that he almost felt tears in his own eyes.

'You are so very kind,' she said sadly. 'If there is anything I can do ...'

Písemsky was silent for a moment. Then: 'There is, in fact, just one little favour I might ask of you,' he said hesitantly. 'I have arranged for a crate of costumes and other items to be delivered to Havana and it is too late now to stop them. Do you think that when they arrive they could be stored here in the theatre until I can make other arrangements? There will be just one crate, but it is rather precious and I would like to have it stored somewhere secure.'

'But of course ...' (For God's sake don't say 'No problem', Písemsky thought in something like panic, but she didn't.) 'We have a number of very secure storage rooms in the basement. Some of our props are very valuable, you know. I could let you have one of those if you like.'

'That sounds perfect,' he said. 'Actually, there are one or two little items of my own I shall need to take out,' he went on. 'I expect to be in Cuba for some time; would it be possible perhaps for me to have the key so that I can help myself without bothering you?'

'Certainly. Just let me know when the crate arrives and we'll make arrangements then. It's the least I can do for you.'

Písemsky left the theatre rather later than he had intended but in high good humour. 'Nice old bird,' he said to himself. 'I rather liked her.'

As he crossed the square towards the Plaza, he saw from the corner of his eye that a lanky youth had detached himself from a group of young men gossiping near the main entrance of the theatre and begun to walk in the same direction, a few paces behind. He could have sworn he had seen him before; several times, in fact. The hair on Písemsky's neck began to bristle; his training had taken place long ago, and in any case he had never treated it very seriously, but he could still sense when he was being followed, and remembered a trick or two. Continuing to the entrance of the Plaza, he went in through one door and straight out through the other, turned into the colonnade at the left of the door, ducked behind a pillar and waited. In a matter of seconds, the youth came hurrying past, looking anxiously around. Písemsky promptly fell in behind him and without any attempt at dissimulation, began to follow him, almost treading on his heels. The youth hesitated, glanced several times over his shoulder, then broke into a run and sped off, at which Písemsky turned and went back to the hotel. He sniggered as he walked again through the entrance, but he was nevertheless quite disturbed. Who the devil was he?

Almost his first words when he met Pérez later were to ask if he had anyone following him. Pérez laughed, a little sheepishly.

'Yes, I heard you gave him a hard time. I thought you might need looking after. This can be a rough town, you know. So I put one of my boys on the job of keeping an eye on you.'

There was a pause while Písemsky thought about this. It might be useful to have a 'minder', but it could also be rather unwelcome. He made no attempt to conceal his displeasure, but there was more to come.

'But what I didn't know,' Pérez was serious now, 'was that there is someone else watching you, too.'

'Who?' Písemsky asked sharply.

'We don't know yet. We'll soon find out. But in the meantime, perhaps you'd better give my boy a clear run. Anyway, don't worry about it. We'll look after him.'

Now where, thought Písemsky, have I heard those words before?

\* \* \*

That afternoon a meeting took place in the back room of the Floridíta, this time around a conference table on which the only refreshments were some bottles of mineral water and a plate of dry biscuits. There was no alcohol. Gorbachóv would have approved.

There were two others present. Pérez introduced Písemsky to them: Diego Macías, a Mexican who he described as his 'business associate', and 'the Major', who commanded the task force. Písemsky looked at them with interest.

Macías was short and plump, with slicked-back hair and the mandatory bandit mustachios. He wore startlingly pink trousers and tunic shirt, and exuded a sort of sweet, sickly perfume that Písemsky mentally labelled 'whore's bedroom', though his knowledge of such places derived purely from hearsay. The Mexican's hand, when Písemsky shook it, was soft and slightly moist, but his voice was firm and surprisingly deep.

The Major – if he had a name it was never divulged – presented a total contrast. Tall, very black, with close-cropped hair just beginning to grey at the temples, he had an unmistakably military bearing, though not wearing uniform, and when he shook Písemsky's hand, the latter could almost feel the bones crunch. His voice, however, was incongruously high-pitched, with a suspicion of a lisp. Písemsky restrained himself with difficulty from giggling: something had gone very wrong here – Macías and the Major had exchanged voices. This thought never quite left him and distracted him throughout the meeting.

Macías spoke Mexican Spanish and American English, making them sound very similar. The Major spoke Cuban Spanish, barely intelligible English and quite fluent Russian, with a good accent. Moscow trained, Písemsky decided, and nobody's fool. I must keep on the right side of him.

There was no small talk. The early part of the meeting consisted largely of a recapitulation by Pérez of the present state of the shipments, including that from Odessa. He then broached the subject of the changes of organisation in Moscow, and it was Písemsky's turn to speak. The meeting quickly became something of an interrogation of Písemsky by Macías and the Major, with Pérez sitting silently by. Having himself begun to wonder what his own role was to be, Písemsky found himself exaggerating in a transparently self-deprecatory way the central part that he had played in setting up the system, recruiting Perdéyev from the military side and Khúyin from the new governmental body. Rightly assuming that their understanding of current political affairs in the former Soviet Union was even less than his, he made it sound as though powerful figures of state and army were behind the scheme. 'I think I can safely say,' he told them, 'that whatever you can sell, we can supply.' He several times caught Pérez casting somewhat enigmatic glances his way, but there was no interruption or contradiction. I suspect he's going to need me as much as I'm going to need him, Písemsky thought. We're in this together. At all events, his two interrogators seemed satisfied and became distinctly warmer in their manner. It was now the Mexican's turn.

Macías reported with evident satisfaction that he had received the first firm enquiry concerning a supply of light automatic rifles and ammunition. He was confident that it could easily be translated into a firm order, the first of several. It came from the neighbouring island, from Haiti. It was common knowledge, he told them, that supporters of the deposed priest-president Aristide were planning an uprising against the illegal military regime. They now wished to arm themselves with a fresh supply of weapons, hence the enquiry. The beauty of it was, he went on, that it was equally common knowledge that the Haitian army was training a special counter-insurgency police force, and they, too, required arms. 'So with any luck,' he said gleefully, 'we can supply both sides. Let's hope it's a long war!'

You are a thoroughly nasty little man, Písemsky thought to himself, and I'm damned glad old Perdéyev didn't hear you say that.

The problem (What, a problem!), Macías was continuing, was going to be one of delivery. Official interchange between Cuba and Hispaniola was minimal. There was, however, a highly sophisticated smuggling network – 'For you Cubans, smuggling has always been a way of life' – and it should be possible to plug into that. He looked interrogatively at the Major.

'Agreed,' the Major said curtly. The task force were already working on this. As a preliminary step, he proposed moving an appropriate consignment of arms from El Morro in Havana to the port of Baracoa, on the eastern end of Cuba, From there he would be able to liaise with the Haitians and make the deliveries. They were looking now for a suitable place to store them. No doubt the meeting would agree to leave the details of the planning to him and his men.

They were, indeed, happy to do so, and it was agreed that Macías and the Major should follow up this initiative with all speed and report back at a further meeting in two weeks, to be held this time in Varadero. At this they all looked meaningfully at Písemsky, who nodded gravely. 'Good thinking,' he said, recalling a film he had seen on TV. 'Let's do it.'

The final item on the agenda was the question of finance, which lay squarely in Pérez's province. First, he said, they need have no worries about the ability of the Haitians of either side to pay for whatever they ordered. As everyone knew (except me, Písemsky thought, but I'm certainly learning), Haiti was now the entrepôt for the illegal Colombian drugs traffic and the place was awash with dollars. The question, therefore, was how to make the transactions. Without giving away too many details, he explained that he had found a way of 'burying' the transfer of dollars within the existing trading arrangements, paltry though they were. Handling this first order would be a sort of test case, of course, but he had complete confidence in its outcome. 'You can safely leave that side of things to me,' he concluded.

My God, though Písemsky, this is really going to work! Up to this point, the whole scheme had seemed distinctly unreal, but these people really knew their business. They were real professionals. It was actually going to happen ...

In this state of euphoria, he said a few laudatory words 'on behalf of the organisation', and the meeting broke up. As he left the room to return to the Plaza, Pérez handed him a sealed envelope.

'Have a look at that when you get back to the hotel,' he said. 'Perhaps we can have a chat about it later.'

Alone in his room, Písemsky opened the envelope. It contained a press cutting from the new independent newspaper *Nezavísimaya Gazéta*. He began to read it with foreboding.

### WAR HERO FOUND DEAD

Great Patriotic War hero, tankist General Valentín Ilích Perdéyev, has been found dead at his desk in his Moscow home. He had been shot once through the temple. His pistol was lying near him. Until recently, General Perdéyev had been responsible for liaison between the Soviet Union and Cuba in the sphere of military supply. It is understood that these duties will in future be handled by a newly formed consortium headed by People's Deputy Geórgy Khúyin.

Speaking to our correspondent from his office on the New Arbát, Deputy Khúyin said that General Perdéyev had been a much respected and valued colleague whose dedication had been an example to all. 'He had for some time been very depressed,' Khúyin said, 'by political developments which he confessed he was unable to understand. We shall miss him,' he continued, 'but we shall ensure that his work will go on.'

'Well,' Písemsky said aloud, 'you certainly "looked after" him!'

Rereading the newspaper cutting, he felt a growing unease. It was certainly less than clear exactly what had happened to the old buffer. Surely they hadn't...

He swayed his head from side to side, then shrugged his shoulders. I don't know why I should feel guilty about it, he thought. Whatever happened, it was nothing to do with me. I wasn't even in Moscow at the time.

But the feeling of unease would not let him rest and he went in search of his usual remedy.

In the hotel bar he became engulfed in a group of British tourists who insisted on chatting and began, eventually, to dispel the mood of dismay that had seized him. He talked about Soviet literature with an ageing Welsh writer of the neo-'mother-was' tendency, whose reputation, he was to discover when the Welshman had temporarily left the bar, rested largely on one rather sentimental novel officially entitled *The Scent of Wales* but known in the trade as *Sheepshit on My Shoes*.

He went to bed laughing.

# 8

Varadero was in another world. Towering luxury hotels with every kind of facility for enjoyment and entertainment, standing, as the publicity brochures put it, in spacious grounds, with emerald-green lawns, sky-blue swimming pools and vast reaches of gleaming white sands, dotted with rush-thatched sunshades and reclining chairs, and all – because of the hugeness of the area – incredibly uncrowded. Avenues of royal palms, the national tree of Cuba, soared in stately majesty to a height of ten metres or more, their smooth, matt-grey trunks crowned with deep-green fronds, with dangling bunches of nuts, decorative but inedible.

A burgeoning tourist trade was beginning to bring in groups from the former Soviet Union (where Cuba had always been a popular playground), increasingly from Western Europe, Australasia and Japan, but primarily from Latin America and Canada. The Canadians, in particular, taking refuge from the ice and snow, would stay for weeks without ever leaving the grounds of their hotels – El Paradiso, Bellamar, Siboney and the rest. Together, the tourists brought in millions of dollars annually, making a significant contribution to Cuba's straitened economy. They were exclusively non-Cuban; work in the hotels was a much sought-after privilege, and the few lucky applicants made up virtually the only section of the island's population to approach, even by proxy, a standard of living quite outside their everyday ken. They were proud and never grovelled in the hope of tips, and even when a few dollars did come their way, they were not legally able to spend them in the hotel foreign-currency shops. Indeed, the only favour they would ask of hotel guests was to purchase something for them with the dollars they had acquired. If their concept of actual costs was sometimes wildly optimistic, and the good-natured tourists topped up their few dollars with some of their own, this was only a sort of unofficial subsidy that no one begrudged them.

Also strung along the shore of the peninsula and reflecting the hotels in miniature were a number of tastefully designed white villas, again with their own well-managed and secure grounds, with lawns, swimming pools and gardens. The walls were festooned with riotously blooming purple and scarlet bougainvilleas, echoed in the flaming orange hibiscus and white oleander, and the slightly sinister beaky heads of the bird-of-paradise flowers. Constructed in two or three basically similar styles, they had essentially two storeys, with a garage and storage space underneath. Each villa faced away from the road, toward the sea, and had a separate flat above the garage, with its own entrance, for the chauffeur-cum-security guard. Though hardly on a par with Soviet dachas in the Crimea, they nevertheless provided extremely comfortable and well-appointed holiday retreats for high-ranking party dignitaries (though Fidel Castro eschewed such bourgeois decadence) as well as most agreeable temporary dwellings for their guests. It was one such villa that Písemsky had at his disposal for an indefinite period.

The feeling of unreality that he had experienced before the meeting with Pérez and his colleagues in Havana had now returned and was further heightened by the irresistibly holiday atmosphere of Varadero. He arrived from Havana after a two-hour drive along the coast, through the industrial town of Matanzas, over a wide-span concrete bridge, built – so Miguel, his driver, reluctantly informed him – by Sergeant Batista, and past the nodding donkeys at the root of the peninsula, laboriously pumping up Cuba's meagre oil reserves and preparing to pollute the beaches.

Conversation with Miguel, who was by nature as loquacious and jolly as most Cubans, had been minimal, since the driver's knowledge of English was practically nil and he spoke little Russian. Písemsky became more than ever determined to improve his own command of Spanish, a necessity underlined when he arrived by difficulty in communicating with the cook-housekeeper, Dora. As though reading his thoughts, Pérez telephoned him very soon after his arrival to check that the journey had been without incident and in general to confirm that arrangements were to his taste.

'Your Spanish tutor can call on you at three tomorrow afternoon,' he said. 'Will that be OK?'

'Splendid. I look forward to meeting him.'

Pérez laughed as he rang off.

Seated in the sunny dining room with a light lunch of smoked sea bass, a cheese omelette and salad, followed by an assortment of fruits, some of which were quite new to him, Písemsky sipped his chilled beer and reflected that things might have been decidedly worse. Definitely so. Not at all unpleasant, all this. Precisely what he thought he was doing there, he would still not have been able to say. His status in what he mentally labelled 'the gang' was almost worryingly good. It couldn't last, he realised; something awful was bound to happen sooner or later. But in the meantime, the thing to do was to enjoy it all and settle down to await the arrival of the Odessa shipment. He still had to make arrangements in Cienfuegos: he'd get Miguel to take him down there in a day or so. All I need now, he sighed, is a good... But he thrust the thought away. I expect I'll manage that, too, one of these days.

At the bookshop near the Plaza in Havana, Písemsky had bought a Russian grammar of Spanish and a colloquial English–Spanish phrasebook. Being an unusually competent linguist and accustomed to highly inflected languages, he spent the next morning reminding himself of the structural system of Spanish and reading bits of the phrasebook aloud, determined to impress the tutor when he arrived that afternoon. After a post-prandial doze, he resumed this activity, becoming by now a little bored, until promptly at three, just after Dora had left, there was a tap at the door and the tutor entered. Písemsky leapt to his feet and thrust out a hand to greet what simply had to be the most beautiful woman in the world.

He stood and gazed. All the prepared phrases of welcome disappeared from his mind. No word of any language would come out of his mouth. It was she who broke the silence.

'*Buenos días,*' she said. '*Me llamo Jina.*'

'*Um... Buenos días,*' he eventually managed to blurt. He offered a chair.

'*¿Habla Usted español, señor?*'

'*Um... Poquíto,*' he hazarded.

She beamed. '*¿Como se llama Usted, señor?*'

'*Ah! Me llamo Iván Písemsky.*'

'*Muy bien. ¿Como está Usted, señor Písemsky?*'

'*Muy bien, gracias.*'

The ice was broken and they sat for a moment smiling at each other, his looks of obvious appraisal not causing her the slightest embarrassment. No doubt she was accustomed to the effect she had on men, and not displeased. She was petite, he supposed was the term, perhaps 5 feet 3 inches tall, with long, jet-black hair, European features in a face that would probably be called dusky, a full bust, much of which was on view, a slim waist, shapely legs, surprisingly long for one of her height and, no doubt, a delectable little bottom. When she smiled, her eyes twinkled (when she was angry they would undoubtedly flash) and the pink tip of her delicate tongue peeped out between even ivory-white teeth. Her lips were blood-red, without the aid of cosmetics. Písemsky wriggled in his chair. Christ, it's been a long time...

'I see you already speakin' ver' good Spanish,' she said mendaciously. Perhaps, he thought, on a par with your English. And indeed, as it soon became apparent, she spoke a dialect of English known to her alone, and sometimes wildly funny. As they continued a surreal conversation in two broken languages, he began to see that his Spanish lessons were going to be rather more fun than he had expected. Not very productive, perhaps, but certainly not dull. After the usual exchange of inane banalities, with questions about health, age, families, likes and dislikes, all answered with shameless dishonesty, dictated not by what he wanted to say but by what he was able to, they switched again to English as he repeated the catechism, applied this time to Jina. She had, he discovered, drunk too much rum the night before:

'Today I got squeasy tummy,' she said.

I'll bet you have – and a few other bits, too, sprang to his mind but not, fortunately, to his lips. *Tíshe yédesh'*...

Two hours flashed by, until Jina at length got up to leave. '*Mañana*,' she said. Then, correctly interpreting his despairing look as she moved towards the door, '*Mañana*...' She giggled. 'Maybe. *Hasta la vista!*'

In the evening, Písemsky asked Miguel to drive him to the El Paradiso hotel, where he released him until the morning. 'I'll walk back.' Miguel swayed his head from side to side, then shrugged and drove off.

At tables set out beneath the palms, the tourists were drinking their sundowners; rum, as Písemsky had flippantly told Perdéyev just a few months ago, with everything. As he entered the main bar he was greeted by the Welsh writer, whose group had moved down from Havana to recover over a few days' lounging in the sun before continuing their programme of visits to other Cuban centres.

'Come and join us, *bychan*,' he called to a bemused Písemsky, who had been called many things in his time, but never before *bychan*. It was, no doubt, marginally better than 'boyo', which seemed to be the alternative. He joined the group without enthusiasm but quite willingly and ordered a *mojito* for himself and anyone else whose glass was empty. Apart from the Welshman, there was only one taker, a rather silent woman of indeterminate age, dressed somewhat more conservatively than the younger women in the group, but with infinitely greater style. She seemed a little out of place and took no part in the good-humoured but essentially frivolous banter that flowed back and forth across and around the table. She was in no way stand-offish, smiling and replying politely when directly addressed, but she did not initiate such exchanges and looked, when caught off guard, a trifle bored. Písemsky began to talk to her, ignoring the Welshman's knowing grin.

The conversation became three-cornered, and in spite of himself he began to find it genuinely interesting. The writer, Gareth, was very well informed about contemporary literature, had met many of the leading figures of the moment and was an amusing if slightly malicious raconteur, and Jennifer – as she invited him to call her – was an art historian with a particular interest in the Impressionist school, who divided her time between Oxford and London, but also travelled as much as she could afford. Joining a tour was her only means of visiting Cuba. She spoke with obvious expertise but complete lack of pomposity about the influence of French painting on the canvases she had seen in the Havana museums. There were many more she hoped to see in Cienfuegos and, especially, in Baracoa, because of its proximity to Haiti. The mere mention of Haiti threatened to ruin Písemsky's increasingly relaxed mood, but as the trio moved from the bar to the à la carte restaurant, where he insisted on buying them dinner, together with two bottles of startlingly expensive French wine, he again thrust all thought of it from his mind. It was such a relief to be with genuinely intelligent and open-minded people intent on something other than simply making money by fair means or foul. There had been a time – Oh God! so long ago – when he would have shared their enthusiasm and aspirations. As they began a lively discussion of a literary competition of which he knew nothing, he felt a growing disquiet at the realisation of the curious byways down which he had himself strayed.

The group was moving off in the morning to Cienfuegos. More living out of a suitcase . . . As they parted, with profuse thanks for an excellent dinner and fascinating conversation, he was able to employ with complete sincerity the words that all too often became merely a routine formula: '*Spasíbo*,' he said, '*Spasíbo za kompániyu*. Thank you for your company.'

Reluctant to see them go, he was left with a feeling of despondency that was profoundly disturbing. Indeed, for the first time he felt cut off from his own kind, an exile. All right, in Moscow he had been a sort of internal exile, too, playing the system simply because it *was* the system, but here he was a stranger in a strange land, and this evening's brief contact with beings from the outside world had struck a chord of sadness that was new to him. He did not want to go back to his lonely villa; it wasn't really his, anyway. He was there just as much on sufferance as he had been in the Kutúzovsky apartment. But the most corrosively degrading emotion is self-pity, he told himself sternly, probably quoting someone, but he couldn't think who. And I'm not going to fall for that.

In an upstairs hall there was the sound of rhythmic music, punctuated with cries of *Olé!* or something of the sort, the kind of sound he would normally have run away from with all speed. But tonight it beckoned him; there would be people and laughter and warmth and company. He climbed the open wooden stairs to the second floor and marched boldly towards the sound of guitars, maracas and tapping feet. It was a cabaret show, featuring precisely the sort of concert performances or arrangements of recently invented 'traditional' folklore that was – had been? – so popular in official artistic circles in the Soviet Union. God knows, he'd had to sit through enough of those in his time. Phoney, of course, but colourful and gay. It was the done thing, he knew, among the purists, to pour scorn on such a genre, though in his deliberately limited experience the 'genuine article' might certainly be interesting but was rarely actually enjoyable. Tonight, in any case, was different. He entered and stood at the back of the hall. Suddenly, he became aware that a large man in a baseball cap was waving to him and pointing to an empty chair at the nearby table where his group was sitting.

'You wanna join us, Mac?'

I seem to be collecting strange names today, Písemsky thought, but he smiled gratefully. 'Thank you very much.'

There was a certain amount of shuffling of chairs and moving about of bottles and glasses to make room for him at the table, followed by friendly murmuring of strangely abbreviated names: Bud, Don, Ed, Marge, Dot, Liz.

'John,' he said, nodding to them collectively. Well, why not...

'Hi, Jaahn.'

'Glad to know ya, Jaahn.'

'Hi there,'

Without further ceremony a glass was placed before him. He raised it to eye level and nodded again to the group: 'Chin chin.'

'Chin-chin,' they replied, and resumed their previous chatting and laughing, accepting him now as one of them. The table was laden with bottles of seven-year-old Havana rum and cans of Coca Cola. No doubt he would be able to make a contribution at a suitable time.

Conversation with his neighbours began in the usual staccato fashion. He wasn't really very good at this, he realised, he had no small talk. But when he was asked where he came from, his bald reply 'Moscow' caused a flurry of interested comment bordering, indeed, on excitement. A further question about 'what's goin' down over there' provoked, as it invariably did, a torrent of opinion from everybody present except the one to whom it had been addressed. This he always found most convenient, since it enabled him, as it were, to get the feel of the meeting before having himself to make any sort of statement. It soon became obvious from what they all said that he would find little in common with them, so when his turn eventually came, he remarked simply that it was all very confusing.

'You can say that again!' they chorused, though not, he gathered, actually expecting him to do so. Funny habit, that.

To deflect further discussion and display polite reciprocal interest, he asked his neighbour where in Canada he lived.

'Traano,' he replied. 'You ever bin there?'

Písemsky did a sort of aural double-take.

'Toronto!' he exclaimed, sounding as though this were a startling item of information. 'No, I've never been to Canada. But I'm thinking of taking a trip there soon. To

Toronto, in fact.' This was news to him, too, but he always left doors open. You never knew...

As the music restarted and a new act began, the company fell silent and turned to watch, their faces eager with anticipation, lips faintly smiling and mouths half-open.

On the brightly illuminated centre stage a line of four women and four men, all dressed in brightly coloured, designer-traditional costumes, broke into a fast, raucous chorus, turning now to their partners on the right, now to the left, swaying and kicking in time with the music of guitars, maracas, claves, *guayo* and *tumba* voodoo drums, shrieking and ululating in skilfully simulated frenzy. The audience loved it.

Then the mood changed: the lights were dimmed, the men retreated several paces and the tempo of the music was transmuted to an insidiously erotic rhythm. Tiny spotlights caressed the coffee-brown bodies of the four women, clad now in only the narrowest of kerchiefs around their busts, straw skirts slung low from their hips, and phosphorescent G-strings in different colours. Their feet were bare. Slowly, almost imperceptibly at first, they began to sway their hips, then – as the tempo increased – faster and faster, gyrating in time with the throbbing beat, which rose in a crescendo and then fell away, only to rise again to a pulsating climax as the women's breasts bounced and swayed and their bare buttocks thrust and heaved, until it receded again to a gentle, trembling murmur. It was pure and unashamed sexual provocation, and the audience was both exhilarated and slightly shamefacedly provoked. As the music sank to an exhausted whisper and died, there was a hushed pause, followed by a storm of applause.

As the lights came up, Písemsky looked with fresh interest at the company in which he now found himself. There were perhaps 200 people grouped around the various tables, all of them, as far as he could judge, Canadians, and all resolutely intent on 'having a good time' and evidently succeeding. Without wishing in any way to criticise them – they had, after all, extended to him a warmth of welcome that was positively life-saving – he simply could not help observing how enormously fat, if not indeed grossly obese, so many of them were, especially the women. In Russia, women past a certain age became either lean and wiry or rather stout, but rarely had he seen the likes of these. They reminded him of the traditional Russian *matryóshki* wooden dolls which fit inside each other; they came in a variety of sizes, but they all had the same shape. This impression was reinforced by their penchant for dressing in garish tracksuits or tight trousers, which exaggerated their proportions, so that a rear view could properly be compared only with that of an agricultural mare. This was all very uncharitable and ungrateful, he knew, but did they never look at themselves in a mirror? The men, too, though generally taller and therefore more able to carry it, were almost equally overweight. As Písemsky looked at the couples at his table, their flushed faces bearing unmistakable traces of recent sexual arousal, he tried to imagine them in the act of making love. As far as he could see, it simply couldn't be done. Being himself also in a state of mild arousal, his thoughts turned not to Jina, but to Raya. My God, he said to himself, I'm getting maudlin. Damn Raya! How could she walk out on him like that, after all he'd done for her! Not a word of warning. Just a two-line note. . .With a sigh he rose to take his leave. 'Thank you, again, for your company.'

'You ever come through Traano be sure to call by,' his neighbour said, thrusting a business card into his hand.

'I surely will,' Písemsky replied. 'I surely will.'

At the time, of course, neither of them meant it.

Walking along the corridor to the stairs, Písemsky glanced at the card before stuffing into one of the many pockets of his Guayabera.

Macinaw Enterprises
Sports Installations and Equipment
*Toronto – Kingston – Gananoque*

*1003A Blair Avenue South*          *tel: Toronto 179 638 4444-9*
*Toronto, Ontario S5V 3S8*

He reached the head of the stairs and descended into the middle of a group of exhausted-looking new arrivals, glassy-eyed and laden with baggage. They were speaking Russian. It was music to his ears, but he slunk away.

# 9

To Písemsky's surprise, waiting impatiently in the darkness outside the main entrance to the hotel was Miguel. Písemsky's objections that he had undertaken to find his own way back were brushed peremptorily aside.

'Señor Pérez wanna talk. He call much times.'

He waved towards the limousine, parked beneath a palm tree in the drive. There was a woman in the front passenger seat. Písemsky's heart missed a beat. Jina? But no, it was a large African-looking woman, Miguel's wife.

Feeling unaccountably like a naughty schoolboy who had stayed out too late, he climbed into the back seat. Not a further word was spoken as they returned to the villa.

At the entrance, the security light flicked on and Miguel's wife keyed in the code to open the tall wrought-iron gate. They drove rapidly to the front door, stopping only long enough for Písemsky to alight before moving off again to the garage.

As Písemsky let himself into the house, the telephone was ringing. To his surprise, it did not stop as soon as he reached it. He picked up the receiver.

'*Alyô?*'

Pérez was clearly in a state of some agitation. There was no preliminary greeting.

'Have you heard the news?'

'No. What news?'

'Listen to the radio. I'll be with you at eight thirty for

90

breakfast. Warn Dora.' He rang off.

Mystified, Písemsky switched on the television in the dining room. All stations had ceased broadcasting for the night. He went up to his bedroom and turned on the bedside radio, which was permanently tuned to the BBC World Service. Like all British expatriates and most thinking English-speakers throughout the world, he relied on this station for credible news, and prayed every night that an uninformed and insensitive government would not carry out the threat to cut it back.

. . . '*still not quite clear what the precise current situation is. Mr Gorbachóv has been on holiday with his wife Raísa at the presidential dacha in the Crimea, where he is said to be suffering from nervous exhaustion, making him unable to continue his official duties. A State of Emergency has been declared, administered by a committee which is known to include the Prime Minister, Mr Valentín Pávlov; the Defence Minister, Marshal Dmítri Yázov; the Vice-President, Mr Gennádi Yanáyev; and the KGB Chairman, Mr Vladímir Kryuchkóv. All newspapers and other media channels have been taken under central control...*'

The BBC special correspondent in Moscow had little firm news to add. Tanks had been seen on the streets of the capital, and rumours abounded: Gorbachóv had been brought back to Moscow in chains; Raísa Gorbachóva had died of a heart attack; troops loyal to the President were converging on Moscow; etc. etc. Moscow must be one of the world's greatest rumour factories. Everyone recognised the formula of 'ill health' as signifying a *coup d'état,* and heads were shaken at Gorbachóv's foolishness in leaving the Kremlin at such a difficult moment. It was all a classic case, and could easily have been foreseen. The fact that none of the pundits actually had foreseen it was tactfully not mentioned.

What did it all mean? Pávlov was a sort of Mossadeq figure who took to his bed at the first sign of trouble; Yanáyev was a drunkard, normally incapable of rational thought after about midday; Yázov was a bit of a blusterer, rather in the Perdéyev mould: if he had agreed to take part in such a dubious manoeuvre, it must have been with painful misgivings;

91

only Kryuchkóv was something of an unknown, but the KGB – as Písemsky knew only too well – was universally reviled and hardly likely to be allowed to resume its former activities. None of them had anything like the stature of Mikhaíl Gorbachóv or, for that matter, of Borís Yéltsin. It was all very puzzling, and Písemsky really did not know how to interpret it.

He was, however, called upon to give a considered analysis at breakfast that morning, where he was joined not only by Pérez but by his shadow, Macías, too. With his usual fertile inventiveness, he rose to the occasion, managing almost to claim some role in the affair.

Realising that his companions were concerned not so much with the fate of nations as with the safety of their own nefarious plans, Písemsky began with only a brief analysis of the political events, trying to invest his pronouncements with rather more confidence than he actually felt, as though he, too, found it all quite predictable. It was a question, as far as the party was concerned, of 'heads I win, tails you lose', but with the party on the losing side. He doubted whether the coup would be successful, both because of the personalities involved and because most of the population, while having little time now for Gorbachóv, would not want to see the President deposed in such a crude fashion. And if it failed, he foresaw two consequences: first, the party would lose what was left of its credibility, both inside the country and internationally; and second, Gorbachóv would nevertheless have lost what little authority he had still retained. He hinted that he and Khúyin had seen all this coming, which was why they had set up the original scheme with such haste and planned for a change of *modus operandi* (he liked his Latin tags) after August the first. Rather neat, that, he told himself, and possibly even partly true!

'But what about the military?' Macías asked. 'What will the army do?'

'Good question!' What they had to remember was that the Soviet Union was now in a state of rapid disintegration, and nowhere did this cause more chaos than in the armed forces, which were breaking up into national armies, some even ready to fight each other. Couple that with the end of the cold war and the hasty withdrawal of Soviet forces from Eastern Europe and the Baltic States – almost being chased out, in some cases – and it became obvious that no one was now in overall command and able to take any decisive action. That, after all, was precisely the scenario that he and Khúyin – and, indeed, Pérez (better keep him sweet) – had taken as their premiss when they had laid their plans.

'So nothing has really changed,' Pérez contributed.

'Not as far as we are concerned. I suppose if things go as I expect them to, more authority will devolve on the Congress of People's Deputies and the Supreme Soviet. And here the nigger in the woodpile (sorry! the joker in the pack) will continue to be Yéltsin.' He paused for a moment.

'Still,' he went on airily, 'I have no doubt that People's Deputy Khúyin will have that well under control. A man with his influence...'

For the next hour, Pérez and Macías discussed Písemsky's analysis, putting various questions and receiving blandly reassuring replies. They could find no real fault in his argument: his guess, after all, was not just as good as theirs, but better. They turned therefore to a consideration of what effect the new developments might have on their immediate plans.

It was agreed that Písemsky should consult as soon as possible with Khúyin, and Pérez undertook to arrange a telephone conference with Moscow at the ministry in Havana the following day. They also thought it wise to expedite the fulfilment of their current programme in several ways.

Firstly, although they did not doubt Písemsky's assurance that little would change, at least in the near future, they decided to enlarge their stock of arms as quickly as possible. Písemsky would discuss this with Khúyin when they spoke.

Secondly, they would instruct the Major to bring forward his present arrangements for transferring some of the 'merchandise' to Baracoa and thence to Haiti.

Thirdly, Pérez would take whatever steps he could to

ensure prompt advance payment, so that in case of emergency there would be no bad debts.

Finally, Macías would bring forward his proposed tour of South America in search of further customers.

A final session with TV and radio brought no further news of any significance and by midday Pérez and Macías had departed, leaving Písemsky in a state of near prostration and badly in need of a large shot of vodka.

Somewhere in his subconscious was the uneasy thought that whether or not his hearers believed him, he was always able to convince himself.

When Jina arrived at three o'clock, Písemsky was in a distracted mood and was about to send her away when, with a knowing look, she forestalled him:

'Hokay. Today I make you love, Cuban style. Come'

Betraying an easy familiarity with the layout of the villa, she led him by the hand to his bedroom, removed her shoes and two other items of clothing, and lay down on her stomach on the bed. He'd been right about her bottom. In a state of something like shock, he mechanically took off his own clothes and lay down beside her, reaching to embrace her.

'No,' she said. 'You jus' lie still. I do this.'

As he lay on his back, she knelt beside him and began gently running her fingers through his hair, massaging his temples, probing in the soft places behind his ears and moving her fingers slowly over his forehead, his cheekbones, his lips and his chin, like a sightless person memorising them. Astride him now at the waist, she leaned forward and moved her shoulders slowly from side to side, so that the tips of her breasts brushed his mouth, giggling as he struggled to catch each nipple in his lips. I like this game, he thought.

Tenderly, her hands moved over his neck and shoulders, down his arms to the fingertips and back again to his armpits, as the tip of her tongue traced a pattern on his chest and stomach until it came to rest in his umbilicus, a strangely uncomfortable sensation. She moved her knees down to a level with his, and as her hands continued to outline his waist and hips, she took the glans of his penis in her mouth, probed it with her tongue and slowly released it, grating it with her teeth as she did so.

Ouch!

She was softly massaging his scrotum now, then she took his left testicle into her fingers and held it playfully between her teeth.

God, I hope she's not hungry!

On hands and knees she hovered, poised above his towering erection, then with a slow, smoothly plunging motion she impaled herself on it.

Gotcha!

For a moment she remained motionless, then began almost imperceptibly to revolve her pelvis, gradually increasing the tempo and subtly modulating the rhythm.

What, no music?

He surrendered himself to sensual pleasure as twice she led him up to the point of orgasm and then gently down again. When he approached this point for the third time, knowing that he could hold out no longer, she turned smoothly about so that her back was now toward him, leaned forward to support herself, and with a series of savage, stabbing thrusts brought them both to a simultaneous climax, in which his own groans of pleasure-pain mingled with her throaty exclamations in Spanish and Russian.

Bravo! He half-expected a round of applause.

They lay for a while side by side on the huge bed, her hand clutching his but their bodies otherwise not touching. Gradually his breathing returned to normal and his heart resumed a steady beat. At length, for the first time, he spoke.

'Why did you call me Kóstya?'

From her sharp intake of breath he knew that for a second she was disconcerted, but she replied calmly: 'Because you are very like my ol' frien' Kóstya. 'Eesa Russian writer.'

He pondered this news. A Russian writer called Kóstya? There must be a million of them. But perhaps this one was different.

'Is he a good writer?'

'Mm-mm-mm . . .' the rumble of appreciation came from somewhere deep inside her. ' 'Ees very good!'

With a husky chuckle, she swung her shapely legs over the side of the bed and reached for her clothes.

'But I dunno 'bout 'is writin'!'

After Jina had left, Písemsky remained lying on his back. He felt the glow of physical satisfaction give way to the stealthy onset of post-coital *tristesse*, which was creeping over him much as incipient hangover stealthily displaces the alcoholic exhilaration of lunchtime wine.

I suppose that's what the Americans mean by getting laid.

He watched how the sunlight reflected from the pool broke through the slats in the window blind and drew dappled beams across the ceiling above his head.

She was just using me.

A light breeze swayed the blinds, making the beams dance.

I'm just a sex object.

He stretched his arms and legs as hard as he could, as though trying to wrench them from their sockets. Then he rolled onto his side and drew up his knees in foetal position, composing himself for sleep.

Lovely!

He was awoken an hour later by a call from Pérez. Khúyin was out of Moscow for a while. No one knew how long. They'd have to contact him later.

Since his desire to ask Khúyin several pertinent questions was outdone by his anxiety at what the answers might be, he thought he could live with this. 'Fine,' he said. 'Just let me know when you've arranged something.'

Pérez was in a more relaxed mood. 'How are your Spanish lessons going? Do you approve of your teacher?'

'Oh, I think I can say I've learned a thing or two.'

Pérez chuckled. 'Well, the good news is that the Odessa shipment is due in Cienfuegos in three days. Do you want to be there when it arrives?'

He did indeed. Indeed he did.

# 10

Písemsky's holiday by the sea was coming to a close. The period of waiting would end when the Odessa shipment was safely locked away, but there was much to do even before then and, as is usual after a period of enforced idleness, he would now have to move fast. The prospect was by no means unwelcome; he had never been one for sitting around doing nothing, though the past weeks had made him wonder whether that, too, would not become easier with a little practice.

The projected meeting with Pérez, Macías and the Major was scheduled for the next day, and though there was little that Písemsky could do in the way of preparation, he could not resist a feeling of apprehension, which was intensified by the news that there would be a further participant in the meeting, described enigmatically to him as a 'friend'. In the event, the proceedings went more smoothly than he had dared hope, partly because the most important decisions had already been made at their breakfast session, partly because the Major was not involved in policy-making so much as in carrying out orders, and finally, because the 'friend' turned out to be a client from Haiti, in whose presence, of course, they could allow no note of indecision or doubt.

Introduced simply as Duvalier ('No relation!'), he was a dapper little man who was most at home in French, which Písemsky understood quite well and spoke adequately for the purpose, but he also used an island patois that Písemsky found largely impenetrable, though his colleagues not only understood it but spoke it themselves. The scope for errors of communication, Písemsky thought, was enormous, but as far as he could tell, they did not occur. It was quite a relief for him to speak Russian with the Major.

Any impression of mildness evoked by Duvalier's appearance was quickly dispelled when he spoke. He was uncompromising in his demands, both in types of arms required and in schedules for delivery. But as Pérez had predicted, there was no problem with finances. Payments would be made in dollars, 100,000 in used notes being handed over by Duvalier to Pérez on the spot as an initial instalment. If the first shipment proved satisfactory, Duvalier said, there would be a further order almost immediately. The contents, however, would be quite different.

'We shall never gain our objectives,' Duvalier said, 'until we can destroy the government's helicopter fleet.' Ground-to-air missiles and launchers, plus the services of expert instructors, would be required.

This last added a new dimension, and there was some discussion with the Major about the availability of appropriate personnel. The task force as presently constituted had not been planned to cover such activities but, as ever, there would be 'no problem' in recruiting the requisite experts. Discussion of logistic matters passed largely over Písemsky's head: all this had never been more than peripheral to his personal plans, and he found his attention wandering. He was jolted out of his reverie by direct questioning from Duvalier about events in Moscow, upon which he gave his usual bland responses, once again stressing for the 'friend's' information that there would be no difficulty in obtaining any items of military hardware his colleagues might require, and receiving a disconcertingly penetrating stare in return.

At midday, when the meeting broke up, Písemsky invited the Major to remain for a while to discuss arrangements in Cienfuegos over a beer and a cigarette. In fact, the Major neither drank nor smoked, but was pleased to have the opportunity to relax and chat in Russian, eventually sharing a light lunch.

They discussed the disintegration of the Soviet Union and found common attitudes to the people at the top. The Major had watched the Gorbachóv period from afar, assessing it in terms not far removed from those used by Perdéyev. Písemsky expressed total agreement, and building on this newly established rapport, he led the conversation round to the Odessa shipment and the proposed plans for its reception at Cienfuegos and transportation to Trinidad de Cuba. He was impressed by the arrangements the Major outlined, and said so in the most fulsome terms, registering, to his own interest, that if they had been speaking in English he would not have been able to do this to quite the same extent. From this point it was easy enough to explain that some crates of Bolshói ballet costumes etc., plus a few of his own personal possessions, would be arriving as part of the shipment. One of them he hoped to have stored at the Tomás Terry theatre in Cienfuegos, and the other at the García Lórca in Havana. A request for assistance with transportation, couched in terms of asking for advice, elicited the desired response: Leave it to the Major. It was agreed that Písemsky would be collected by helicopter on the following morning, giving him time to make his private arrangements in Cienfuegos before the shipment arrived. After lunch, the Major returned to Havana.

Jina found Písemsky in an unusually flippant mood. After a half-hour's desultory conversation practice, during which he was clearly not concentrating on the matter in hand, he suddenly jumped to his feet.

'Come on,' he said, 'today it's my turn.'

Whether his lovemaking was Russian style or not, no one enquired. But it was most enjoyable, and though she called him many names, not one of them was Kóstya.

The Director of Ballet at the Tomás Terry theatre, a magnificent early nineteenth-century building that because of its provincial location had mercifully escaped the attentions of modernisers and improvers, was a diminutive gentleman called Roberto Guevara. Standing hardly more than 5 feet tall, he had a completely bald head and, as if by way of compensation, a curly black beard. From a distance, Písemsky thought, he looked rather as if he had his head on upside down. Also, perhaps as a counter to his lack of stature, he wore large, polished jackboots in the Russian *sapogí* style. Shiny black and sharply pointed, they seemed when he walked to have a life of their own and to be taking him where they themselves wanted to go, rather than being directed by him. Písemsky was reminded of a dancer in one of the émigré Don Cossack groups that he had once seen perform in London. This dancer – was he called Sergéi something? – had also been so tiny that it seemed unlikely at first glance that he would be able to negotiate the theatre staircase, but his boots had carried him into extraordinary leaps and gyrations that inspired an audience that mistook gymnastics for dancing into ecstasies of acclamation. When Písemsky was talking with Roberto Guevara, he kept half-expecting him to break into a *gopák*.

He was, however, an informed and vastly entertaining conversationalist whose knowledge of local history and artistic traditions, as well as of art in a larger context, he was so eager to display that for the first half-hour of their meeting, Písemsky hardly got in a word. Písemsky played the willing audience, thus immediately winning Guevara's respect and regard, so that when, eventually, he led the conversation round to the object of his visit, the battle was already won.

He had never met anyone whose use of gesticulation and facial expressions to emphasise meaning was quite so extensive and, he had to admit, effective. Guevara spoke in Spanish, and every pronouncement, accompanied by a drawing back of the lips in what in other circumstances would have been a snarl, displaying tiny, regular, pearly white teeth, was somehow drawn from his mouth with second finger and thumb, almost as though he were pulling it out on a continuous string. Písemsky later swore that he had not so much heard Guevara's utterances as read them, as they hung momentarily in the air between his lips and fingertips. At all events, he understood them and contrived, restraining himself only with difficulty from aping Guevara's gestures, to make appropriate responses. But Guevara, it transpired, was also quite able to communicate in English (which he spoke with his hands more or less in his pockets), so that the danger of misunderstanding was removed.

The ground had been well prepared by Señora Gómez, who had already informed Guevara of Písemsky's mission. Parallel arrangements with those agreed in Havana were quickly made, and Guevara accepted with alacrity Písemsky's invitation to a meal where the local people ate. In fact, the best food was available only where tourist parties were entertained, but Guevara had entrée there: 'Eating, too,' he grinned, 'is an art form.'

The restaurant was in a former colonial residence some distance outside the town, reached after unlikely meanderings on dirt roads by the only taxi still in use. Its driver, declining an invitation to join them, disappeared into the bar; it was a moot point which of them would be the drunkest by the end of the evening, or whether any of the others would be sober enough to notice.

They also began the evening in the bar, where everyone knew Guevara, whom they treated with courtesy and gentleness, while furtively raising their eyebrows over their glasses and grinning knowingly at Písemsky. As a Russian, he was welcomed, if without particular warmth, and he chose to merge as much as possible with the background rather than to attempt to shine. Hogging the conversation when Guevara was present would in any case have been beyond most men.

When they moved to a table on the terrace, they looked out onto a virtual wall of green, in which the broad leaves of bananas and serrated fronds of coconut palms merged with the bougainvilleas and oleanders in one solid mass, through which the royal palms soared almost out of sight above their heads like the columns of a vast cathedral. The inevitable *trovatóres* appeared, but at Guevara's prompting, in place of *Guantánamera* they sang ancient Spanish troubadour

101

romances and Spanish–French *punto campesino*, as well as playing a jazz blues *trovin* that had the entire clientele of the restaurant and bar swaying and tapping their feet. Písemsky was impressed by the delight the musicians took in being asked to play what they would no doubt have called 'real' music, and he watched in fascination as Guevara – reduced at last to silence – followed with rapt attention, nodding in approval at particularly felicitous passages and occasionally allowing the shadow of a frown to flit across his brow at a false note or stutter in the beat, noticed by him alone. He whispered occasional explanatory comments, but in general let the music speak for itself. At the end of their concert the musicians made to move to another table and Písemsky was reaching for his wallet when he felt Guevara's restraining fingers on his wrist. 'If you want to add a little when you pay the bill, that will be fine, but don't insult them by offering anything now. That was not tourist stuff they were playing.'

At Písemsky's bidding, the choice of dishes was made by Guevara, after much discussion and gesticulation with the waiter and in the kitchen with the chef. '*Es un hombre muy importante,*' he heard, '*muy simpatico.*' He pretended not to notice.

They began with fruit, a mixture of guava, papaya and orange, followed by a thick ajiaco vegetable soup made of yuca, turnip, carrot, malanga and herbs, combining to form flavours quite unique in his experience. I don't think even Márfa Timoféyevna could better this, he thought, to his own surprise. Strange how in unguarded moments his mind was increasingly often turning to Russia, as if he had been on holiday long enough and it was time now to go home. He shrugged the thought away.

Determined that his important guest should sample as many of the delights of Cuban cuisine as possible, Guevara insisted also on a small swordfish steak before tackling the main course of the meal, roast pork with black beans and a side salad of cabbage and cucumber. Fortunately, the meal was spread over several hours, with lengthy breaks for music between courses, so that Písemsky did ample justice to each dish without torturing his stomach, even managing a large portion of *Tatianoff* chocolate cake (with a name like that he could not refuse it) and just a taste of grated coconut and cheese in syrup, probably lethal but quite superb.

Having started the evening with the inevitable *mojíto* – properly served with cracked ice, sugar, lime juice and crushed mint, with light Havana Club rum topped up with soda water (Písemsky successfully avoided *Cuba libre,* he hated Coca Cola even when it was renamed Tropicola), they continued for some time with more of the same, before moving on to beer – no wine was even on offer – and after the meal, in honour of the Russian guest, a little ice-cold vodka with the compliments of the chef, and tiny cups of delicious Cuban coffee. It was at this point that Písemsky embarked on a habit that was soon to take him firmly in its grip – the smoking of Havana cigars.

The end of the evening was somewhat confused when Písemsky thought back on it the following morning. It had been a feast in more ways than one, and equally in more than one sense he was suffering from indigestion.

'Today,' he murmured as he shaved a distinctly off-colour visage, 'I definitely got squeasy tummy.'

The vessel bringing the arms and other cargo was due to dock at about midday, which gave Písemsky an hour or so to spend at leisure before the excitement began. He strolled from the Jagua hotel along the Malecon promenade to the Martí park, hoping to see the interior of the cathedral, whose pink dome he had admired from the roof of the Tomás Terry theatre on the previous evening, but it was closed, so he crossed instead into the park and settled on a bench by the Triumphal Arch. For a while he dozed in the sunshine, now pleasantly warm. In an hour or so it would drive everyone into the shade of the palms.

Today, he mused, is the first day of the rest of my life. *Today I become a thief!*

He stirred uneasily at this thought. Well, he reasoned, not really. It's not as if I were going to break into someone's house and steal their personal belongings. I would never contemplate doing anything like that. The pictures in this collection, after all, have probably been stolen at least twice already and then hidden away. It's only right that the public should have the opportunity to see them. I'll really be doing everyone a favour, won't I? And as for the ikons, well, I've seen the documents on their provenance, and it's pretty obvious that no one knows where half of them came from anyway. As far as I can see, they don't really belong to anyone in particular. Whoever I sell them to will know their real worth and look after them – probably a lot better than anyone in Russia would at the moment...

Inevitably, after further indulgence in such devious rationalisation, the Mochítsky method triumphed yet again, and Písemsky, the cultural benefactor, was ready to get to work.

He returned to his hotel, where the Major picked him up at 11.30 and drove him down to the Bahia de Cienfuegos, which in colonial times had afforded shelter to the Spanish galleons, especially after the completion of the Jagua Castle in 1745, to protect them against marauding pirates. A small fleet of tarpaulin-covered Soviet army lorries lined the quay as the ship successfully docked, and without any formalities the unloading began.

Písemsky quickly identified his two anonymous crates, which were carefully transferred to a Toyota pick-up for transportation to the theatre, where they would remain for the night. The Major's men would then convey one of them by air to Havana and thence to the García Lórca theatre. Písemsky would accompany it, being met at the theatre by Miguel and subsequently driven back to Varadero.

At the Tomás Terry, where Roberto Guevara had made his promised arrangements, though mercifully he was not himself in evidence, Písemsky was left, at his own request, to check the inventory. He later returned to the Jagua hotel bearing a locked briefcase. Like clockwork! Wonderful!

In the bar at the Jagua, a group of tourists of mixed nationality were standing around the television, paying more than usual attention and punctuating their viewing with excited comments. Even from the reception desk, which was some distance away, Písemsky recognized the burly figure of Yéltsin. Hurriedly claiming his key, he rushed to his room and switched on the TV. It was there, during the next 12 hours, that he learned the history, somewhat out of phase with real time, of the abortive Moscow coup.

Písemsky watched with rapidly changing emotions the films and reports of correspondents from various countries. He saw that Pávlov had indeed taken to his bed; that Yanáyev had been too drunk to speak coherently at the news conference; that Yázov had confessed to being an 'old fool'. Much as he had predicted, so far. He saw how Rutskói – in his opinion the best of that bunch – had been dispatched to the Crimea to escort back the shattered President: whether Gorbachóv had been suffering from nervous exhaustion originally, he did not know, but he certainly looked as if he were now.

But what startled Písemsky, as it had so many others, was the image of Yéltsin posturing defiantly on a tank before the Moscow White House, surrounded by an ocean of ecstatically cheering supporters. And even in the flickering, snowy picture on the ancient black and white screen, Písemsky could not mistake the smoothly smiling figure in the background, waving at the camera: Geórgy Khúyin . . .

Having satisfactorily completed his dispositions at the theatre, Písemsky had a brief meeting in Havana with Pérez and Macías to discuss the news from Moscow. Modestly reminding them that he had forecast it all with considerable accuracy (which was more or less true), he impressed them even more deeply when he told them about Khúyin's 'close standing' (pretty neat, that!) with Yéltsin, managing also to associate himself in it.

'We could see which way the wind was blowing,' he said, and quoted an old Russian proverb for Pérez's benefit, but the Cuban's command of the language did not extend as far as such niceties. 'You know – "From where the wind comes, happiness comes".' He grinned: in his gung-ho mood he came near to teasing.

Pérez, however, had the last laugh. As Písemsky walked towards his car, where Miguel sat waiting to drive him to Varadero, he accompanied him until they were out of earshot of Macías.

'By the way,' he said, 'we pulled our boy off keeping an eye on you when you went to Varadero. But I have a message for you from the Major: he doesn't know who it is, but there is still someone following you. Would you like the Major to put a stop to it?'

Písemsky reflected for a moment. 'He must do what he thinks fit,' he replied. 'It's really nothing to do with me, is it?'

# RUSSIAN
# INTERLUDE

# 11

As events in Moscow quickened their pace, Márfa Timoféyevna broke the long-established pattern of her life and acquired both a telephone and a TV set. If the world was to become more to her liking, she wanted again to be part of it. Thus it was that in that same sequence of TV newsreel that had startled her husband in Cienfuegos, she recognised not only the egregious Khúyin but another familiar figure, a person of no eminence but whose presence in that context gave her the greatest pleasure, so much, indeed, that she was prompted at last to take a step that she had been contemplating for several months.

Her letter lay unnoticed for three days until Zoya, who had at first been camping in the parliament White House and then sleeping on a friend's floor, returned at last to the flat off the Mokhováya for a leisurely shower, a change of clothing and a few hours of much-needed sleep. When she entered the tiny hall, she tossed the envelope incuriously onto the table, and it was only an hour later, as she was about to get into bed, that she remembered it. Groaning with fatigue, she padded reluctantly across to the hall and retrieved it, settling this time under the blankets, with her head on the pillow. She raised the envelope to her eyes and studied it; it was addressed in a bold, slightly old-fashioned hand and had a Moscow district postmark. Contrary to custom, the panel for details of the addressee had been left blank, except for the barest details: *Sokolóva, Polevóye Seló.*

This meant nothing to her.

Curious now, Zoya neatly slit the envelope open and found a short, businesslike, but most remarkable note:

> *You do not know me,* she read, *though I feel I know you very well. I am your father's wife.*
>
> *We are both now virtually alone, and it seems from your recent activities that we may well have much in common . . .*

There followed a courteously informal invitation to Zoya to visit Márfa Timoféyevna at the family dacha, the location of which was described in much the same terms as Mochítsky had used, but with an important addition:

> *I will put up a sign at the end of the track,* it said, *so that you will know where to turn off the Tula road.*

Márfa Timoféyevna's new telephone number was given, with a suggestion that Zoya would ring to confirm a date and time when it would be convenient for her to visit.

By writing rather than telephoning, Márfa Timoféyevna had given Zoya a clear choice of options, avoiding the possible embarrassment of confrontation, even of a telephonic kind, and the phrasing of the note had equally avoided any sense of conveying a summons. The decision was Zoya's.

In a state of something approaching shock, Zoya decided to sleep on it. But as she eventually surrendered to her fatigue, she knew that she would go.

Márfa Timoféyevna was standing on the veranda waiting to greet her. As Zoya approached, she looked with great interest at this newly discovered stranger, her father's wife.

She saw a greying-haired lady in her early fifties, wearing a tasteful but unpretentious blouse and skirt, in complete contrast to the black, peasant weeds that she had always donned as part of her 'wrinkled retainer' act for Mochítsky's business meals. Her hair was tugged back in a bun, revealing a gently weatherbeaten face, with a network of crow's feet wrinkles from the corners of her eyes and the beginnings of furrowed lines at her mouth and chin. She had a very Russian face, wide and slightly flat, with high cheekbones and cornflower-blue eyes, undimmed, as yet, by advancing years. She had partaken too often of her own superb cooking to retain her former slim figure, but neither had she allowed it to thicken out of control. Perhaps 'comfortable' was the right word. But it was her voice that captivated: that low contralto that comes from deep in the chest – not breathy or pharyngal, like the whine of Prague Czechs, nor shrill like the rasp of the southern English middle classes or uptown New Yorkers; the Russians call it *grudnói* – from a word that can mean 'breast' as well as 'chest', and indeed, such a voice has a nuance of sexuality that can excite, no matter what commonplaces it may utter.

Her smile of welcome lit up her whole face as she held out her hand in greeting: 'My dear Zoya, how very kind of you to come.'

Having wondered throughout her taxi journey from Moscow about the wisdom of coming at all, and having not known quite what to expect when she arrived, Zoya was completely disarmed. She found herself smiling warmly in response and saying how grateful she was to have been invited – all of which was quite genuine and totally unrehearsed. She was charmed, too, by the ambience and soon found herself being given a guided tour of the garden and the dacha, including the kitchen – a rare privilege. She surprised Márfa Timoféyevna by her knowledge of wild fruit and herbs, acquired at a succession of Pioneer and Young Communist summer camps, and soon the two women were chatting and exchanging ideas like old acquaintances. At length, they installed themselves at the table on the veranda with tea, jam, and home-made cakes and biscuits which evoked mumbles of rapture from Zoya, her mouth too full to articulate clearly her delight and appreciation.

'I expect you were surprised to get my note.' Márfa Timoféyevna brought the conversation round to a more serious topic. This was more a statement than an enquiry, and Zoya simply nodded. 'I'd been thinking about getting in touch with you ever since your mother and father left the country,' she continued, 'and when I saw you on television at the White House, I couldn't resist any longer.'

Zoya remained silent, having become a little tense at the mention of her parents. She would let Márfa Timoféyevna have her say before deciding what her reaction would be.

'I never actually met your mother,' Márfa Timoféyevna went on, 'just as I have never actually met you either until today. But I have been following your career with some interest...'

At this, Zoya betrayed open surprise, and there was a pause in Márfa Timoféyevna's monologue.

'I have never had a child of my own,' she said quietly, as though speaking really to herself, 'so you see...' Her hands moved upwards in a sort of shrug. Then she visibly took herself under control and continued almost brusquely: 'So now I have met you, at last, and I'm very glad to have done so. I hope we shall become friends.'

Again Zoya nodded, but this time she spoke. 'I am glad, too. I really did not know what to expect you to be like, but now that I know you, I am delighted that you wrote to me.'

Each felt that she was approaching dangerous ground; there was so much that could but perhaps ought not to be said, aspects of their tenuous relationship best left unexplored, judgements left not articulated, emotions not released. They began, instead, to talk about political developments, on which Zoya took fire and was halted only by the sight of an unmistakable twinkle in Márfa Timoféyevna's eyes. Was she laughing at her?

Sensing what was passing through Zoya's mind, her hostess took great care to dispel any misapprehensions. 'I envy you your energy and enthusiasm,' she said. 'We do so need young people like you. My generation made so many mistakes, not so much in what we did as in what we didn't do. We knew much of what was really happening all around us, but we played the game by the rules that were dictated to us and did not ask too many questions. There are difficult times ahead;

112

the real battle is only just beginning. Not everything we did was bad; not everyone was corrupt and vicious. We need now to preserve what was good and build upon it. It's so sad that words like ideals, principles or vision have been so debased. We need a new terminology in which to formulate the philosophy of the new order we are supposed to be building. No lasting good will come from simply exchanging one ready-made ideology for another. From the corruption of the command economy to the debased morals of the market place can hardly be called progress. We need to move forward, not backward in time...'

Now it was Zoya who was smiling, and Márfa Timoféyevna cut short her tirade and began to laugh. Then she changed the subject abruptly.

'Have you heard from your father?'

Zoya was equally direct. 'No, and I don't expect to.' The look on her face showed a desire not to continue this topic, but Márfa Timoféyevna ignored it.

'Don't be too hard on him,' she said gently. 'He is not a wicked man. Weak, perhaps, and devious in his ways, but he is not a wicked man.'

For a moment they were both silent. Then, almost as though talking to herself, Márfa Timoféyevna went on: 'What fun he was when we were young!' She emphasised the word 'fun' and her face again lit up. 'What a sense of humour he had! Wherever he went there was laughter. And such a voice! As students we would picnic by the stream and sing all night, and...' She seemed lost in a world of her own, a world that Zoya found it impossible to enter.

'I don't know what went wrong,' Márfa Timoféyevna was saying. 'He seemed to enjoy his life, at least at first. He had his disappointments, of course, most of them probably deserved, but I don't think there was any one great traumatic event... Then gradually he changed, until he became almost a stranger to me.'

Zoya said nothing, her face remained closed, but Márfa Timoféyevna persisted: 'We are all – people of my generation, I mean – infected in some way. We have a sort of inherent inability to resist any opportunity to gain advantage, however unworthy, that comes our way. And even worse, we can rationalise our behaviour in such a way that the responsibility for our actions is somehow not our own. It is always someone else who is to blame ...'

Her voice tailed off, and again she changed the subject. 'How is your mother?' she asked. 'Has she written to you?'

Zoya's expression softened: 'Oh yes, several times. She is well and glad to be back in what she calls home.' Again there was a pause, until Zoya continued: 'She's given me quite a lot of news about my father. He seems to be in Cuba, keeping what she calls "bad company", something to do with selling arms.' It was her turn to become lost in thought, as Márfa Timoféyevna sat motionless beside her. 'It's funny,' Zoya said, 'how well informed she is about what he is doing. I don't understand how she knows. I asked her about this in my last letter, but that was some time ago, and she hasn't answered. And the other day, when I tried to ring her I could swear I heard someone saying that "Captain Takasc" was away on a mission. I don't know much Hebrew, of course, so I don't really know what they were saying. I probably got it all wrong. They can't have meant my mother.'

Márfa Timoféyevna looked at her sharply, but Zoya was still engrossed in her own thoughts.

'I see,' she said softly. 'Now I understand.'

To the delight of each and the great surprise of Zoya, friendship between her and Márfa Timoféyevna blossomed apace. Drawn together in a sympathetic relationship which, paradoxically, had been engendered by circumstances to their mutual detriment, they effortlessly bridged the generation gap, finding a complementary, if not identical, attitude to contemporary affairs and managing with a minimum of misunderstanding to speak the same language. Over a remarkably short period a genuine affection grew up between them, and Zoya took to visiting the dacha whenever her busy timetable allowed.

On one such visit she was introduced to the pathway from

the Tula road up to the grove above the dacha, and Márfa Timoféyevna again spoke with unmistakable tenderness of Mochítsky as a young man and of his rapturous reaction to the first view of it. '*Beryóza*,' he had said only half in jest, 'the silver birch, eternal Russia!'

Zoya, too, was thrilled at the sight and made a point of taking that route from time to time. It was only when she saw the silver birch grove that she ever thought of Mochítsky, whose very existence she otherwise did not recognise.

# THE
# CULTURAL
# BENEFACTOR

# 12

Písemsky returned from Havana to Varadero in a state of high nervous tension. On the one hand, phase two of his action plan – retrieval and storage of the two crates – had been satisfactorily concluded, and a first selection of the contents of each was currently 'burning a hole' in his briefcase. But on the other hand, someone was still watching his every move. Who the devil could it be? The fact that Pérez did not know who it was probably ruled out a whole list of potential candidates: the Cuban authorities, exiled Cuban organisations, the CIA, all of whom might in their own terms have a legitimate interest in what he and Pérez were up to. As for the KGB, it was a broken reed: its operatives might still go on working until someone actually got round to telling them to stop, but he would surely have recognised their style. In fact, to be brutally frank, someone would have tried strong-arming him by now. So he came back to the same old question: Who else could it be? The obvious way to find out was to try a bit of rough stuff himself, but that was simply not his way; he was not that sort of man. Well, I certainly didn't encourage the Major to use violence, Písemsky quickly reassured himself, but if he does take it upon himself to 'look after' whoever it is, there's no way I can stop him, is there? After all, his head may be on the block, too. He'd be protecting all of us, not just me.

When he entered the villa, Písemsky immediately poured himself a half-tumbler of vodka, which he drank in one gulp –

with hardly a blink of the eye. He then locked the precious briefcase securely in his bedroom cupboard, closed the windows, locked the door, returned downstairs and took the bottle and glass outside on the terrace. Lying back in a cane rocking chair, he lit a cigar, sipped his vodka and thought over his plans for the next step: phase three – beginning the sale.

His talks in Paris and London on his way from Moscow to Cuba had of necessity been coded almost to the point of incomprehensibility, but the message had seemed to be that the sale of art treasures by anonymous vendors was by no means unusual: many reputedly wealthy people had in fact been selling off the family silver for years. For a reasonable consideration, art dealers could often find private pur-chasers, so that the publicity attendant on auction was avoided. These were usually galleries or museums, but private collectors were also on permanent lookout for certain items. Putting a price on them beforehand was much more diffi-cult, but all dealers took a useful percentage of receipts and could therefore be relied upon to sell only to the highest bidder. This last point had been presented in an unusually specious formula: the relationship between seller and dealer must be one of mutual trust . . . Interpreted à la Písemsky, this meant simply that with the prospect of a hefty slice of the action, not too many questions would be asked. 'Trust me' was not something he ever said or wanted to hear.

So far, so good. The problem now to be tackled was deter-mining which dealers to approach and how to get the items to them. The first half was at least partly solved. In Paris, he had been given the name of a dealer in New York, a Russian émigré, who would 'talk the same language' – a nicely ambiguous statement. That should provide a first, trial outlet for the ikons; to be safe, he would need more than one, of course. For the pictures, he would try London, and for this he had been put in touch with the New York agent of a London dealer, highly recommended by Sotheby's. It was on the basis of these potential contacts that he had selected for his first foray into the market the two Picasso lithographs and one ikon, possibly the work of the great master, Andréi

120

Rublyóv. Each item was small and easily portable. Getting them to New York, in the absence of direct flights from Havana, would have to be done via Canada. There remained now only to familiarise himself with the three items and their provenance, before making the necessary travel arrangements. He determined to wait until night had fallen and everyone else had left the villa before examining them.

As the evening dragged on, Písemsky ate a cold supper without noticing what it was, after which he sat in a slightly alcoholic haze and watched the television reports on the latest developments in Moscow. The recent news of the abolition of the Communist Party of the Soviet Union had left him unmoved, thankful only that he had seen it coming and made provision to cope with the consequences as far as they affected him personally. This evening he saw with a mixture of emotions, primarily contempt, how Yéltsin, now President of Russia, had achieved the final humiliation of a bewildered Gorbachóv in front of the Russian parliament. Revenge may indeed be sweet, but it is not a pretty sight. At length, he was left alone in a darkened house, and having carefully checked all doors and windows, he took out the briefcase and began to examine his treasures.

He began with the two Picassos, reading through the notes prepared for him on their provenance before examining them. He settled himself at the desk, extinguishing all lights other than that of a single angle-poise lamp. Then sitting in a pool of light, he began with intense concentration to read:

*2 lithographs, 12 x 9, Combined technique, dated 24 June and 26 June 1934, Paris.*

*These lithographs, from a series entitled* Bull, Horse and Woman, *became separated from the remainder of the series (dated 20 June and 22 June 1934) and have therefore not been published in any of the collections of Picasso's works.*

*Purchased originally from the artist by the collector Ambroise Vollard, they were acquired in Paris by an émigré Russian connoisseur who returned to USSR in 1939. They subsequently passed to the Hermitage museum in Leningrad.*

121

*Adjudged pornographic and morally harmful, the lithographs have remained since that time in the archives of the Hermitage. Though their existence has been known to experts, they have never been on public view.*

Intrigued by this information, Písemsky took the first of the lithographs from its folder, propped it under the light and began to examine it, initially with little comprehension.

Turning it first this way, then that, he found it quite unintelligible, until, moving his chair a little further away, he began to distinguish in the jumbled mass a woman's head, thrown back, her features delineated by the sketchiest of lines, with brazenly voluptuous open mouth; rounded breasts, with dark, swollen nipples; buxom limbs; hairy shanks; tangles of curly black hair; flashes of pale flesh; a delicate, seahorse-like head; furry ears; horns; flared nostrils; flecks of foam; hovering hooves ... all writhing and twisting before his eyes. And as he stared hypnotised into this heaving mass he seemed to detect faint gasps; rhythmic moans; a subdued whinny; the liquid slap of flesh on flesh; strange sucking noises; a repressed, deep-throated lowing; a dying sigh ... He sensed, too, the acrid, pervasive odour of animal sweat, foetid breath, semen, urine ...

Gasping for air, he felt both revulsion and attraction, making his head spin.

Rising brusquely from his chair, Písemsky shook himself like a hound fresh out of water, then stood with head swaying in bewilderment from side to side.

'*Ai-ai-ai!*' he gasped, 'That's dangerous stuff! It's not safe to look at it for too long.' Then realising the irony of what he had said, he grinned, without amusement, and began pacing the room, unable for a while to settle again at the desk.

A glance at the second lithograph showed it to be very similar to the first. He tucked them both into their folders, poured himself a large measure of vodka and returned again to his task.

Removing a closely typed document from its file, he began

122

to study the notes on the ikon he had selected as the first to be sold.

*Extract from the provenance of the ikon*
*attributed to Andréi Rublyóv (1360/70–1427/30)*

*Rublyóv, like the majority of painters of ancient Russia, did not put his signature on the ikons and frescoes he completed. Moreover, we know that he usually worked side by side with other masters ... who also did not sign their work. In the Russia of the Middle Ages, as in the West, the master usually headed a workshop or studio, which fulfilled its commissions collectively ... hence the difficulty in clearly differentiating the works of Rublyóv himself from those of his fellow members of the workshop... Although Rublyóv was significantly more talented than his contemporaries, it should never be forgotten that he was surrounded by painters who were devoted to the same aesthetic ideals...*

The author of the document, a world-famous art historian who had more than once fallen foul of authority for his refusal to distort the facts in order to conform with ideologically derived theories, continued in this vein at some length, honestly unable to ascribe the ikon definitively to Andréi Rublyóv's own hand, but unhesitatingly attributing it to the master's workshop or 'school' and dating it therefore from the late fourteenth or early fifteenth century. He did not, of course, touch upon such sordid considerations as market value, but Písemsky was confident that whether the ikon had been painted by Rublyóv or by one of his followers was a comparatively minor detail, and that its worth to the right purchaser was very great indeed.

The subject of the painting, Písemsky read, was the head of an apostle, believed to be the apostle Paul because of its close resemblance to a detail of a fresco on the northern arch of the choir in the Uspénsky Cathedral in the ancient Russian capital of Vladímir, known without reasonable doubt to have been executed by the master's own hand in 1408.

Still unnerved by his experience of the Picasso lithographs,

Písemsky adopted a truculent stance, deliberately coarsening his manner and vocabulary in order to reassert his imperviousness to all this artistic nonsense. Taking another swig of Stolíchnaya – why wasn't there any *stárka* on this benighted island? – he began with uncertain fingers to remove the layers of wrapping in which the ikon was painstakingly swathed. At length he revealed an oblong of ancient wood, some 40 centimetres by 25 and perhaps 3 centimetres thick, on one side of which was an indecipherable rubric in what looked like Old Slavonic, and on the other a faded head-and-shoulders portrait, darkened with age and slightly chipped at the edges. He propped it against a pile of books under the spotlight of the lamp and stood back to view it. So what's so special about this, then? he thought.

As he later confessed, the excitements of the day, and up to a point the vodka he had consumed (he had not been drunk: he never got drunk), must have begun for a second time to play tricks on him. As he peered through an alcoholic mist, he saw the face of an old man – or perhaps not such an old man – at all events grey-haired and grey-bearded, inclined at a curious angle, turned slightly to the right on full-frontal shoulders, and with eyes that stared straight into his own and instantly dispelled all hint of bravado. The face was the stylised visage of an ascetic: fine features, with skin drawn tight over the cheekbones, a thin, straight nose, mouth downturned beneath melancholy moustache, and chin sunken beneath the curling waves of his beard. It was the eyes that held him: sunken and hollow, as though from suffering and anguish, but piercing, penetrating as they peered deep into the innermost recesses of Písemsky's being. He saw in them inexpressible sorrow, pain, compassion and, most of all, reproach.

'Don't look at me like that!' he blurted, hastily throwing a sheet of the wrapping over the face. He rose from his chair and retreated several paces. 'Leave me alone!'

He drained his glass and floundered up the stairs to his room, where he flung himself face down on the bed and sank into merciful oblivion.

He awoke at four in the morning with a bursting bladder, a blinding headache, a raging thirst, and a foul taste in his mouth that nothing would disperse. Blundering down the stairs, he thrust the ikon into the case and locked it away. Then he swallowed several aspirins, switched off the light and retired again to the slow torture of an early-morning hangover.

# 13

For more than a month Písemsky haunted El Paradiso hotel, seeking a group of Canadians that would suit his purpose. Trading on his experience with the first group, which had by now returned to Toronto, he found no difficulty in striking up an acquaintance and, as before, enjoyed a simple and undemanding welcome. By careful questions dropped into casually opened conversations, he gradually built up a picture of the way in which such groups operated, and on this basis he began to lay his plans.

His Soviet passport was still valid, and as a citizen of the former Soviet Union, resident only temporarily in Cuba, he should experience no formal restrictions on his movements. Enquiries also suggested that obtaining a Canadian visitor's visa would likewise present little difficulty. He therefore began to plan a sortie to Toronto, hesitating only through fear of having his precious burden intercepted and confiscated by Customs on entry into Canada. What he needed was an innocent tourist who would act as courier.

Several new groups arrived during that time, but for three weeks Písemsky's search was in vain. Either they came from the wrong part of Canada – from places as far apart as New Brunswick and British Columbia – or they did not offer any suitable candidate for the role he had in mind. But after nearly a month of hunting, during which he consumed gallons of undoubtedly toxic rum and Coca Cola, sat through countless performances of the same floorshows and manfully played his part in endless repetitions of the same banal conversation, he eventually found a mark.

Judy, on her second visit to Varadero, was a woman of a certain age, recently divorced – apparently without rancour or regret – relentlessly intent on having 'a good time' and openly on the lookout for the male partner essential for the consummation of this desire. Having unfortunately fallen in with a group composed either of devoted married couples or of pairs of elderly spinsters even more firmly attached to each other, she welcomed with open arms the advent of a personable male of comparable age. She was pleasantly good-looking, with a blooming complexion, well-dressed, and endowed with rather more social graces than most of her compatriots but, like so many of them, she was extremely fat. Jolly without being inane, with a sense of humour that did not find it necessary to express itself in strident laughter, she was tolerably agreeable company, and her conversation, while hardly intellectually demanding, did just occasionally border on the interesting.

For three evenings Písemsky sat with Judy, drinking *Cuba libre*, smoking Havana cigars, which she enjoyed, exchanging mildly flirtatious banter and watching the floorshow. When, after a particularly erotic dance routine, he intercepted a frankly speculative stare, he decided the moment had come to strike. It was simplicity itself to hint at pleasures more properly shared in private, and in due course he found himself alone with Judy in her room.

Having been given to wondering about the mechanics of sexual congress with a woman of her proportions, a venture thus far beyond his ken, he was at first at a loss as to how best to approach her. But without any preliminaries, she retired briefly to the en suite bathroom, returning wearing only a brassière, straining under the burden of her massive bust, and knelt on the edge of the bed, presenting him unceremoniously with her posterior. Viewed from this aspect, her hindquarters did indeed remind him irresistibly of a mare, on which, to his surprise, he took a most joyful ride, repeated – after some amazingly skilful oral stimulation – only a short

127

while later. One subsequent glance at her bloodshot eyes confirmed the conquest: he was in business.

Over a last cigar Písemsky led Judy to talk about the organisation of the departure of her group. They were due to leave Varadero by bus in a week's time, taking the mid-morning Air Canada direct flight from Havana to Toronto. He made a mental note of the flight number and time of departure. Their main baggage would be collected at El Paradiso, identified by each of them at the airport, and then checked in all together. They would go through passport control individually, and on arrival at Toronto they would be responsible for claiming their own baggage and taking it through Customs and Immigration. Effectively, therefore, a group ceased to exist as such as soon as it boarded the homeward flight.

As Písemsky rose wearily to take his leave of Judy, explaining that he would be away from Varadero on business for several days but would seek her out as soon as he returned, he saw her crestfallen reaction to the fact that there was to be a hiatus in the 'good time' she had been so enjoying. Never mind, he told himself, she'll be even more glad to see me when I get back.

'Be good!' he said playfully. 'And please don't go off with any strange men. I mean it!'

She forgave him.

Promptly at 8.30 the following morning, Písemsky set off with Miguel in the limousine, and by 11 o'clock he was at the Air Canada office in Havana requesting a ticket for Toronto on the same flight as Judy's group. He was fortunate in obtaining the one vacant seat: someone in one of the Toronto groups had failed to turn up for the outward flight, so the seat was available for the return leg. 'Fortune favours the brave,' he said to the smiling assistant, not entirely appropriately, but like all Cubans she welcomed a joke, however obscure. You wouldn't laugh, he thought, if you knew what I've had to go through to set this up. Payment in dollars on the spot caused a raised eyebrow or two, but dollars are never refused.

128

His next port of call was the visa department of the Canadian Consulate, where he completed a complicated application form for a visitor's visa that would be valid for seven days. He gave his Toronto address as the Sheraton hotel (there was bound to be one) and though he was momentarily nonplussed by a request for details of someone resident in Canada who would vouch for him, he suddenly remembered the business card that had been thrust into his hand and which he had later stored away in his wallet 'just in case'. 'Don Macinaw', he entered boldly in the appropriate space, copying also the Toronto address. It seemed most unlikely that it would ever be followed up, and if it were, he had no doubt that Don would be pleased and flattered that he had displayed the confidence to quote him.

In the afternoon, Písemsky had a brief talk with Pérez alone: Macías was still on his sales tour of Latin America, where he had already obtained a large order from Gustava Espina Salguero, who was plotting the overthrow of the legitimate government of Guatemala. In accordance with the devious philosophy he had outlined at their first meeting, Macías was hoping now to obtain a similar order from the government itself.

Písemsky's proposed visit to Canada elicited no comment. It was understood that when procedural details had been settled with Pérez, he would need to arrange his personal financial affairs with a Canadian bank. His share in the first down payment from Duvalier would not be great, since it had been agreed that priority should be given to satisfying the Cuban government's demands and to paying the dollar bonus promised to the task force. Both measures would guarantee smooth running of the system when what Pérez called the 'really big money' started coming in. The conversation was both businesslike and amicable, and Písemsky, whose mood had been rather frenetic for the past week or so, began to settle into a more equable frame of mind.

What he found so difficult was the perpetual waiting. Always, it seemed to him, there was something beyond his power to control, and no matter what he achieved, he was constantly being compelled to contain his impatience until the time was ripe for the next move. The feeling of impermanence that was so strong at Varadero did not allow him even for a short space of time to relax completely. The prospect of returning now to sit out a week at the villa dismayed him. His Spanish lessons with Jina had become routine and less interesting or amusing. Having satisfied each other's sexual curiosity, they had entered a period of quiescence, when neither of them took any initiative. And as for Judy, her peculiar charms would have to wait if absence were really to make the heart grow fonder, so that he could exploit it to the full at the optimum moment.

In these circumstances, he seized with alacrity on Pérez's suggestion that he should accompany the Major to Baracoa, from where the first arms assignment for Haiti was about to leave. The Major would arrive at Varadero by launch the following morning, and they could take the scheduled flight on the little Russian Yak-40 plane to the tiny Gustav Rizo airfield outside the town. So pleased was Písemsky with this prospect that on the drive back to Varadero he astonished Miguel by bursting into a Russian folk song, and was in turn himself astonished when Miguel joined him in perfect harmony. They sang all the way home.

When Písemsky and the Major arrived in Baracoa the following evening, the Major had a room waiting in a Cuban hotel in the old harbour area, but for Písemsky a reservation had been made at El Castello, formerly a fort, now a tourist hotel, on the hill overlooking the bay. Písemsky's ignorance of Cuban *moeurs* was underlined when he began mildly to object to this segregation, only to learn that whereas the Major would have been perfectly welcome at the tourist hotel, Písemsky's own presence at the Cuban establishment would have been the occasion for unwanted attention and comment. 'Here it is I who am the barbarian,' he murmured ruefully.

The return of the arms smugglers from Haiti was not expected until the following evening, the Major informed him. Perhaps he would like to take advantage of a free day to explore Baracoa? They agreed to meet at the harbour at nine in the evening, and Písemsky left by taxi to claim his room.

Sitting alone in a corner of the terrace of El Castello was Jennifer, watching the sun sinking toward the headland below La Yunque table mountain, where Christobál Colon had first set foot in the New World almost exactly 500 years earlier. She welcomed Písemsky with a smile as he took a seat silently beside her, and as the huge disc of the sun disappeared with astonishing rapidity they seemed both to hold their breath, listening for the hiss.

He recalled the witticism regretting that the Pilgrim Fathers had landed on Plymouth Rock rather than the other way about and tried to adapt it to this case. It did not really work but she took the point and nodded vigorously her agreement.

'Yes,' she said sadly, 'it was the beginning of a dreadful period. Such cruelty. Such wickedness. Such greed...'

They sat in silence until she again took up the theme.

'Yes, and still it goes on. Violence has bred violence. We are all still suffering the legacy of the conquistadores. There is not a single country in the whole of Latin America that has not been or is not still racked by internal strife in consequence of the tensions created by the conquest. I expect you've heard about this frightful man Salguero who is organising a military uprising in Guatemala?'

'Um, yes,' Písemsky almost whispered. 'I seem to have heard that name mentioned just recently.'

Jennifer was silent now. They sat a little longer as the breeze that accompanies sunset began to stir the palms, and the cicadas momentarily ceased their stridulating chorus. The afterglow set the sky ablaze above the bay, its reflection in the calm water etching the silhouettes of the fishing boats, anchored for the night. Somewhere out there, thought Písemsky, in the 77-kilometre Paso de los Vientos between Cuba and Haiti, one such boat was at this very moment bearing materials to fuel precisely the sort of violence that his companion so deplored.

Damn Jennifer! Why did she always make him feel so ill at ease with himself, so *dirty*? What did she and her like, in their comfortable North Oxford suburb, know about social tensions in the real world? What right had she to pontificate about violence, when the nearest she ever came to it was a television programme? How could she and her little bourgeois coterie appreciate that in a rat race it was only the biggest rats that survived?

Perhaps something of his irritation hung in the air. At all events, Jennifer smiled apologetically. 'Oh dear,' she said, 'I do get carried away, don't I? You must forgive my little homilies.'

She looked at her watch. 'Almost time for dinner. I promised to meet Gareth for an aperitif. Will you join us?'

Over drinks and then dinner, Písemský was unwontedly morose and silent, studiously avoiding Jennifer's puzzled eyes. She had no right to make him feel guilty, especially when he had done absolutely nothing wrong. It wasn't as if he were in some way inciting people to violence. Nothing of the sort. He was a peace-loving man. But if people were determined to be violent, there was no way in which he could stop them, was there? All he was doing was selling them what they wanted, as any enterprising businessman would. If he wouldn't sell them the arms, they would simply go to someone else who would. It was as simple as that. So why should he feel guilty? And why was it, damn it, that for no reason at all, he did?

Since it was impossible in such a small company to remain totally silent – there were only six left in the group, the others having gone back to sun themselves on the beaches of Varadero – Písemský fell back on his old technique of chairing the meeting. By putting a few leading questions, he induced the others to do all the talking, so that when he eventually retired early to bed ('Had a very busy day...') they all told each other what a splendid conversationalist that Russian chap was.

Not that he saw much prospect of sleep. His nerves were so

taut that he found it impossible to relax. As he sat on the balcony overlooking the bay, smoking yet another cigar, he tried to visualise what might be happening to the arms shipment somewhere out there, but in fact he knew so few details of the expedition (which, he hastened to tell himself, was probably just as well) that he could not really conjure up any picture clear enough to hang onto. His mind kept turning to children's stories and Hollywood films about bold pirates on the Spanish Main, swarming up rigging with daggers in their teeth, skewering pot-bellied bourgeois merchants and carrying off raven-haired damsels (hardly, he supposed, maidens in a technical sense) along with the rest of the booty. It was something of an effort to realise that this was in fact the Spanish Main, and that in these very waters Blackbeard, the Welshman Henry Morgan and the infamous Captain Kidd had been the violent scourge of dishonest and honest seafarers alike and had visited their dubious attentions likewise on the good citizens of Havana, Santiago, Trinidad and Baracoa. 'Well,' he murmured to the shadows, 'nothing much has changed. I'm just a fly on the surface of life's rich tapestry. It's not up to me to change the course of history.'

The problem of how to pass a nerve-racking day was solved at breakfast by an invitation to join in the programme of the British group. Písemsky had been reminded with some asperity that it contained both a Welshman and a Scotswoman and was therefore not 'English'. They grudgingly forgave him when he explained that there is no commonly used Russian word acknowledging this distinction, though the Czechs had *Britský*, which was now being taken up by other Slavs.

In their little Toyota minibus, they went first to see a small cigar factory – 'Not one of the big, automated ones,' Domingo, their guide informed them, though nowhere in their travels throughout the island had they seen the slightest evidence of the existence of such installations. 'Hand-made cigars are in much greater demand,' Domingo added, as though reading their thoughts. And did they know that the origin of the word 'cigar' was the Amerindian *sik ar*, meaning 'to smoke'? Or that *tobacco* was the word used by Indian shamans for the forked reeds by means of which they used to inhale smoke through their nostrils? The word for the plant, *cohiba*, was now the name of a brand of cigar; no doubt they had seen it in the shops? They liked to be given this sort of information: so much more interesting than a torrent of dubious statistics that in any case no one would remember a half-hour later.

The factory lay a little outside the town, along a winding dirt road lined with sweet-smelling acacias and eucalyptus, beyond which could be seen the thatched roofs of peasant huts, even today made largely of palm fronds, peeping through the jumbled sea of banana, tobacco and bamboo, broken here and there by sturdy coco palms and stately yagrumas. It was a much larger structure, with wooden walls and corrugated iron roof, sited in a grove of truly regal palms, whose silvery-grey trunks made Písemsky gulp involuntarily in near recognition, and surrounded by neat beds of white mariposa butterfly-blooms, the national flower of Cuba.

Filing slightly shamefacedly in, feeling like not entirely welcome beings from another world, they stood for a moment accustoming their eyes to the gloom inside the primitive factory and adjusting also to the temperature and smell. There was no form of air-conditioning, not even a fan, so that the only means of fending off the sun's heat entailed also excluding a great deal of its light. They could, however, make out a room arranged like a conventional classroom, with desk-like tables in rows facing front, and a supervisor's desk like a teacher's table turned towards them. The rank odour of perspiration blended with the sweet aroma of the cured tobacco to produce a smell that was strangely not unpleasant, at least after the initial shock.

Seated at the tables were men and women of all ages and colours, each with a little heap of tobacco leaves, a pot of flour paste, a wooden rack and a semicircular knife blade. With practised hands they smoothed the leaves flat and rolled them, filling the inside with scraps cut from other leaves, forming a long cigar with untidy ends. With fingers dipped in the paste they glued the final leaf, and by rolling the knife blade sliced the ends neatly and placed the finished article in the wooden rack. Easy! For the most part, the workers made no acknowledgement of their visitors' presence, though when addressed directly they responded, perhaps rather wearily, with the usual flashing smile. Písemsky noted with an ironic grin a torn, dusty poster of Fidel Castro and, incredibly, a yellowed, printed notice advertising *Havana cigars as smoked by Winston Churchill.*

Having tried without success to communicate in Russian or English, he was suddenly addressed by the foreman in good though heavily accented French. He came originally, he said, from Haiti. For want of any other question (it can be extraordinarily difficult in such circumstances to make spontaneous conversation without sounding either condescending or slightly inane – or conceivably both), Písemsky asked about health regulations, wondering whether constant contact with the tobacco leaves caused skin diseases, and received a polite but firmly negative and quite untrue reply. The conversation died, but as the group was about to leave, the Haitian touched Písemsky's elbow: '*Monsieur, mon fils va commencer ses études à l'université,*' he said, '*mais il n'a pas de stylo. Si vous pourriez. . .*'

From his breast pocket Písemsky took a ballpoint pen of the sort that used to be distributed as souvenirs to foreign guests at the House of Friendship and thrust it silently into the Haitian's pink palm. Printed along it was the inevitable slogan, this time a quotation from Khrushchóv: 'The Soviet Union' it said 'is a bastion of peace'. Then in an unwonted flash of unpremeditated generosity, he added a 50-dollar note, leaving the Haitian gasping with pleasure, a friend for life.

'Well,' one of the group muttered as they walked back to the bus, 'now I know what a sweatshop is. What did you think of that, Gareth?'

'Oh, very disappointing, mun,' Gareth chuckled. 'Not a sweaty thigh in sight.'

They lunched on the balcony of a tiny hotel on the shore of a deserted bay, where the water inside the coral reef was almost a milky white, while out to sea it shaded from blue to violet. Small boys as nimble as spider monkeys shinned up coconut palms and presented them with freshly picked nuts, chopping off the heads with single strokes of lethal-looking machetes. Písemsky winced at every blow, expecting to see amputated fingers and spurting blood, but there were no mishaps, and soon a dash of white rum was added to the milk in the nuts, and the incredibly refreshing liquid drunk through a straw. This was the life!

After lunch the group split up, one or two of the company wandering off along the white sands, gathering huge shells and chunks of coral to adorn their bathroom shelves at home. The remainder, including Písemsky, lay drowsily on long chairs in the shade of the palms, where their fellows eventually rejoined them, talking in desultory snatches among themselves. For the first time for some days, he felt fully at ease. There was something about these people that made them congenial company, quite different from the Canadians, despite the latters' easy manner. He had noticed before that with North Americans, although they spoke more or less the same language, there was always an element of doubt as to whether the words meant quite the same things. It was a matter of cultural loading: words and structures might be common, but the underlying assumptions were sometimes rather different. He was sure the British felt the same way; he and they were Europeans, and despite the veneer of Soviet culture that he naturally wore, their apperception of reality was much the same. American culture might have had largely European origins, but it had gelled into something distinct and different. Soviet culture, because of the European origin of its ideological basis, had never become deeply rooted in the multi-ethnic Soviet society, remaining superficial and somehow ramshackle, so that now it was disintegrating and virtually disappearing with disconcerting rapidity.

Písemsky's companions were discussing arrangements for their journey home in two days' time.

'When are you going home then, Iván?' Gareth suddenly asked him.

Písemsky was taken aback, suddenly overcome by a wave of *toská*, a misty-eyed nostalgia, not so much for what has been as for what might have been, indeed, for what ought to have been.

'Home?' he said faintly.

'Well, you know. Russia, or whatever it's called now.'

'Ah.' He pondered a response, realising that whereas almost the first question the Canadians had asked him was about his 'line' or business (with Russians, it would have been 'How much do you earn?'), the British group had shown no obvious interest in the details of his private life. Even the present enquiry had been made more to include him in the conversation than to fish for actual information. There was no real need for him to reply, yet he somehow thought he should.

He began tentatively enough. 'That's a very difficult question, Gareth,' he said, 'because I'm not sure any more where "home" really is.'

The company was silent, listening; there was obviously more to come.

'Technically, I suppose "home" is Moscow, but I now have no family ties there and no job to go back to. In a broader sense, "home" was the Soviet Union, and that no longer exists. I came away because I had begun to feel so out of sympathy, as if I were standing still while everything around me was changing. I don't suppose I should find it any easier if I went back there now.'

As he spoke, Písemsky had been, as it were, listening to himself. He had never before attempted to formulate his thoughts in this way, and was himself uncertain what conclusion he would eventually reach. But his companions were obviously intrigued, and each was anxious to question him further, while at the same time hesitant about being thought to be prying. It was Gareth, who had initiated the topic, who again took it up.

'That must have been pretty weird,' he said sympathetically, 'but don't you think things will be better there now, since they've got rid of the Communists?'

Písemsky smiled bleakly. 'Ah, but I suppose, to be honest, you would have to count me as one of the Communists they've got rid of...'

The silence was almost tangible. Regretting he had ever begun in this vein, he could clearly not leave the topic now.

'Don't misunderstand me,' he went on. 'I am not an unreconstructed Stalinist, to use the jargon everybody seems to love, and I don't think we could have gone on much longer as we were. But not everything was bad, you know, just as not everything in your country is good.'

At this, there were a number of rueful nods and grunts of assent.

'We made a lot of mistakes, and we did some awful things. But we also achieved a great deal, and now the chances are that absolutely everything – good and bad – is being swept away.'

'Ah! The baby and the bathwater,' somebody said.

'Exactly. A sort of vindictive determination to destroy everything the Communists put in place, simply because of its origin, and regardless of its worth.'

He paused, then continued with a sigh. 'The pity of it is that very few people in the West – and this includes your own government – seem to have any real idea what things were like in Russia before the Bolshevik Revolution, or for that matter in Eastern Europe before the last war. They seem to think that before the wicked Communists took over, everything was wonderful, and that if they only got rid of those wicked Communists it would all be wonderful again.

'They are wrong on both counts. They have made the same mistake as we did: they have believed their own propaganda.'

Then realising that this was perhaps not the place for a political tirade, he made what was clearly intended to be his final comment.

'It may be easy for anyone to see what we have gained, but only we can appreciate how much we have lost.'

Shocked at the vehemence of the outburst he had provoked, Gareth used his favourite ploy to take the heat out of any conversation.

'Discuss!' he said, as though in an examination paper. There was a general guffaw, more of relief than of amusement, and for a moment silence again prevailed. It was Jennifer who drew a line beneath the discussion.

'That was extremely interesting, Iván,' she said mildly. 'Thank you very much.'

When the heat of the day had subsided, the group climbed again into the minibus and returned to Baracoa for a brief tour of the sights of the town. As at Cienfuegos, the general dilapidation that had so shocked Písemsky in Havana was less extreme here, and many of the old Spanish houses, less grandiose or pretentious than their counterparts in the capital, were well restored and displayed their own special type of elegance and charm. The party came at length to the cathedral, a singularly unimpressive building, in spite of its age, both inside and out. The one focal point of the interior was a glass case, standing on a marble table with curved mohogany legs, near the altar. On a scarlet embroidered brocade background, and with a recently added silver base, was an ancient cross, some 4 feet tall, rough-hewn in gnarled hardwood, said to have been erected by Christopher Columbus himself, and therefore the oldest cross in the Americas. It was not a thing of beauty, but the visitors regarded it with due reverence, tempered, for at least two of them, with rather less favourable assessments of the benefits accompanying the faith that it symbolised.

The point was emphasised to deadly effect as they emerged from the main door of the cathedral to see directly opposite, as if trying to peer into the church, the carved stone bust of an Amerindian, with the legend:

*Hatuey, Primer Rebeldo de America*
*Immolado en Yara de Baracoa*

'This is the Ciboney Indian chief, Hatuey,' Domingo

informed them, 'the first American revolutionary, burned at the stake at Baracoa in 1512 by order of Governor Diego de Velasquez, the man who later founded the settlements of Trinidad de Cuba and Santiago de Cuba, and who sailed from Santiago in 1514 to begin the conquest of Mexico.'

'What did Hatuey do to deserve such a fate?' one of the group enquired.

'He objected to the way the Spaniards treated the Indians. They used to hunt them like animals, just for sport. There is a famous saying attributed to him' (Domingo struck a pose and recited it with appropriate expression): '*If torture and murder are the wishes of your God, I cannot be part of that religion* ... So they burned him at the stake for refusing to embrace Christianity. He was the first American martyr.'

'*Duw mawr!*' exclaimed Gareth, with unconscious irony. 'Great God!' But the others stood speechless, shaking their heads.

Jennifer looked directly at Písemsky. 'Violence breeding violence,' she said. Písemsky turned away.

After a light and hasty supper, at which the conversation stayed carefully away from international politics, Písemsky made his farewells. There were hearty handshakes all round, and expressions of goodwill.

'Best of luck then, *bychan*,' Gareth said, clapping him heartily on the shoulders.

Only Jennifer hung back, coming last to offer her hand. On impulse, Písemsky raised it to his lips. She smiled sadly: 'I hope you find peace.'

By 8.30 Písemsky was already down at the waterside in the old harbour, where he found the Major pacing in military fashion up and down the quay. Nervous tension, it seemed, was not his own prerogative. In the event, they had not long to wait. Shortly before nine, faint lights appeared at the mouth of the harbour, and a large fishing boat took up station in line with other boats already riding in the calm water of the bay. It cast its anchor, and three figures in fishermen's gear rowed to shore in a dinghy and reported formally to the

140

Major. They spoke in a patois that Písemsky did not understand, but the message they gave was clear: 'No problem.' He later learned that the mission had gone completely without incident, and that the boat would have returned even earlier if they had not stopped en route to catch some fish. 'Not just for the sake of appearance,' the Major told him, 'but for their supper.'

Before they parted for the night, Písemsky at last made up his mind to ask the Major the question that had been trembling on his tongue.

'You remember you told Pérez there was someone following me,' he said. 'Did you ever . . . um . . . ?'

The Major laughed. 'Oh, yes. We don't have to worry about that any more.' He paused. 'As a matter of fact, it was all a bit of a surprise.' He paused again. 'Did you deal with anyone in Moscow connected with Mossad?'

'Mossad? Not as far as I know.' Písemsky was equally mystified.

'Well, one of their people was taking a particular interest in you.'

'What do you mean, "taking an interest"?'

'Well, keeping an eye on you . . . And on the rest of us at the same time, unfortunately.'

'But who? Who was he?'

Again the Major laughed. 'Not *he*,' he said. '*She.*'

But that was all he would say.

# 14

At first light on the following morning, Písemsky set off with the Major in a pick-up van from Baracoa, across the eastern end of the Sierra del Plurial and along the southern coast, skirting the US naval station at Guantánamo and taking the inland spur to La Maya and then across the Sierra Maestra to the ancient port of Santiago de Cuba, where they arrived at about nine o'clock. The Major was a fast but skilled driver, and Písemsky was as exhilarated by the vertiginous mountain passages as he was charmed by his first glimpses of the Caribbean. Both men were in a state of mild euphoria at the success of their first venture.

As he drove, the Major recounted some of the history of the Oriente, the eastern half of Cuba, which, he said, had always been a focus of dissent and rebellion and which was where the peasants and slaves had first learned to use the traditional symbol of their subservience, the machete, as a weapon of war. 'You Soviets say "the cobblestone is the weapon of the proletariat",' he reminded Písemsky, 'and we might say the same of the machete.' He related in glowing terms the course of the victorious campaign of Fidel Castro, whose tiny remnant of survivors of the landing from the yacht *Granma* from Mexico had swollen to an army that ousted the tyrannical Batista. 'In Europe you had a problem with a corporal,' he said, smiling. 'Our problem was a sergeant.'

He spoke scathingly, though without heat, of the American presence at Guantánamo, which he was sure would soon be coming to an end. 'There is already more communication between us than there used to be.' In one of the few remarks Písemsky ever heard him make concerning his personal attitudes, he made it quite clear that he owed his allegiance to Santiago, not to Havana, which he regarded as a centre of bourgeois decadence. He was fiercely loyal to Fidel Castro, but less so to the other members of the government. Písemsky made no comment.

At Santiago, the Major dropped his passenger off in Cespedes Square, arranging to collect him there at 11. They would then take the midday flight to Havana, where Miguel would be waiting to drive him to Varadero.

Písemsky breakfasted on the terrace of the café overlooking the square, with the cathedral to his left and the house built by Hernando Cortéz in 1520 immediately opposite. The cathedral – the oldest in Cuba – was closed to visitors, a phenomenon all too familiar to Písemsky, since so many of the most interesting places in the Soviet Union had inevitably been closed for renovation – *na remónt* – a phrase engraved on the frustrated hearts of a million tourists. (Restaurants, on the other hand, closed only at mealtimes, so that the staff could eat.)

The Cortéz house, later occupied by that same Diego de Velasquez who had burned the Indian Hatuey at the stake in Baracoa, was similarly under repair. From the outside, it might have reminded a Western visitor of, say, the governor's palace in Funchal, but to Písemsky, who was ignorant of Iberian architecture, its graceful archways and latticed balconies overlooking the square were reminiscent of old Turkish merchant houses in Plovdiv, in Bulgaria, or in those lovingly restored 'museum towns' like Gjirokaster or Berat in Albania. Peering through the arcaded entry, he saw a cool, cloistered courtyard with palms and trumpetwood, and an elegant central fountain, and marvelled again at the dedication with which the old conquistadores had fashioned such tranquil oases in the hostile wilderness of an unknown island, populated, when they first arrived, by Carib cannibals, as well as more peace-loving Indian tribes.

Somewhat piqued at being denied entry to the two most interesting monuments of local history, he wandered aimlessly along the street named after the revolutionary poet Heredia until he came to the inevitable Casa des Troves, where local jazz musicians in scratch combinations were jamming to an appreciative audience, all swaying and rocking in perfect time. A girl looking remarkably like Jina invited him to dance, but he declined in some confusion and retreated back to the square, where the Major was already waiting. They had time, he said, to make a quick check of the helicopters stored at the airport before boarding their Yak-40 for Havana. Shortly after 12, they were in the air.

In Havana, Písemsky went first to the Canadian Consulate, where his visitor's visa was ready for collection, and Miguel drove him smoothly back to Varadero. He paused at the villa only for a quick shower, a change of clothing and a light snack, before going on to El Paradiso hotel to seek out Judy and 'protect his investment'.

He found her sitting alone by the pool, reading a paperback and sipping a *mojito*. She tossed the book aside as he approached and gave him a smile of welcome.

'So you did come back,' she said. 'I wondered if you really would.'

'But of course,' he replied in mock indignation. 'I told you I would.'

He waved to a hovering waiter, but Judy forestalled him. 'Don't bother,' she said. 'I've got a bottle of vodka in my room.'

From the window on the sixth floor, they watched the enormous, glowing orb of the sun dipping rapidly toward the horizon, laying a golden trail across the placid water that seemed to lead right into Judy's room. Together, they rode happily into the sunset.

After a strenuously enjoyable evening, with dinner and a great deal to drink, Písemsky laid the final bait. 'Tomorrow is our last day at Varadero,' he said, 'and I want to make it

144

something special. Would you like to have dinner with me at my villa?'

Judy was both saddened and pleased: saddened, because her good time was coming to an end, and inordinately pleased that despite her fears that he had simply taken his pleasure of her and disappeared, he had indeed returned and was setting out to entertain her in such a special manner. An intimate dinner at his villa would surely be far superior to yet another evening at the hotel.

'I have various things to attend to during the day,' Písemsky continued, taking her obvious pleasure as a sign of assent, 'but I'll have you collected at reception at 7.30.'

Písemsky's 'things to attend to' included shopping at the hotel, where he went first to the jewellery counter in the main foreign-currency Intur shop. There, after much giggling, the sales assistant produced an Aztec-style silver chain and pendant, which had to be wide enough, as Písemsky explained with unambiguous gestures and a hilarious demonstration on the young lady's person, not to disappear from sight within Judy's cavernous cleavage. He bought also a decorative wooden box to hold them, beautifully wrapped and ready for presentation. That should provide the final touch.

For himself, he bought what he had begun to think of as his Canadian disguise: an unbelievably garish T-shirt bearing the words I LOVE CUBA in very large letters on the chest and back, a Mexican-style sombrero, a pair of macho sunglasses, and a baseball cap (made in Taiwan) of the sort that seemed glued to the shaven heads of so many visitors.

Lastly, he visited the art shop on the first floor, where he flicked through a stack of prints of historical scenes of sailing ships and pirate raids on various Cuban ports, and another of colourful if not particularly talented drawings of Cuban flora and fauna. He finally selected some 20 items, plus a stout cardboard folder tied with ribbon. Then he returned to the villa to make his preparations for the flight to Toronto.

At 7.30, Miguel had Judy paged at reception and with charming formality escorted her to the waiting limousine.

She was suitably impressed, and by the time the villa gates swung open and she saw Písemsky sitting at a table with drinks and snacks at the poolside, she was as pink and pretty as an embarrassed débutante. This is going to be a doddle, Písemsky thought, recalling an expression he had learned from Gareth.

Drinks at the poolside were served by a grinning Dora, who approved of Judy's proportions, which closely resembled her own. They watched the sun go down, smiling mischievously at each other at the memory of how they had been occupied at that time on the previous evening. Then Dora summoned them to dinner by candlelight, with Cuban music playing softly in the background.

'This is too good to be true,' Judy murmured to herself, but true it was. And when she opened the package lying on her plate at the table, she was totally speechless. As Písemsky fastened the clasp behind her neck, softly caressing the lobes of her ears as he did so, and arranged the pendant equally tantalisingly over her partly exposed breasts, she gasped aloud, unable even to murmur her thanks.

Details of that dinner, Judy could never subsequently remember. She knew only that she had both eaten and drunk a great deal, and she would recall how at one point Písemsky had leaned over and placed his hand over hers: 'It really is such a pleasure to be with you, Judy.' And when he told her he would be accompanying her to Toronto, her joy was complete.

When Dora had served coffee and brandy and left them alone at the villa, they sat side by side, holding hands. Oh God! Písemsky thought, I can't keep this up much longer. I'm going to die laughing. A guided tour of the villa ended inevitably in his bedroom, with breathless coupling in the familiar position. Well, Písemsky consoled himself, with a wolfish grin, at least she can't see my face.

As Písemsky prepared to escort Judy back to the hotel (with a silent giggle he had baulked at the idea of taking her into his bed for fear that she might roll on him in the night), he made his final play.

'Oh!' he exclaimed. 'I've just had an idea. Do you think I can ask you to do me a little favour?'

There was no need to await an answer.

'It's about this,' he explained, taking the precious ikon out of a drawer and contriving to unwrap it without actually looking at it. 'It's a religious painting that I promised to take to my cousin in New York. It isn't worth anything, but it's of great sentimental value to her. She's very old. I don't suppose she can live much longer...' (Damn, he thought, I'm making very heavy weather of this. And indeed, it was obvious that Judy had no idea where it was leading.) 'The fact is, because I've got a Soviet passport, I'll probably have my bags searched when I enter Canada tomorrow, and if they see this, they may think it's valuable or something and confiscate it. Do you think you could take it through for me? I'm sure they won't even look at yours...'

He hesitated, then began to reprimand himself. 'But I really shouldn't be bothering you with my little problems,' he said, making to thrust the ikon back in the drawer.

'Don't be silly, Iván!' Judy snatched the ikon from him. 'Of course I'll take it. I'll put it in the top of my case and give it to you when we get to Toronto.'

'Judy, you're an angel!' Písemsky exclaimed. (But you sure as hell will never fly, he wanted to add. Fortunately, he restrained himself.)

When the Canadian groups checked in at the airport the next morning, they were joined by a figure who, to an outsider, was indistinguishable from the rest. He sported a T-shirt announcing I LOVE CUBA and a baseball cap, and carried a canvas holdall to which was tied a large sombrero. His face was partly hidden by dark sunglasses, and a fat, unlit Havana cigar protruded from his lips. Only his paunch, while swelling alarmingly, was still less gross than those of the others, male and female, and perhaps a slightly incongruous note was struck by the smart leather briefcase, with a combination lock, that he also carried in the holdall which was his only item of luggage. But on inspection by bored Customs officials this proved to contain nothing more interesting than a newspaper, a couple of paperback novels, a folder of tourist prints of Baracoa and other ports, some personal documents, a packet of Kleenex and a half-empty box of cigars. The bearer's passport was stamped with hardly a pause – Soviet passports were still a familiar sight – and Písemsky passed through to the departure lounge and mingled with the crowd. He had watched Judy's suitcase moving smoothly off on the conveyor: the first hurdle had safely been jumped. He saw her scanning the hall as though looking for someone, but managed to hide behind a pillar and avoid detection until, remarkably punctually, the flight was called.

On the plane, their seats were widely separated and there was mercifully no possibility of their sitting together. Safe in this knowledge, Písemsky walked back to where she was sitting and took her a drink.

'I couldn't find you in the crowd,' he said. 'Never mind.' He raised his drink in a toast: 'To Cuba!'

Still starry-eyed, she echoed the toast: 'To Cuba!' If she was surprised at his unusual garb, she did not remark on it. Returning to his seat, he fell instantly asleep.

Awaking later to torture his palate with a tray of plastic food, which he in fact ate with something approaching relish, he struck up a conversation with his neighbour (it would have been difficult not to) and asked about Toronto hotels. He found that there was, indeed, a Sheraton, as well as a Hilton, an Inter-Continental and numerous others, with a Holiday Inn (Crowne Plaza) near the airport and another downtown.

From the in-flight magazine he learned the general layout of the downtown area, supplemented by his neighbour, especially in reply to his queries about the location of the main banks. By the time they landed, he felt as though he already knew the town well. 'City,' his neighbour corrected him when he said so. 'In Canada, anywhere with more than two streets is a city.'

At the baggage reclaim, Písemsky joined Judy at the

carousel and gallantly carried her suitcase to the Customs hall. As he had predicted, his holdall was searched, while her case was nodded through. The Picasso lithographs, nestling among the tourist prints (which had seemed quite attractive in Varadero but were already beginning to look like kitsch) excited no comment. They went together to an obscure corner of the bar, where the ikon was removed from Judy's luggage and locked safely in his briefcase. Mission accomplished.

After a final drink, Písemsky bid Judy a fond farewell. '*Au revoir*,' he said, feeling extremely foolish. 'I'm booked in at the Sheraton, so you know where to find me.'

Installing her in a taxi, he waited until it had disappeared from view before hailing another for himself.

'Hilton,' he said.

# 15

Taking a room for four nights, Písemsky began to orientate himself in Toronto, facilitated by the almost inescapable sight of the CN tower, and to plan his visit to New York. Through the hotel travel desk, he booked a short-hop flight by Air Canada to Detroit for the following midday, noting that about an hour after arrival there was a Delta flight to La Guardia. A two-day visitor's visa could, he discovered, be obtained at Toronto airport. There remained only to make appointments with his New York contacts and to book a room there for a couple of nights. He was fortunate in finding someone in authority at the Madison Avenue office of Mulrooney, the agent recommended to him in London for the sale of pictures, and arranged a meeting for late the following afternoon. A room was booked for him at the Yorkshire hotel on Central Park South, in easy walking distance on the one hand of Madison Avenue and on the other of the Lincoln Center. The remaining appointment would have to be made on the spot.

Satisfied with his progress, Písemsky had a leisurely dinner at the Hilton, with excellent Californian wines. By the time he had reached coffee and liqueur and lighted a fat cigar, he felt sufficiently relaxed to sit back and take stock. On impulse, he called for a telephone and selected Don Macinaw's Toronto number.

'Well hiya, Jaahn! Whaddya know!' a hearty voice bellowed in his ear. The man doesn't need a telephone, Písemsky thought, I could hear him without one. After murmuring a fairly incoherent explanation of his presence in Toronto, in response to a torrent of questions, none of which seemed actually to require answers, he agreed to call again when he had returned from New York so that they could 'have a few beers' together on his last evening. Surrendering at last to fatigue and alcohol, he retired to his king-sized bed.

At 9 a.m. Písemsky entered the imposing lobby of the Royal Great Lakes Bank and requested an interview with a senior manager. To a young man who was clearly not senior in any sense, he mentioned casually that his business concerned opening an account with a first deposit of half a million dollars, at which he was ushered with commendable alacrity into the presence of the Deputy Director (the Director was 'in conference' on the golf course). There followed an hour of detailed discussion, including perusal of documents taken from Písemsky's briefcase and an exchange of faxes with Pérez in Havana and the Bayer-Hofmann bank in Zürich. As a consequence, Písemsky was issued with cards and documents granting him credit to the sum of a quarter of a million dollars. An appointment was made for about a month ahead, by which time the bank would have prepared a portfolio of investments for his approval. He was escorted personally to a waiting taxi, in which, after a brief stop at the Hilton, he proceeded to the airport.

There, he obtained a visitor's visa for the US, and prompted by an unwonted twinge of conscience, he dialled Judy's number. To his great delight, she was not at home, and he was able to dictate a fond message to her answering machine and to bask in the righteous glow of having done the right thing without having to suffer the consequences. An hour later he was in Detroit, where he took the Delta flight to La Guardia and a limo to the Yorkshire. This, he thought, is where the fun really starts.

Písemsky had previously visited New York on several occasions and had always found the city exhilarating and congenial. Some of his Soviet colleagues, he knew, had found it hostile and intimidating, but whereas he could understand

151

how such a reaction could arise, he did not to the slightest degree share it. To him, it was a wonderful place, where everything worked and anything could happen. Of course, he had moved only in a small area – in fact seldom going outside Manhattan, or even only the central area of Manhattan, with the occasional visit to Greenwich Village – and this was hardly a typical cross-section. Yet the same, surely, applied to most people in most cities, which were basically just conglomerations of villages, only a few of which were ever visited by the average person in their daily life. So he was glad to be back and was looking forward to some excitement.

At the Yorkshire, he deposited the ikon and lithographs in the hotel strongroom and by 5.15 had presented himself at Mulrooney's office. Once again, a polite but unenthusiastic reception was quickly transmuted into rapt and respectful attention.

Making a great play of the need for absolute confidentiality, Písemsky explained that he was acting on behalf of senior governmental figures of the former Soviet Union, where, as Mr Mulrooney knew, there was an acute shortage of hard currency.

They had decided, he said, to dispose discreetly of certain little-known items from state-held treasures of art and painting. A condition of sale, therefore, would be that the source of the items must never be revealed. Full documentation concerning the provenance of each item was available for inspection. Cash payment was required in US dollars, in two equal instalments, one when a legal agreement to purchase was signed, and the other when the items were actually handed over.

Thus far there was little for anyone to get excited about, but then Písemsky stated in a matter-of-fact tone but to Mulrooney's almost fatal astonishment that the first two items for sale would be hitherto unseen Picasso lithographs from the series *Bull, Horse and Woman,* and that the asking price would be 2 million dollars. At an agency fee of ten per cent, a sale even for that price would net the agent no less than 200,000 dollars, and the price, he knew, was low.

Písemsky made it clear, without actually stating it, that he might reasonably have raised the price, but that the requirement for a rapid sale was paramount. If Mulrooney wanted to purchase the items himself and sell them for rather more, this was of no concern to Písemsky. This oblique appeal to the man's greed would, he was sure, clinch the deal, as well as discouraging him from asking too many awkward questions about the vendor.

Leaving a speechless Mulrooney with Xerox copies of the provenance and of the two lithographs, Písemsky gave him until the following afternoon to make his bid. There were, he implied, other potential purchasers to whom he could turn, and with this parting shot he took his leave.

By 6.30 Písemsky was back at his hotel, partly uneasy at the near irrevocability of what he had done, part elated at his undoubted success. Over a stiff drink from the minibar in his room he recalled with a shudder his reaction on his first examination of the lithographs. They still disturbed him and he would be glad to be rid of them.

After a light supper, he strolled across to the Lincoln Center, where he was fortunate enough to obtain a ticket for the Metropolitan Opera. Less fortunately, the programme was Wagner's *Siegfried,* sung by indifferent artistes in almost total darkness. Whether he would in any case have been able to concentrate on the unlikely plot was doubtful; as it was, he slept soundly until the first interval, paid sporadic attention until the next, and then left.

As he turned into Broadway in the growing darkness, he saw a solitary figure approaching along the sidewalk and wondered, in spite of himself, if he were about to be mugged. But it occurred to him at the same time that it was entirely possible that the other fellow was having identical doubts about his own intentions. He therefore adopted a swaggering gait and stared malevolently at the other man, who seemed somehow to intercept his gaze, shrank visibly and faltered for a second or two before scurrying across the street to the safety of the far side. 'Well, whaddya know!' Písemsky said aloud. He was still grinning when he entered the bar of the Yorkshire for a goodnight vodka to send him safely off to sleep.

But sleep, when eventually he lay in his broad bed, would simply not come. The music had not worked its magic, and the vodka had stimulated rather than dulled his senses. He switched on the bedside light and tried to read, but the words seemed to crawl about the pages. He tried the television, but only trivia, and not even entertaining trivia, appeared on the screen. Eventually, he lay in the semi-darkness, involuntarily reliving the events of the day. He was reconstructing his conversation with Mulrooney when the telephone suddenly rang. With surprise and trepidation, he lifted the receiver.

'Hello, Mr Písemsky,' a langourous female voice drawled in his ear. 'Aren't you a little lonely tonight?'

'Um... Well...'

'Wouldn't you like a little company? Let me take your mind off things. I'm just along the corridor. I'll be with you in one moment.'

Before he could utter a coherent word, his mysterious caller had hung up, and in what seemed like only a few seconds there was a discreet knock at the door. Still in something of a daze, he hurriedly put on a dressing gown and opened the door, admitting not one girl, but two; a tall graceful blonde and her shorter, stockier, black-skinned companion.

'Hi there!' they said in unison, placing a bottle of champagne and three glasses on the table. In a trice the bottle was opened and the glasses filled. He accepted one, still without speaking a word.

'Chin-chin,' said the blonde. 'Call me Gigi. And this is Tara.'

'Um.. .John,' he managed at last to mumble.

'Chin-chin,' said Tara, opening a silver pill box and proffering it to him. 'Just take a snort of this with us,' she said, herself sniffing a pinch of the white powder, as also did Gigi, 'and the world will be a different place.' Mechanically, as though he had no will of his own, he followed suit.

'OK, John,' said Gigi. 'Now let's all get acquainted.'

In a remarkably short time, the two girls had removed not only their own clothes but his, and what took place from then on seemed to be happening not to Písemsky himself but to someone else, someone familiar but to whom he could somehow not put a name.

Sprawling together on the bed, they titillated him and each other, inducing him also to participate with them in exploring each other's every orifice, stroking, probing, sucking, until they rode him in turns and he mounted each of them, and with dildos strapped about their loins they mounted him and each other in a writhing, panting, moaning mass, which he seemed to be observing from somewhere above, looking down on them, until they froze in exhaustion and lay still, and what he saw was the *Bull, Horse and Woman* of Picasso's wild fantasy, with his body and theirs substituting the original protagonists...

With a frantic heave he extricated himself from the welter of limbs and shrieked at the girls: 'Go away! For God's sake leave me in peace!'

As the startled couple wriggled into their scant clothing, he fumbled in his wallet, thrusting a 500 dollar bill into Gigi's hand and physically bundled them out of the door, which he fastened by its chain.

He spent the night slumped in an armchair, trembling and whimpering softly, until as dawn broke over Central Park, he collapsed at last onto the bed and slept.

As soon as the hotel was stirring, Písemsky requested a change of room: another room on another floor. There were several vacancies and the change was quickly made. Still in a state of some distress, he went down to breakfast in the hotel dining room, where, as in all American restaurants, he was immediately served with a cup of lukewarm, undrinkable coffee that tasted as if it had been made several days earlier and reheated a number of times. After Cuban coffee, it was a rude shock. Abandoning it after a few mouthfuls, he switched to tea, which he drank neat and very weak. He would dearly have liked a glass of vodka, but at that hour not even he would dare to order it. After several cups of hot tea, he felt his blood beginning to circulate again and shaped up to face the day.

A quick call to the Russian ikon dealer resulted in an appointment for midday in Greenwich Village, which in the event taxed his powers of persuasion and deception to the full. He subsequently realised that in fact his two very shrewd hosts, father and son now called Green (the old man, ironically, had hailed originally from Odessa), had not for a moment believed his story but had, for their own reasons, decided to play along with him by appearing to accept it. His opening spiel, which on the previous evening he had almost believed himself, was met with knowing grins. There was, they told him, a glut of ikons on the market; so many Russians had been rummaging in their attics and selling off the family heirlooms in Vienna, Paris and New York. As a consequence, prices were low and it was a bad time to sell. His best course – that is to say, the best course for his principals – would be to defer all sales for a year or so, though there was, as a matter of fact, a risk that the market might take even longer than that to recover. Of course, if he really insisted on an immediate sale, the Greens might be able to take the merchandise off his hands, just by way of a favour, and to take their own chance on whatever profit they might be able to scrape together. Could he perhaps give them some idea, however approximate, of the total that he – that is to say, his principals – were hoping to dispose of?

Hoist neatly with his own petard (Písemsky had often wondered what that actually meant), he had to make a rapid decision. The more times he went through this exercise of selling, the more risk there was that something would go horribly wrong. As things stood, he had already acquired more money than he could ever reasonably need; should he not just grab what he could get, and run?

Pleading the necessity to confer with his principals (Of course, of course.), he hedged. As a matter of fact, he told them, he did have a list of a number of items that would at some point be offered for sale. Perhaps if he gave them sight of the provenance, they would like to make a bid for them all together? The only justification for such a step, of course, would be immediate payment in cash. But a further complication would be the problem of getting the merchandise to them in bulk. He might be able to persuade his principals to agree to have them delivered to, say, Cuba, but to import them into the States would be extremely difficult.

'From Cuba?' they grinned. 'Leave it to us. No problem!'

The haggling began in earnest when the two men had examined the document of provenance. Despite strenuous efforts to disguise their delight, they positively drooled, rocking back and forth on their chairs and stroking their wispy beards. '*Nu da,*' the old man said at length, mumbling scarcely audibly in Russian. 'Well, yes, not at all bad, I must admit.' Of course, they would have to do some checking, to consult their expert colleagues, and so on ... but it was clear to Písemsky that they were hooked. How was he to exploit the situation?

'Perhaps,' he suggested, 'we can handle this in two stages, instead of one. I have with me the ikon attributed to Andréi Rublyóv (*Possibly* by Rublyóv, they reminded him. *Possibly* by Rublyóv.) and I am empowered (Yes, yes!) to sell it immediately. If you would like to think about a reasonable price, perhaps we can meet again tomorrow? Then in a week or so we can get together again to discuss the rest.'

Heads were again rocked, this time from side to side, but at length this approach was agreed and an appointment made for the morning of the following day, since Písemsky would be leaving New York that evening.

When he left the two ikon dealers, Písemsky began to suffer a nervous reaction that made his head spin and his legs weak. Stumbling into the nearest bar, he swallowed two double vodkas – there had been no alcohol to fuddle brains at the meeting – which enabled him to collect his thoughts sufficiently to face the follow-up session about the sale of the Picasso lithographs. Fortunately, this was rather easier than he had feared. Mulrooney had clearly decided to accept his proposition, and despite an unconvincing attempt to lower the asking price, which Písemsky resolutely blocked, he soon produced a ready drawn-up legal document for signature, formally witnessed by a woman whom he described as his 'partner', who did not, however, attend for longer than was required to write her name. The sum of 1 million dollars was wired to Písemsky's Toronto bank, and verification of receipt was duly supplied. Though taken aback by Písemsky's request to complete the deal the following morning, Mulrooney could hardly withdraw now and, taking a deep breath, he agreed.

Returning to the Yorkshire, Písemsky slumped before the TV, flicking through the channels in search of something interesting. So many channels and nothing worth seeing: the US cavalry, manes flying and bugles blaring, rode to the rescue in the nick of time; policemen beat up a black man in the name of law and order; so-called singers and groups bawled and gyrated; several soaps acted out the same situations in different costumes and accents; a crimson-robed priest sang mass to a congregation of Hispanics; some chattering Brits discussed the latest Broadway musical (Písemsky hated musicals); cartoon dogs inflicted unspeakable violence on indestructible cartoon cats; Yéltsin sat glowering as Khasbulátov harangued Congress, with Khúyin smirking in the front row... Písemsky hastily moved on. It was extraordinary how unrelated to his present life all that business in Moscow had now become. On top of the TV set was a separate panel; for 5 dollars, an 'adult' film could be watched. Písemsky operated a switch so that the charge would be automatically added to his bill, and sat back: a series of grunts and moans accompanied a sexual act being performed by a macho muscleman on a kneeling woman... He hurriedly switched off, groaning and shaking his head as though in pain: Why am I being persecuted like this? He poured himself a large measure of vodka to steady his nerves.

Having soaked himself for half an hour in a bath full of water so apparently muddy that he wondered if it would clean him or stain his body brown, Písemsky dressed with meticulous care. After the disreputable performance of yesterday evening, he wanted to feel fresh and respectable, expunging it from body and mind as though it had all never happened. In this pristine and virtuous state, he went down for dinner.

Munching an *amuse bouche* with his aperitif, he acknowledged a decision he had unconsciously made earlier in the day. All this wheeling and dealing was not really his style. He was a reasonable man; he must take whatever he could get, even if the prices he accepted were ridiculously low, and find a legitimate use for the money. His life was somehow running out of control again; each move predetermined the next, but there was no overall direction, or – if there was – it was not a direction in which, in his saner and more sober moments, he really wanted to go.

He saw again the glowering face of Yéltsin, the ex-party boss turned scourge of the Communists, poacher turned gamekeeper. This was the man who had compelled him to embark on this dangerous new course, who had finally made it impossible for him to return to the only other way of life he knew. Then the visage of Khúyin took the place of Yéltsin's, so vividly that he gasped in horror when a voice addressed him, only to find a waiter asking to take his order.

Mechanically, he gave it, then returned to his reverie. Compared with New York, even Cuba and arms-dealing was a world of calm and serenity. But Khúyin, with whom he would soon be called upon to renew contact, was quite another matter. It was now absolutely clear to Písemsky that he wanted no further dealings with him. Cutting off his links with Moscow meant cutting them off with Khúyin, too. In fact, from the arms trade as well as from the sale of art treasures, he simply wanted out. After all, he had never really wanted to do this sort of thing; he had been an honest and successful functionary, working hard and having no particular vices, when suddenly, from no fault of his own, the whole basis of his lifestyle had been swept away and he had been forced to carve out a new livelihood by his own enterprise and wits. Well, he'd managed to scrape together a few million (he was still honest enough to choke a little at this figure), and now all he wanted was to eke out whatever years he had left to him in a quiet and undramatic way. His colleagues in Cuba would surely understand; after all, they would be able to keep a larger share of the profits for themselves. As for the ikons, well, he would not be greedy; the Greens could have the lot for just a few million. And the paintings could stay in the García Lórca in Havana until he could calmly and sensibly decide what to do with them.

Písemsky began to feel better. He congratulated himself on the immaculate logic of his argument and signalled the waiter for another large vodka to accompany his oysters. So that was all settled, then. He'd simply go back to Havana, thank Pérez and Macías for their cooperation, and bow quietly out. Perhaps he'd take Canadian citizenship and move to Toronto. It seemed a reasonable place; a bit provincial, compared with European cities, but not such a backwater as Havana or Varadero. Yes, that's what he'd do. He might even get a job of some sort, in business, for example . . .

But a germ of doubt persisted. Would Pérez, or especially, Macías, be happy to see him back out now, when he knew so much about what they'd been doing? He would have no intention – far from it! – of reporting them to the authorities, even if he had the remotest idea of which authorities would be interested, or of buying himself any sort of immunity. That was not at all the sort of thing he would ever do. He was quite simply not that sort of man. But did the others realise this? Macías, he was sure, was a nasty, vicious little man, the sort who would probably never be able to understand that not everyone was as crooked and unscrupulous as he was. The more Písemsky thought about it, the more he began to realise that simply walking away from it all might not in fact be so easy. Another kind of behaviour might be called for. He sighed. What awful people he seemed to be getting involved with these days.

As for the ikon business, the two dealers certainly hadn't believed a word of his story, nor had they tried particularly hard to pretend otherwise, but Písemsky had no real choice

160

but to stick to it and follow it through to the end. If he more or less gave the ikons to them at some ridiculously low price, they would be quite sure that he had stolen them and was desperate to get them off his hands, in which case they would either drive the price down lower or even have him arrested in the hope of gaining some sort of reward. So he must bargain with them for the best price he could get. He would, however, try to sell the ikons as one lot, except for the Rublyóv, instead of piecemeal, as he had originally intended.

So by the time he reached his pudding, Písemsky had talked himself in a complete circle, ending with very much the same dilemma as when he began. But at least he had made conscious decisions, striving to formulate an intelligent interpretation of the situation in which he found himself and to follow its inherent logic. The shattering effect of his nightmare experience with Gigi and Tara had begun to dissipate and he already felt more firmly in control of his destiny.

In this mood, he decided to have a night 'on the town' (if anybody still said that). Recalling an evening spent at a jazz club in Greenwich Village some years earlier, during a visit to New York with a delegation to UNO, he consulted the fount of all such knowledge, a taxi driver, about where it might have been.

'Village Vanguard or Blue Note,' the oracle replied 'Whedyawannago?' Písemsky chose the first, and enjoyed a 15-minute drive through lower Manhattan, where the darkened, towering blocks, dotted with intermittent lights like stars against the background of a still deep-blue sky, seemed as unreal as a magic, fairy-tail scene. Just like a stage set, he thought; nature imitating art, or something. He couldn't quite sort it out.

Entering the club, he found himself in a long, narrow room, with a low ceiling and intimate (otherwise, bad) lighting, a bar at one end near the door, tables and chairs filling most of the space, and a stage at the far end, on which a trio of black musicians were playing a slow, sweet blues. There were as yet few clients about; just one or two seated at the bar, drinking, smoking and chatting to the barman, turning only half an ear to the music. Two or three tables were occupied by couples; a few singles sat drinking alone with their thoughts. Písemsky perched on a bar stool, ordered a double vodka with a beer as chaser and lit a cigar. The music began to soothe him, though he felt that at this early stage the musicians were doing little more than tuning up and practising.

After about an hour, when things were becoming more lively, he moved to a table and began listening more intently to the now augmented band, as it shifted from cool jazz to Chicago and eventually to classical New Orleans numbers that exhilarated musicians and audience alike. During the last number before the interval, he was conscious that he had been joined at the table by someone else, a woman, whose musky perfume was overpowering, but certainly preferable to the pungent Red Poppy with which Russian women used to strive unsuccessfully to mask their body odours. He stole a sidelong glance at her as he rose to refill his glass. She seemed attractive enough, though her dark hair, hanging down in a thick mass, was hiding much of her face.

'You wanna buy a girl a drink, honey?' she said.

Oh dear, here we go again, he thought. But why not? What's wrong with buying someone a drink?

'Surely. What will you have?'

'Vodka and lime,' she simpered.

Písemsky approached the bar. 'Same again for me,' he said, 'and a vodka and lime for the lady.' He nodded with his head toward the table.

The barman looked across and gave him a pitying smile: 'That's no lady, bub. That's a feller.'

'What!' Písemsky grabbed at the bar to steady himself, as his head reeled with shock and embarrassment. 'Forget the drinks,' he said, brushing aside several indignant newcomers as he forced his way out of the door.

He dashed into the little square opposite, where a line of taxis was waiting.

'For God's sake!' he muttered as the cab whisked him rapidly uptown. 'Isn't anything in this place really what it seems?' He was still trembling with indignation, turning rapidly to anger. 'I must get away from this horrible town. I hate New York . . .'

*'When are you going home then, Iván?'* He heard the echo of Gareth's question, and he recalled also his own reply – *'I'm not sure any more where "home" really is.'* To his chagrin, he found he was near to tears.

But the Mochítsky technique came again to his rescue. To hell with this! If that's the way it is, then I have to beat these people at their own game. He muttered a Russian proverb: If I'm going to live with wolves, I'm going to howl like a wolf. It was time to put a stop to all this unhealthy introspection and take charge. He recalled, with a ghost of a smile now, the pious resolutions he had been making over dinner, and in an ironic tone he cited aloud the two talents proudly proclaimed by Chátsky's rival, Molchálin – *moderation and correctness* – which only an hour or two earlier had seemed so admirable.

Then he let Gareth cap Molchálin (Chátsky's riposte had put it more elegantly, but the message was the same): 'Bugger that for a lark!'

# 16

Písemsky's morning appointment with Mulrooney was for nine o'clock. Deliberately delaying until 9.30, he walked briskly into the office, looking ostentatiously at his wristwatch. 'Sorry I'm late. Afraid I'm in a bit of a hurry. Got a plane to catch.'

Brusquely refusing the proffered seat, he opened his briefcase, took out a folder and spread the two Picasso lithographs casually on the agent's desk. 'Here you are,' he said briskly. 'Wonderful work. I hate to see them go.'

Mulrooney leaned over to examine them, not daring to touch, hardly daring, in fact, even to breathe on them.

'If we can just settle the finances, I'll be on my way,' Písemsky said, looking again at his watch.

Hardly bearing to take his eyes off the lithographs, Mulrooney authorised the wiring of a further 1 million dollars, this time to Písemsky's Swiss account. When the transaction was completed, Písemsky assumed an air of barely transparent nonchalance and prepared to take his leave.

'Goodbye,' he said, thrusting out a hand to be shaken. 'It's been a pleasure doing business with you. Please don't bother, I'll see myself out.'

Thirty minutes later, he was in the Greens' office in Greenwich Village, going through the same pantomime with his watch and the business about catching a plane.

'Of course, of course,' father and son chorused, showing not the slightest sign of urgency.

With them was a stooping, wrinkled old man, wearing pebble-glass spectacles and mumbling to himself through wet lips. 'Dr Vernádsky,' the elder Green introduced him reverentially, 'the world's foremost authority on the Rublyóv school of ikonography.'

Dr Vernádsky nodded gravely, modestly acknowledging his eminence. Písemsky also nodded, and without a word took the ikon from his case, removed the baize wrapping and placed the ikon on the table. Also without a word, all three men leaned over to examine it, rocking heads and shoulders and mumbling sounds of appreciation. Then Dr Vernádsky began his expert appraisal, viewing the painting from all angles, studying the pose, the colours, the shape of the head... At length, he took out a tiny knife, screwed a jeweller's glass into one eye and scraped a tiny sliver of wood from the back of the ikon, examining it at some length. Then the same procedure was repeated, this time with a speck of enamel from the border of the painting. All this was punctuated with mutterings of *N-da!* and *Tak-s!* and various indeterminate sounds, as the Greens sat barely able to contain their excited impatience and Písemsky strove to disguise his rising anxiety by concentrating on a growing desire for a large vodka and a cigar. At length, Vernádsky gave Green the elder an almost imperceptible nod, bowed low to the ikon and left. The relief in the air was almost tangible.

For some reason, Písemsky wanted to laugh. What would now follow was all so archetypical, so utterly predictable. In his new mood of callous cynicism, he watched the charade being acted out like a spectator at a familiar drama, observing the unfolding of the plot with interest, even though the denouement was long since known.

When Vernádsky had left, the elder Green launched into what essentially was a repetition of what he had said at their first meeting, plus a grudging admission that the ikon did in fact seem likely to date from somewhere about Rublyóv's time and might therefore be of a certain interest to some people. Eventually, with much hesitation, he named a price.

'No,' said Písemsky.

The looks of frozen horror on the faces of father and son were like a scene from a Gogol farce. Once again, Písemsky found it difficult not to laugh. Everyone waited for someone else to speak.

The elder Green sighed deeply. 'You are a hard man,' he said, shaking his head sadly. Then he named a slightly higher price.

'No,' said Písemsky again.

Again they were silent. The younger Green beckoned to his father, and with muttered excuses they both left the room.

Some five minutes later, they slunk back in. 'What figure did you have in mind?' the older man enquired.

'Three-quarters of a million US dollars, now,' Písemsky stated baldly.

With an even deeper sigh, the old man nodded to his son, who unlocked the wall-safe and took out a faxed authorisation for payment of precisely that amount. Písemsky dictated the address.

'I like you, Mr Písemsky,' the old man said as he sent off the fax. Both he and his son were now grinning broadly.

When receipt of the money had been wired from Toronto, Písemsky once again assumed his blasé mien.

'A pleasure to have met you,' he said. 'I'll contact you again in about three weeks.'

Two hours later, Písemsky was en route by Air Canada to Toronto, richer by 2.75 million dollars and a wiser man.

'Howl like a wolf . . . !'

Having reclaimed his room at the Toronto downtown Hilton, to the relief of the reception staff who had been wondering what had become of him, Písemsky rang Don Macinaw's number.

'Don?'

'Yup.'

'It's John.'

There was a pause.

'Jaahn. Well hiya, fella! Whaddya say?'

Písemsky had been caught this way before. He said nothing.

'Where are ya?'

'I'm at the Hilton. I've just got in from New York.'

'You're in Traano, Jaahn!'

Yes, I know, Písemsky wanted to say. Instead, he said: 'Yup.'

'You want we should eat, Jaahn?'

'Um, yes. That would be nice.'

'You got it!'

'What?'

There was a longer pause. 'Whaddya mean what?'

'You said I got it.'

'Yup.'

'Got what?'

There was an even longer pause. 'Jesus Holy Christ! We gotta teach you ta talk Canadian, Jaahn.' Don laughed. 'You eat Greek?' he asked suddenly.

'I beg your pardon?'

'You like Greek chow?'

'Um, yes, I do . . . I think.'

'That's just fine. We got the best l'il old taverna this side of Athens, Greece. I'll stop by the Hilton in one hour. OK?'

'You got it!'

Here endeth, thought Písemsky, the first lesson.

As Macinaw drove through downtown Toronto, talking without a pause for breath, Písemsky looked at the names on the shops and offices: MacKenzie, Blair, Fraser, Thompson . . . the Scots were everywhere in evidence. With a name like Macinaw, Don should certainly feel at home here, he thought.

The vine-roofed Taverna Niko was crowded, but as the two men entered the portly host came bustling up.

'*Kalispéra!*' he said warmly, shaking their hands. '*Kalispéra sas!*'

'*Kalispéra!*' Don replied. '*Ti kánis?*'

'*Kalá, kalá! Kai ésis?*'

'*Kalá!*'

Niko signalled to a waiter, who escorted them to a table at the end furthest from the *bouzouki* orchestra.

'So you speak Greek?' Písemsky said, as they took their place at the table.

'Sure. My pappy came from over there.'

'But your name is Macinaw!'

Don grinned. 'We-e-ll. . .'

'And Niko? Do you always speak Greek together?'

Don guffawed loudly. 'Hell, no. That was the whole bag. All the Greek he knows.'

'With a name like Niko?'

Don shook his head at his companion's naivety. 'Niko's no Greek. He's a polack.'

And indeed, Niko's voice could again be heard, this time saying goodbye to departing guests: '*Dziękuję bardzo. Do widzenia!*'

Now, Písemsky thought, I know how Alice felt in Wonderland. Nothing, absolutely nothing, is really what it seems to be. And that, he added soberly, includes me.

Partly from genuine curiosity, but largely in order to avoid the sort of interrogation that would almost certainly have begun when the usual exchange of banalities was over, Písemsky began himself to quiz Don about his business. Something to do with sports equipment, he seemed to recall.

The transformation in Don was remarkable: from a blustering semi-buffoon he became a serious, articulate and obviously shrewd businessman, evidently successful but just a tiny bit worried by the universal problem of every fast-growing concern, cash flow.

He operated on a scale far greater than Písemsky had imagined and had even more ambitious plans, to which, during the course of an absorbing discussion, Písemsky almost accidently added a vital new dimension. In fact, the whole thing, as he later realised, was a classic example of serendipity.

A former fisherman in the Cyclades, Don's father had

settled in Canada just before the outbreak of World War Two and begun a little business hiring out fishing gear and boats in the Thousand Islands area of the St Lawrence, a long way from Naxos but a familiar enough environment. By the time the old man died, leaving his business to his only son, he owned a chain of such concerns all along the river and into the Great Lakes, extending, as pollution killed off the fish stocks, into more active water sports – speedboats, water-skiing and windsurfing.

In his turn, Don further extended the business's activities into winter sports: skiing (mostly cross-country) and, especially, ice-skating, and thence to the great Canadian winter pastime – the 'real man's game' – ice hockey. The next step was to broaden the company's scope even further into building the actual installations for these sports: they built ice rinks in London, Windsor, Kingston and Gananoque, as well as in Toronto itself, and were in the process of negotiating contracts in Ottawa, Quebec and Montreal. But competition, especially from the States, was fierce, and Don had begun to look further afield, to other areas of Canada: New Brunswick, perhaps, for cross-country skiing, Manitoba for schools of equestrianism. 'You name it,' he said. 'Canada's a big country.'

'But not the only country,' Písemsky interjected.

'Pardon me?' Don paused, his eyebrows slightly raised, and Písemsky began his usual process of unravelling a line of thought that had never consciously occurred to him before.

'Just think of somewhere like Cuba,' he said. 'A paradise in the sun, just waiting to be developed. All those fantastic beaches . . . Varadero's only a small part, you know. There are lots of others. And tourism is Cuba's potentially biggest industry. From Canada alone it must already be making millions, and when the Americans start coming . . .'

'Jeez!' Don exclaimed. 'I know what you mean. Don't think I haven't wondered about that myself.' (You are really a bit of a piss artist, too, Písemsky silently commented.) 'But capital, capital . . . It would take a few million bucks to get a scheme like that off the ground. Who's going to put in that kind of money?'

Into the silence that followed this apparently rhetorical question, Písemsky dropped a calm, hardly audible reply.

'Well, I may just be able to help you there . . .'

Don was clearly startled. 'Are you kidding?'

'Just let me think about it,' Písemsky added. 'I'll be back in Toronto in a few weeks. Maybe we can have another talk about it then. But you might like to think it over a bit yourself.' He changed the subject.

Before he left for the airport next morning. Písemsky rang the Deputy Director of his bank. Certainly, they said, a full report on the financial and managerial viability of Macinaw Enterprises would be dispatched to him in Havana within a week.

# 17

Nothing significant had happened in Cuba during Písemsky's absence. He had himself experienced such trauma and achieved so dramatic a change in his fortunes that he felt almost offended that his absence seemed hardly to have been noticed, and that nothing had changed. Not that he regretted the prospect of at least a few days of peace and relaxation after the excitements of his first foray into Canada and the United States, though he had begun by now to acknowledge that it was not in his nature to relax, except for the briefest of periods.

At this time, in particular, he could withdraw only *pour mieux sauter*: the unfinished business with the ikons would not allow him to sit back for too long, and there was the necessity also to develop a legitimate cover for his increasing wealth. Even so, he did little during the next two weeks but sit in the shade, dozing and hazily planning his next moves, and making a feeble attempt to take a little systematic exercise by regular swimming in the villa pool. He was conscious of putting on weight at an alarming pace.

'You gettin' very fat,' Jina had told him in her blunt fashion, the apparent discourtesy stemming more from the absence of command of nuance in her rudimentary English than from a desire to give gratuitous offence. 'You gettin' like Canada man. I don' like Canada men.'

He was suffering, too, from the heat and, especially on his visits to Havana, from the enervating humidity, which left him gasping and listless, and increased even further his fluid intake – mostly rum, in various cocktails, when he was with Cubans, and vodka, chased with beer, when he was alone. He was aware that he was beginning to take his first shot of vodka progressively earlier in the day; it seemed to be the only thing that would make him fit for any sort of action after generally unsatisfyingly sleepless nights. But this did not worry him unduly. It's not as if I were becoming an alcoholic, he told himself. I could give it up at any time if I really wanted to. But why should I? I'm not doing anyone any harm.

In the second week after his return he received from the Toronto bank a complete dossier on Macinaw Enterprises which confirmed the impression he had gained in his conversation with Don at Taverna Niko. The business had been developed with acumen and flair but had reached a critical stage, when only a large injection of new capital would enable it to achieve its logical ambitions. The report was careful not to cast the slightest doubt on the viability of the business nor on the skill and conduct of the management. The problem, insofar as a problem could be said to exist at all, was one of undercapitalisation. In fact, in the bank's opinion Macinaw Enterprises – provided there were judicious controls – might constitute a perfectly sound investment for the new client. They awaited Mr Písemsky's instructions.

Písemsky acknowledged his own lack of expertise in such matters; in Moscow he had administered the spending of a large budget, but the question of balancing this against revenue had simply not arisen. It he had needed a supplementary sum, he had only to request it. He needed sound advice, and when the second payment for the Haitian small-arms shipment came through he became even more aware that the wealth he was now accruing would need skilful management, not least *vis à vis* tax demands, which he was naturally anxious to avoid. He needed a legitimate activity involving both income and huge reclaimable expenses. He believed the term was 'laundering', though the mechanics of this process were a mystery to him. Added to this, Písemsky had become fired with enthusiasm for the ideas he had floated with Don Macinaw for

172

expanding tourist facilities in Cuba. On all these matters, there seemed to be only one person in Cuba to whom he could turn – Pérez, not least because to some degree they shared the same problems and had similar aspirations.

He was pleased, therefore, when in the third week, just as he was beginning to think about his next visit to North America, a meeting was called at Varadero to hear a report by Diego Macías on his sales tour of Central and South America. Písemsky arranged that Pérez should stay an extra night at the villa after the meeting, so that they could talk privately, without the inhibiting presence of Macías. In the event, circumstances contrived to bring other matters also into conjunction at what proved to be something of a turning point in their cooperative affairs.

On the morning of the scheduled meeting with Pérez and Macías plans were suddenly changed and Písemsky was informed that for the first session they would be joined briefly by Duvalier, and by the Major. Pleased as he always was to see Pérez and the Major, he found Macías and Duvalier severally unsympathetic and jointly almost more than he could bear. But you had to hand it to them; they certainly knew what they were doing.

The delivery of the shipment of small-arms had been, in the words of a satisfied Duvalier, '*formidable*', but such was the seamy underworld of intelligence networks in Port au Prince, with the constantly mutating relationships between insurgents and government, that the latter had rejoiced almost equally with the former at the appearance of a new source of arms that seemed, as yet, impervious to any kind of embargo. Indeed, as Macías later announced with a malicious smirk, he had been able to obtain what he called 'complementary orders' from the two sides: from the illegal government of General Raoul Cedres, an order for six helicopter gunships – all that were currently in store at the Santiago de Cuba airport; and from the supporters of Jean-Bertrand Aristide, as many batteries of the ground-to-air missiles as they could supply from the stock held at Trinidad de Cuba, plus instructors in their use.

At the Major's suggestion, the logistics involved in fulfilling these two orders could be harmonised, in that the pilots and navigators who flew the helicopters to Port au Prince could subsequently join Aristide's forces in order to train them to shoot them down. The order from the government side was perfectly legal and could be fulfilled quite openly, and the Major's scheme for the subsequent deployment of the personnel involved would obviate the need to smuggle in men, which was inherently more difficult than delivering hardware. The whole scheme had a sort of awful symmetry, thought Písemsky, who found in it an element of poetic justice. And as for their own role, well, it wasn't as if they would be interfering in someone else's war in order to give one side an unfair advantage over the other. On the contrary, the logical result of such a trade would be that each side would end up more or less where it had started. Rather neat, really. Crazy, of course, but if these people wanted to behave in that way simply because they had more money than sense, it was hardly up to Písemsky and his colleagues to prevent them from doing so.

A further order, Macías reported, had been received for various arms, this time from the Guatemalan revolutionary Organisation for National Unity, which was in a constant state of guerilla warfare with the increasingly dictatorial regime of President Jorge Serrano, from whom Macías hoped also to obtain an order. The Major was asked to devise a means of delivery, in the knowledge that this might involve the risk of military opposition. In the Major and his professional troops such a prospect aroused no fears; indeed, it was difficult to avoid the impression that the Major positively looked forward to some real action. In both Písemsky and Pérez, however, it caused a tremor of apprehension. Neither welcomed the possibility, however remote, of this new dimension in what had so far been a deceptively simple operation.

Duvalier had left the meeting after reporting on the Haitian situation, and when the Major had also departed after the discussion of Guatemala, the three remaining protagonists were left to tackle another problem, consequent, ironically enough, on the success of their schemes so far: if the three new orders were filled, the stocks of ex-Soviet arms currently held in Cuba would be virtually exhausted. The projected conference with Khúyin was now a matter of urgency. He was known from TV reports to have been absent from Moscow for some ten days on honeymoon in the Crimea, but he had now returned and an attempt to contact him was to be made that afternoon.

'You just pin him down as firmly as you can.' Macías said, handing Písemsky a list of *matériel*, ranging from side arms to tanks, for which he anticipated receiving orders in the next few months, 'otherwise we shall have to find an alternative supplier.' He paused. 'Or,' he said portentously, though neither Pérez nor Písemsky understood the import, 'we shall have to diversify...'

Over a largely liquid lunch, a morose Písemsky prepared himself mentally for the coming telephone conference, trying vainly to decide how best to approach Khúyin. At length, an idea occurred to him that caused him to laugh aloud, but to Pérez's request to share the joke he replied that it concerned a ploy that he might not have to use, but that if he did in fact use it, Pérez would certainly understand.

When the time for the telephone link-up came, there was – to Písemsky's dismay – no technical hitch of any sort, and Khúyin's voice came over loud and clear. He spoke in English:

'Hello. This is George Khúyin speaking. Can you hear me?'

'*Da, da. Slýshno. Otlíchno...*' Písemsky confirmed, but Khúyin interrupted him brusquely.

'Speak English, old boy. More secure this end, you know.'

It's an extraordinary thing, the listening Pérez thought, before Gorbachóv's time there didn't seem to be anyone in the entire Soviet apparatus who spoke anything but Russian, but suddenly they are all speaking English as though they had done so all their lives. Where on earth had all these characters been hiding?

Písemsky was speaking again, reminding Khúyin in simple though thinly coded terms about their agreement and explaining that he and his colleagues now wished to place an order for a further consignment of merchandise.

There was an awkward silence. Had the phone gone dead? 'We have a problem,' Khúyin said slowly. (My God, he's changed his tune!) 'Too many orders to fill, all at the same time. Iraq and Iran, various African chappies, the Serbs via Bulgaria and the Croats from the old DDR... You know. Everybody wants our stuff. So I don't really think I can help you, old boy. Question of priorities, you know...'

Pérez looked shocked, but Písemsky was ready with his ploy.

'I hear you've just got married,' he said calmly, apparently going off at a tangent. 'Congratulations. Anybody I know?'

'No, I don't think so,' Khúyin answered automatically. 'But she knows your daughter. As a matter of fact, they are both working in Yéltsin's office.'

This last remark almost threw Písemsky off his stroke, but he rallied to the attack.

'*Vash syn slávnyimál'chik,*' he said. '*Ochen' khoróshii páren'!*'

'*Podozhdíte minútochku!*' Khúyin bawled into the receiver, and Písemsky duly waited a moment, listening with a grin to someone being asked to wait outside, followed by the slamming of a door. Then Khúyin returned.

'Speak English, damn you. Now, what was that you said?'

'I was down in Cienfuegos a few days ago,' Písemsky said brightly in an even, conversational tone, 'and I met your son. He's a lovely little boy. Very like you, though with Lola's colouring, of course. He thought I was his Russian daddy and wanted me to take him to Moscow. I knew you'd like to meet him, so I said I'd try to arrange for him to go over to stay with you and your wife. Lola would also love to see you, I'm sure...'

'Son? What son? I don't know anything about a son.' Khúyin's voice was trembling.

'I took some splendid photographs,' Písemsky went on. 'Would you like me to send you them?'

'For God's sake!' Khúyin exclaimed. 'Just wait a minute, will you? I have to think about this...'

'Of course, of course,' said Písemsky, visualising the grinning faces of the Greens, *père et fils*, and grinning back at them into space. 'By the way,' he went on, 'about that merchandise. We really do need it quite urgently.'

Khúyin groaned. 'Oh, I'm sure something can be done,' he snapped. 'Just let me know the details and I'll see what I can arrange.'

'Well, that *is* decent of you.' Písemsky winked at Pérez, who was now enjoying the joke. 'I was sure you would help us if you possibly could. Here are the details. Have you got a pen handy?'

'Has Khúyin really got a son in Cienfuegos?' Pérez asked him when the conference was over.

'I've no idea,' Písemsky said blandly. 'But I do know one thing – he can't be sure he hasn't!' He grinned wickedly. 'And I dare say we could find a possible candidate if we had to.

'Now, let's drink to Lola. She moved very nicely for us today.'

When the two men later set out to discuss the questions that had been hitherto at the top of Písemsky's agenda, it soon transpired that from the morning session and the telephone conference with Khúyin there were new and possibly more urgent topics to be aired. Písemsky was pleased to discover early in the conversation that whereas Pérez had previously been fascinated (unhealthily so, in Písemsky's opinion) by the personality of Diego Macías, his attitude had now been transformed into one of growing distrust, tinged with fear. This, in turn, served to reinforce Písemsky's own scarcely concealed dislike, and he was reassured by the knowledge that in the aversion that he instinctively felt for Macías he now had a potential ally in Pérez. The morning's meeting had done nothing to restrain their swelling antipathy.

Both Písemsky and, especially, Pérez were uneasy that so

much of their arms trade seemed to be with an island only a few miles from Cuba itself. Pérez despised the present Haitian government and was quite indifferent to its fate, but he saw a danger that, on the one hand, the Americans would inevitably begin to have suspicions about the source of the *matériel* that had led to the sudden rise in the scale of armed conflict and, on the other hand, the Cuban authorities might begin to cast a wary eye on the potential influence of Haitian unrest in Oriente, not a particularly stable area at the best of times. The proposed switch to Guatemalan markets was only marginally better; it would still be too close to Cuba for comfort. Moreover, Pérez said unusually formally, disposing of unwanted arms is one thing, but importing arms expressly for resale is quite a different matter. On all these counts it seemed unlikely that their operations as at present conducted could continue for very much longer.

On a more personal level, what was really worrying both men was the possibility of violence. They had entered the murky world of arms-dealing almost by accident; an opportunity had presented itself that was too good to be ignored. They had thought of it simply as a matter of commerce, and the realisation that it might soon involve bloodshed had come as something of a shock. The Major's attitude had neither surprised nor disturbed them; he was a professional soldier, trained for action. But the callous indifference of Macías had increased their disdain for him and for everything he stood for. They had come a long way since that exhilaratingly facile conversation at Silver Woods and they were beginning to fear that they were getting out of their depth.

They were, they realised, being less than logical. Písemsky developed this theme, gesticulating forcibly to drive home his points, as they strode along the seafront between the villa and the line of hotels. People bought arms, he said, in order to forward their aims by force, and when force was employed, someone was liable to be hurt. Men had always behaved in this way and always would. It was only human nature. And if they were determined to use arms, they would go out and buy them – 'from someone else, if not from us... Guns don't kill,' Písemsky declared passionately, as if propounding some eternal verity, 'people do!' Pérez may not have been entirely swayed by Písemsky's arguments, but he said nothing. His own problem was not so much that his conscience was troubling him, but that he was scared.

As they reached El Paradiso, they turned and retraced their steps towards the villa. Písemsky felt a reluctance now to enter the hotel. It was not exactly that he was ashamed of his treatment of Judy – why should he be? No harm had come to her. On the contrary, she had had a really 'good time' and would undoubtedly be eternally grateful to him – or ought to be. But the business with Judy had been the beginning of a traumatic period, the details of which he would prefer now to forget. The time would come, of course, when he would be able to laugh at such a silly attitude, but not yet. So he resisted any possible desire that Pérez might have had to observe the Canadians at play and led the way firmly back to the villa.

Recalling the telephone conference, they chuckled at the recollection of Khúyin's discomfiture but, as Písemsky put it: 'I may have scored a few points, but I don't think I made any friends.' It was clear to both that Khúyin attached little importance to the agreement reached in Moscow and they realised that Písemsky's clever little ploy was not likely to work a second time. Moreover, the prices they would have to pay for arms under the new dispensation would so reduce their margin of profit that the whole business would become less attractive for everyone concerned. So once again, it seemed likely that the dealing would soon come to an end, and both men took heart from this prospect.

However, they had no illusions about the attitudes of Macías and the Major to a cessation of trading, which were likely to be rather different from theirs, especially as the latter commanded a highly trained and disciplined force that might not take kindly to the loss of congenial and lucrative employment. Pérez speculated about the 'alternative source' of arms that Macías might have had in mind. The Cuban army arsenal, perhaps? This was a line of thought he simply did not dare to follow further. Taking his cue from Písemsky, he reasoned that since Macías and the Major had been recruited in the first instance only to assist in the sale of the unwanted Soviet *matériel*, then as soon as that sale was completed, their task would equally have been achieved. What they did with themselves afterwards was of no concern to either Pérez or Písemsky. So what were they worried about? But secretly neither of them was convinced by this argument, and each feared that they might have created a monster that would eventually devour them.

As they reached the villa, the two men decided to leave further discussion to the morning, not attempting to solve their problems now but resolving to sleep on them. Ridiculous concept, Písemsky said to himself. How can I sleep on them when I know perfectly well that they are going to keep me awake? And they did.

The conversation next morning began rather cagily but soon moved into a more positive and even enthusiastic mode. In discussing financial matters, Pérez was on more familiar ground and he spoke with clarity and authority on banking arrangements in Cuba and in Canada, the movement of capital between the two, and other technicalities which, though the word was never uttered, constituted 'laundering'. In this he was motivated also by the fact that in some respects he and Písemsky had common needs. Together with what he had learned in Toronto, this gave Písemsky the reassurance he craved, but he surprised both Pérez and himself by the vehemence with which he expressed the frustration that had been building up within him.

'Whenever I ask advice on what to do with my money,' he exclaimed testily, 'I am always told how to use it in order to make even more. But I want to use it to *do something*, something that will give me a purpose in life, something that I can be at least partly in charge of.'

Continuing this untypical plunge into honest expression of what was really in his mind, Písemsky told Pérez about his talk with Macinaw in Toronto and about his notion of developing more tourist facilities in Cuba by employing Cuban (his own) capital and Canadian know-how. He made it all sound extremely tentative – as, indeed, it was – but Pérez instantly took fire and launched himself into a maelstrom of orbital thinking, from which Písemsky had great difficulty in hauling him back to earth.

Písemsky's plans (Pérez had already promoted the hazy ideas into something far more grand) coincided precisely with the aspirations of the Cuban authorities, who – he was sure – would be extremely cooperative. When Písemsky spoke vaguely of Santiago de Cuba as a possible area for development, Pérez quickly adduced a counter-proposal: Trinidad de Cuba, he insisted, was the perfect spot – white sands, beaches sheltered by coral reefs, the blue Caribbean, waving palms... To Písemsky's barely concealed amusement he waxed positively lyrical. 'Stop!' Písemsky said. 'You sound like a glossy brochure. For God's sake let's be a bit more practical.' Nevertheless, he was himself infected by the other's enthusiasm, though he was careful not to let this be seen.

Together, the two men began to draw up a preliminary checklist of the main features that would have to be discussed – by Pérez, with various departments of the Cuban Government, and by Písemsky, with Don Macinaw. Obtaining any required planning permissions should certainly present no obstacle; cheap labour would be plentifully available; some materials might have to be imported, as would fuel... In the event, it soon became quite obvious that they lacked the technical expertise to take such a discussion much further on their own; preliminary meetings with the other parties would be the next necessary step, and telephone calls to Havana and Toronto were made to start the process of setting them up. It was decided that Písemsky would go to Toronto for deliberations with Macinaw and his bank, and that subsequently, if the scheme still seemed practicable, Macinaw should be invited to Havana for talks with the authorities, with a visit to Trinidad de Cuba as part of his itinerary.

At midday Pérez left for Havana, leaving Písemsky marvelling at the almost mystical patriotic fervour that had invested Pérez's arguments and at his unconcealed relief at being able to devote his nervous and emotional energy to planning a project that would be both legal and morally proper, as well as eventually bringing some material benefit to the people of Cuba. Quite touching, Písemsky thought cynically, experiencing nevertheless more than a twinge of envy. None of this, he reminded himself, was anything more than an informal conversation, with no legal status and no enforceable obligations, but since he had no fundamental objection to doing well by doing good, he would play along, as proposed, and see what happened. Meanwhile, there were other matters disturbing him, not the least of these being his health, which was beginning to cause him real concern.

There was little specific that he could complain of: he simply felt unwell. Sometimes at night he would wake up bathed in sweat and with a persistent buzzing in his ears. His temperature would certainly be above normal, but yet hardly constituting a fever. Many days he felt listless, disconnected in some indefinable and not entirely unpleasant way from reality – as though, he thought with a shudder, he'd been sniffing more of that white powder or smoking something. At such moments, concentration on even simple tasks for any length of time demanded enormous effort. None of this was constant: it came and went, so that he did not feel justified in making the effort of attending a clinic, since he was sure that the symptoms would disappear as soon as he crossed the threshold. This very unpredictability added to the general feeling of malaise, which was doubly unwelcome in that now more than ever he needed to have his wits about him.

Perhaps, Písemsky thought, the trip to Canada, where there would already be an autumnal bite in the air, would reinvigorate him. The Canadian climate mirrored that of his native central Russia and would surely refresh him, in contrast to the steamy hothouse atmosphere of Cuba, which seemed to suck every vestige of energy out of his body.

So it was with high hopes, if lesser expectations, that he

arrived in mid-October in Toronto. He recognised the possibility of an accidental encounter with Judy, though Toronto was a large city so he considered this unlikely, and for the first time he realised that since his visit to New York he had completely lost any trace of sexual drive. He had never had the predatory libidinous instinct of, say, Khúyin but had what he thought was the normal interest of a healthy male. Now even that seemed to have been subdued. Well, that was hardly anything to worry about. It probably would not last, and, in fact, it might make life a good deal simpler if it did.

Písemsky's first task was the disposal of the remaining ikons. This, he decided, must be handled by telephone: under no circumstances would he go to New York. The mere thought of such a trip induced a fit of anxiety hardly distinguishable from the physical malaise with which he was periodically afflicted. At the third attempt, he did eventually establish contact with the Greens and was both gratified and a little suspicious at the warmth of their response. I must have undercharged them even more than I realised, was Písemsky's reaction, but I should be able to make up for that on the next round.

The Greens had been hoping to hear from him and would be happy to fall in with whatever procedure he would care to suggest. Typically, having said this, the younger Green immediately hastened to put forward his own plan, which was even more acceptable than anything Písemsky might himself have proposed. If Písemsky would inform them when the merchandise had arrived in Cuba, he said, keeping up the pretence of believing his original story, they would arrange to have it 'taken off his hands' on the spot. The inventory could be checked, a price agreed and payment made, all in one operation. 'I am sure we shall have no difficulty in agreeing the terms,' Green added, giving the astonished Písemsky a Baracoa telephone number through which messages could be channelled. Much encouraged, if bemused, Písemsky forecast possible delivery in perhaps six weeks' time. There was no good reason to give such a false impression of the date of delivery – the 'merchandise' was already safely stored away in Cienfuegos – but it seemed to be in the conventions of the game they were all playing that nothing should ever be quite what it seemed. Anyway, it would give him ample time to attend to the other purpose of the present visit to Canada, his negotiations with his bank and with Macinaw Enterprises.

A first contact with Don Macinaw's secretary led to a series of formal meetings with Don alone and later with his colleagues, followed by a tour of the various sites where the company had constructed or developed sports facilities. For Písemsky, the tour had a secondary function of acquainting him with much of Ontario and Quebec, giving him a broader picture of Canadian life and thus helping to mould his attitude to the question of possible naturalisation as a Canadian citizen. He was as yet unclear about the relative advantages of taking such a step as opposed either to remaining as he was, though with his Soviet passport he was in one sense stateless, or seeking some official status in Cuba or South America or elsewhere. He still hankered after the indefinable atmosphere of Europe. Once again, he noted that such cultural activities as theatre and concerts had no role in the lives of the sort of people he was now consorting with.

At their first meeting, Písemsky astounded Don by his knowledge of the company's affairs and by the pertinent questions that the bank's dossier and his discussions with Pérez had enabled him to formulate. He, in turn, was impressed by the answers he received and by what Don had to show him at the Macinaw sites. As they ate and drank their way around the two provinces, Písemsky and Don talked incessantly, so that by the end of his three weeks Písemsky had quite detailed proposals to put to the Cuban side, and Don could already make preliminary estimates of probable requirements in manpower, materials and finance.

Instead of large luxury hotels on the Varadero model, they proposed colonies of lodges, on a pattern derived from traditional Amerindian settlements, clustered around a central pleasure-dome. (Písemsky teased Don by reciting Coleridge when they hit upon this title, only to be capped by Longfellow and a string of possible names like Gitche Gumee for the settlements. Giggling like schoolboys, they declared a truce.) For each colony there would, of course, be a water sports base, as well as the facilities in the pleasure-dome. Such a project would, Don reasoned, appeal to a different kind of clientele, whom he described as the 'safari set' as distinct from the package trippers, and when Písemsky indelicately enquired how Don had himself become a package tripper he learned to his surprise and with grudging respect that all employees of Macinaw Enterprises were given an annual trip of this sort to Cuba, and that in the interest of what he called industrial democracy, he always took part in one of the groups himself. 'But I don't always meet such far-out guys as you,' he said. Písemsky, who did not understand this description, decided to take it as a compliment and changed the subject.

He realised not only the soundness of Don's analysis of the market but the fact that by splitting the building projects into small units, Macinaw Enterprises would be able to handle them all without the necessity of going into unequal and probably uneasy partnership with other, major building contractors. A possible exception, he supposed, was the pleasure-domes. From his own point of view, this had also the added advantage that the outlay of capital would similarly be staggered and could, in case of necessity, be cut off at any point. Finally, he had been struck during Pérez's lyrical outbursts by his concern for environmental conservation; Don's proposal would surely go a long way towards assuaging fears on that score.

In general, Písemsky was much encouraged by the outcomes of his visit to Canada, though the later stages were marred by an inexplicable attack of dizziness which led to hasty cancellation of a proposed meeting and a half-day in bed. It must have been all the drinking we've been doing, he thought. I'll give it up for a while when I get back to Cuba. That's all it is.

In a final session, it was agreed that Don would visit Cuba in six weeks' time for discussions with the appropriate authorities. A preliminary date was fixed, and after Písemsky

185

had indulged in an orgy of shopping for clothes that would fit his increasingly portly figure, he returned to Havana in a calmly optimistic mood. There he reported his discussions to Pérez, who was suitably impressed. His own preliminary enquiries had also met with positive reactions and it was agreed that arrangements for Don Macinaw's visit should go ahead as suggested. The invitation would be attended to by Pérez, together with accommodation and transport for the visit to Trinidad de Cuba. Satisfied, but somewhat exhausted, Písemsky was whisked off by a smiling Miguel to Varadero.

# 18

Cuba is a very large island. Whenever Písemsky consulted his map before going on an expedition, he was always surprised at how big it was. All he had culled from the various guidebooks, in Russian and in English, were typically useless snippets of data (he refused to dignify them as information) such as the fact that Cuba is the seventh largest island in the world – somewhere between Australia and the Isle of Wight, he supposed. Meaningless, totally meaningless. In fact its area, he had discovered, is roughly the same as that of England: or did they perhaps mean Great Britain? Not really very helpful.

Its shape, he read, had been variously compared to that of a scythe, a shark, a lizard and a crocodile. Or a banana, he thought. There must surely be some sort of symbolism at play here, but he could not quite work it out. Anyway, it is 1,250 kilometres long and from 191 kilometres, at the widest part, to only 32 at the narrowest. At the nearest place, it is only 27 kilometres from Haiti, which is occasionally visible from certain vantage points. In the south, Jamaica is only 140 kilometres, and in the north, Key West roughly the same distance. Add Mexico's Yucatan peninsula at 210, and you are pretty well boxed in or, if you prefer to look at it that way, you could get to lots of other places very quickly.

But what you couldn't do, which was Písemsky's problem, was to get very easily from one place inside Cuba to another without going by air, which was not always possible, and never easy. And since Havana was quite close to one end of the island, it was by the same token a long way from the other places that interested him, like Santiago and Baracoa, with Trinidad and Cienfuegos about a third of the way along. As he sat by his pool watching the omnipresent aura vultures soaring overhead, he envied their apparently effortless mobility. Did they actually enjoy flying? he wondered. They certainly gave that impression. His mind went off again at a tangent: what sort of country was it that made such a ghastly scavenger a protected bird? Was there more symbolism at work here? He pulled himself out of his reverie and returned again to his map. He had a lot of travelling to arrange, and no energy to expend on it. He could hardly be bothered.

Once again, it was the Major who came to his rescue. At Trinidad de Cuba he had to organise the transfer of the missiles to Baracoa, ready for smuggling into Haiti, and at Santiago he had similarly to arrange the flight of the helicopters, with their crew-cum-instructors, to the same destination. Naturally, therefore, he planned first to transfer the missiles to Santiago and then to fly them to Baracoa in the helicopters that they were intended later to shoot down. This somewhat roundabout route had the added advantage of keeping the helicopters well away from the US naval station at Guantánamo. All very logical. And since Cienfuegos was no great distance from Trinidad, he could leave Písemsky there for a day or so to check his inventory, or whatever other business he had, and Písemsky could then rejoin him at Trinidad, making a first acquaintance at the same time with potential sites for tourist development.

At a brief session at the Varadero villa soon after Písemsky's return, the Haitian orders from both sides had been confirmed and a notional timetable set for the movement of *matériel* and men. Písemsky's call to the Baracoa number had been answered at first in Spanish, quickly switched to American, and his suggested date for a rendezvous at the Jagua hotel at Punta Gorda accepted within the hour. The Greens must have a client ready and waiting, he thought, mentally raising the price he would ask. Planning the itinerary thereafter presented no problems.

188

But the temporary uplift that Písemsky had received from his Canadian business holiday very quickly subsided. No sooner had he settled into the villa than the same malaise again afflicted him: vague headaches, dizziness, sweating, a wretched cough that seemed to have developed for no obvious reason, and now a stiff and slightly swollen neck that made it quite impossible to sit, lie, or, for that matter, even to stand in anything like a comfortable posture. The sunlight, too, seemed to have become much brighter, hurting his eyes, so that he took to wearing intensely dark sunglasses like the ones he had adopted in his Canadian disguise.

'I don't know what the hell's the matter with me,' he said to Pérez at one point. 'I'm all aches and pains, and I can't think why.'

But Pérez had no real words of wisdom for him. 'Perhaps you're just getting bored with being on your own in Varadero,' he suggested. 'Why don't you find somewhere in Havana where you could spend part of your time? Would you like me to look for an apartment for you?'

In his more reflective moments Písemsky did in fact admit to himself that he was both bored and lonely. Cuba was no longer exotic: it was just strange. It was no longer bathed in glorious sunshine: it was simply hot.

In Moscow now it would be time for the third fall of snow, the one that stayed for the winter. The air would be crisp and clean, and the crackling frost and ice on the river would sparkle and gleam in the winter sun. Your breath might freeze on your chin, and the tiny hairs in your nostrils might turn into needle-sharp icicles, but you would breathe pure draughts, straight from the frozen steppes, the blood would surge through your veins and you would hold your head up high, glad to be alive... Yes, and you would keep yourself warm with vodka, Písemsky scoffed at his own fancies, pouring himself half a tumblerful. This is the stuff that made us Russians what we are today!

At Cienfuegos, he thought, he would have another fabulous meal with Roberto Guevara and see if he could recapture the zest and buoyancy that had characterised him when they first met. He'd arrange to have a private examination of the crate in storage, and then to exhibit the contents to whoever it was that the Greens would send. He would demand payment on the spot, before anything would be allowed to leave the theatre, and since the Major would be in the vicinity, he'd organise a little armed security, just in case. The elder Green called me a hard man, he thought, and that's just what I'm going to be. He was curious, too, about the method that would be used to take the ikons out of Cuba and, more especially, into the States – unless, of course, they were destined for somewhere else. The more he thought about it, the more curious he became. After all, if they had a route they could use once, they might well be able to use it again… Písemsky subscribed wholeheartedly to the principle enshrined in the untranslatable word *avós'* – from which is derived the name of the net shopping bag *avós'ka* that one always carried, *just in case* one happened to see something useful in the shops. He wanted to know how the Greens would operate – *just in case…*

During the 250-kilometre drive from Havana to Cienfuegos, mostly along the one main road that runs like a spine through the length of the island, Písemsky and the Major renewed the cordial relationship they had developed on their first trip to Baracoa. Although Písemsky's use of English was effortless, his relief at being able to converse in his native Russian seemed to move his whole behaviour into a higher gear. For the first time since his return from Canada, he felt totally in charge of himself – physically, mentally and emotionally.

It was therefore an unexpected shock when the Major began to speak of the dangers that would inevitably result from their adopted trade when established arms dealers began to be aware of their existence. 'They won't welcome competition on their own patch,' he warned. Then, as Písemsky sat silent, he asked him: 'Can you use a handgun?'

'I haven't held a gun for twenty years or more. Why? Do you think I should have one?'

'It wouldn't be a bad idea. As a deterrent, if nothing else.'

190

The Major pulled up at the side of the deserted road, opposite a coconut grove. He took a revolver from under the dashboard and gave it to Písemsky. 'Let's see what you can do with this,' he said, nodding toward the nearest tree.

Getting out of the car, Písemsky took careful aim. The first shot hit the trunk squarely. The next five went wide.

'Well, it's the first shot that counts,' the Major commented. 'If you ever need to use it, make sure you're so close that you can't miss.'

'Close enough to see the whites of his eyes, you mean.' Písemsky gave a nervous giggle.

'Just as long as you don't spend too much time looking into them,' the Major replied more seriously, restarting the engine.

For several kilometres they rode in silence. Písemsky had thrust the revolver into his holdall on the back seat, and from time to time he glanced back at it, as though hoping it had disappeared. He could think of no possible circumstance in which he would ever use it. He might already be doing things he would never have dreamed of a year or so ago, but killing someone – that was different. Unless, of course, he was going to kill me, he reflected. I suppose everyone has the right to defend himself. That is only reasonable. But he couldn't ever see it happening. Not to him. I'll just hide the thing away somewhere. I'm sure I'll never need it.

His mind, however, would not abandon the theme of violence that had so disrupted his earlier relaxed mood. Perhaps this would be the time to turn this to advantage.

'Actually,' he said suddenly. 'I've got a business meeting arranged in Cienfuegos. Something left over from Moscow. Nothing to do with our affairs. But I'm a bit uneasy about it. Do you think one or two of your men could keep close to me, just for one afternoon?'

The Major chuckled. 'Well, I can't bring your guardian angel back! But I dare say we could manage something for you.'

They arranged that for the vital period of the handover of the ikons and verification of payment, two of the Major's men would remain within earshot at the theatre, and they could take Písemsky on to Trinidad afterwards. If the Major was curious about Písemsky's business, he did not say so. Písemsky was debating with himself how much more to reveal, but the Major himself resolved the issue. Explaining his own plans for the forthcoming operation, he described the system of checkpoints that he had set up along the road from Trinidad de Cuba to Santiago, which after the first 50 kilometres was also the road to Baracoa, to monitor the progress of the lorries transporting the missiles and launchers. It would be a simple matter, he agreed, to monitor at the same time the route taken by any other vehicle.

At Cienfuegos Písemsky went first to the Tomás Terry theatre, where Roberto Guevara was awaiting him. After a rapid verification that the crate of ikons was intact, Písemsky invited Guevara to meet him that evening for dinner then took a taxi down the Malecon to the end of the Punta Gorda peninsula to the Jagua hotel, in the grounds of the Valle Palace, whose lavishly decorated interiors and art treasures he proposed to visit whenever time allowed. His meeting with the emissary of the New York art dealers was not due to take place until early on the next afternoon, so it was with considerable surprise that no sooner had he entered the lobby than he heard himself hailed by name. It was the younger Green, in person, his face contorted in the familiar half-grin, half-smile, and his hand outstretched. 'My dear Mr Písemsky, how splendid to see you.'

To the invitation to drinks and dinner that followed, Písemsky replied curtly that he already had an appointment, then relented and suggested that Green might join them. He and Guevara might cancel each other out a little, he thought, and since they would all be 'off duty', as it were, there might even be an interesting conversation and possibly some hard news – both commodities for which Písemsky was beginning to yearn.

Such did prove to be the case. They went again to the same restaurant and had roughly the same meal, over which

Guevara and Green quickly found a common interest in medieval music and painting. Their erudite exchanges occasionally left Písemsky a little out of his depth, but in general he was able to make an intelligent contribution to the conversation, and by the time he and Green had deposited Guevara in the centre of Cienfuegos and returned to the Jagua, a subtle change in relationship had taken place between the two men.

Green, however, was not one to allow his sympathies to interfere with business. Though going as far as to desist from simulating disappointment when he came to examining the ikons – in fact, he made no attempt to disguise his wonderment and pleasure – he nevertheless indulged in some shrewd bargaining, until a cheque for 7 million dollars changed hands. The technical means for verification was less easily arranged, and it was not until the next morning that the deal was clinched. Then, with an unknown companion, Green arrived at the theatre in a pick-up, the crate was loaded by the Major's men, who had been lounging nearby, and with a cheery wave, Green drove off. The number of the pick-up was passed to the Major, who later reported its itinerary. Rejoining the main arterial road north of Rodas, it had turned right and continued down the length of the island to Santiago de Cuba and thence to Guantánamo. But instead of then continuing to Baracoa, it had suddenly veered off onto a dust track and, at a border post which had to all appearances been awaiting it, had quickly disappeared into the US naval station. 'Very neat,' said the Major. 'And not, I think, the first time it has made such a trip.'

'Very interesting,' Písemsky said pensively. 'You never know. . .'

The beauty of the coast road from Cienfuegos to Trinidad was largely wasted on Písemsky. As the elation engendered by a stimulating social occasion followed by an extremely satisfactory business deal drained away, he began once again to feel the incipient onset of his malaise as they trundled slowly along in an ancient Soviet army *villis* jeep. He feared that his aching eyes were becoming seriously defective when the road

193

in front of them suddenly seemed quite distinctly to be rippling up and down. It must be an optical illusion, he thought, a trick of the lowering sun on the metalled surface, but quite soon the driver slowed to barely a walking pace and eventually stopped altogether. Peering through the dusty windscreen, rendered largely opaque by the deflection of the slanting rays on the spattered bodies of countless insects, and over the side of the vehicle, he saw that the entire surface of the road, as well as much of the verge on each side, was a mass of blue-backed, pink-bellied land crabs of all sizes, scuttling out of the mangrove swamps of the coast into the sugar cane on the land side, clambering relentlessly over each other in a living, heaving, eerily soundless layer. Barely visible beneath them were two parallel lines of carcasses squashed by a previous vehicle. But the crabs plodded heedlessly over the remains of their brethren, following a suicidal path from which nothing would deflect them. The driver was clearly reluctant to continue and looked helplessly at Písemsky as though seeking advice or perhaps approval to proceed. At the same instant, they both shrugged their shoulders and the jeep moved slowly on, leaving trails of carnage behind them. As the mass of crabs slowly thinned, the driver weaved his way at a snail's pace, reducing the slaughter as much as he could.

This is a mad world, Písemsky reflected. This man is a trained killer. For all I know, he has already killed many times. But he hesitates to run over a crab. Well, I rather sympathise. I sometimes think I prefer dogs to people myself.

The hotel at Trinidad reminded Písemsky of the Soviet-built blocks on the Black Sea coast of Bulgaria, at Golden Sands or Varna, which, he now admitted ruefully, by comparison with Varadero were quite definitely substandard. All the better: this demonstrated the necessity for the sort of development he and Macinaw were planning. The beaches were wonderful, but in his present state of physical discomfort he was unable to give them more than a cursory glance. He saw enough simply to confirm that Pérez had been correct in his assessment, and took the first available plane to Havana, where, through the good offices of the Cuban Government, he was seen without delay by a senior medical officer and subjected to a thorough examination. The veracity of all that Písemsky had been told of the vaunted Cuban health service was confirmed.

You eat too much. You drink too much. You smoke too many cigars. You don't take enough exercise. You're a mess. This is not what the medical officer said, but it is what she meant.

What she actually said was that Písemsky was rather overweight and must cut down on alcohol and smoking, and that he should take more physical exercise. His excess weight probably accounted for the dizzy spells, bouts of sweating and occasional breathlessness that he had reported, and the smoking might explain the cough that racked his lungs, especially first thing in the morning. The sweating might account for the sore armpits and groin, and sleeping in an awkward posture for the stiffness in his neck.

Well, if that's all it is, a much relieved Písemsky thought, there's really nothing for me to worry about. I can easily lose weight if I want to; that's never been a problem. 'It's my metabolism,' he used to say. 'I only have to look at food, and I put on weight. But I don't believe in all these fads about dieting. All I have to do is eat less. It's the quantity that makes the difference.' As as for alcohol, he could give that up at any time. Smoking, too. So he'd lose some weight and start taking regular exercise – swimming, and maybe windsurfing or something a bit more demanding. No problem.

The doctor disrupted this inner monologue. 'But, of course, we can never be sure. You have an unusual combination of symptoms, and I think we should do a few tests. We mustn't take the risk of missing something more serious.'

'Tests?' he exclaimed. 'What sort of tests? What do you expect to find?'

The doctor smiled reassuringly. 'Just routine,' she said. 'A few simple blood tests,' she explained, 'and your blood pressure – that sort of thing.'

This was the signal for a series of extractions of blood

samples, an ECG involving walking a treadmill until he almost expired of exhaustion, peering into his eyes, his nose, his ears and his throat, and subjection to a catechism of searching questions about every detail of his most personal and private habits. Why all this, he wondered, if I'm just a bit too fat? Just think of all those obese Canadians. Do they have to go through all this, too?

While he awaited the results of the tests, Písemsky spent two days at the Plaza in Havana, now almost empty of tourists and noisome with the sounds and smells of renovation. At length he was summoned to the hospital, where he was interviewed by a group of specialists in various fields of medicine.

They began gently, pointing out that his blood pressure was rather high: did he know what it normally was? He did not. Some people, they explained, have a naturally rather high pressure, so nothing could be concluded from that. More importantly, perhaps, his blood count showed a raised lipid value, and from the printout of his tortured session on the treadmill it could be seen that there was some cardiac ischaemia. In other words, they explained, he had a mild heart condition, exacerbated – if not, indeed, caused – by excess weight, smoking and lack of exercise. Yes, this could be controlled; it was not, as yet, serious, but could, unless he changed his lifestyle, become increasingly dangerous.

There was a pause, and the members of the group looked uneasily at each other, but not, Písemsky noted, at him. Eventually, the medical officer he had first seen began to speak.

'Our problem is,' she said calmly, 'that none of the tests have given a convincing explanation for the cluster of symptoms that you have presented. There are other tests that we think you would be wise to take, but we are not in a position at this hospital to conduct them. Our advice to you is to seek help from a clinic in North America.'

Mystified and deeply troubled, Písemsky returned to Varadero. Don Macinaw was due to arrive in some ten days' time. He would return with him to Toronto.

\* \* \*

Early in 1992, after a delay of about a month while he attended to his business affairs in Quebec province, where an exceptionally severe winter had disrupted his building schedules, Don Macinaw arrived in Havana laden with preliminary plans, sketches and calculations for the proposed Trinidad de Cuba development scheme. After a series of meetings arranged by Pérez with relevant governmental departments, most of which Písemsky did not attend, it was formally decided to proceed with raising the finance and drawing up definitive plans as soon as possible. Ten million dollars from Písemsky's various bank deposits was paid into a Cuban holding account, subject to strictly secret legal control, giving him a monthly interest described officially as consultancy fees, on which he could live comfortably without drawing on his remaining capital, most of which had been transferred to the Zürich bank, with a contingency reserve in Toronto. The arrangement with the Cubans could be terminated at six months' notice by either side. The remaining finance for starting developments was contributed by the Cuban Government (partly on behalf of certain expatriate bodies in the United States), by Pérez and by Macinaw Enterprises, of which both Písemsky and Pérez were made directors.

Informal meetings followed, first at Varadero, where Macinaw Enterprises was to enter the Cuban scene by installing water sports facilities in conjunction with the existing hotels. This arrangement would allow profitable use of Canadian services during the period of run-up to the beginning of construction at Trinidad, giving Macinaw Enterprises hands-on experience of work with Cuban labourers in a Cuban environment, as well as being a viable financial venture in its own right. Don, as Písemsky soon realised, never missed a trick.

From Varadero they moved to Trinidad, where a Canadian team began a major survey, enthusing over its findings and foreseeing no insuperable problems. As usual when the two men were together, they rode on a tidal wave of alcohol, which served to anaesthetise Písemsky's ailments so effectively that he was even heard to allege that he had never felt better in his life. As for restricting his intake in order to lose weight, how could he possibly be so unsociable at a time like this? Certainly, when Don had returned to Canada, he would do as the doctors had advised. Postponing the regime for another month or so would do no harm at all. And anyway, he reflected with an instinctive spasm of unease, he still had to consult the Toronto clinic that they had told him about. For all he knew, they would give him a clean bill of health. So why worry prematurely? Life was too short for that.

# 19

Despite all his confident hopes, Písemsky was found by the Toronto clinic to be HIV positive. His reaction to this shattering diagnosis displayed the naivety engendered by his background, where the stock reply to enquiries about the prevalence of venereal disease, drug abuse and other social problems that so afflicted the Western world was 'We don't have that sort of thing in the Soviet Union.' He had, of course, heard and read about AIDS but had never knowingly met anyone infected with the HIV virus. Even to a man with his experience of foreign travel, it was the sort of thing that didn't happen in the world he knew. It only happened to other people, whose lives were quite different from his, who lived in another sphere. His initial shocked reaction therefore was precisely what might have been predicted: 'There must be some mistake!'

At the clinic, they were accustomed to such outbursts. Gently, sympathetically, they spelled it out to him, respecting his feelings but concealing nothing. He had become infected with a virus that lowered his ability to create antibodies to resist what they termed *opportunistic infections* – any other malady that came along. In some 60 per cent of persons so infected, this progressed to the condition commonly referred to as AIDS, when the body finally lost its inherent ability to resist, resulting in death from one or a combination of diseases that would otherwise be curable, such as tuberculosis and pneumonia or, most often, from cancer. Advances had been made and continued to be made in the treatment of patients affected with the HIV virus. The use of reverse transcriptase inhibitors could often slow down the advance of the virus, and vigorous treatments for opportunistic infections could also delay the onset of full-blown AIDS. There was no way of predicting whether the virus would develop to this stage, or how long it might take to do so. They gave him a glimmer of hope, but the message was nevertheless quite clear: it was a sentence of death.

As part of their investigations, the clinic put to Písemsky a question that he did not at first understand: *Do you belong to an at-risk category?* Here, too, he displayed the naivety that the party line had encouraged. 'At risk?' he asked. 'What do you mean "at risk"? At risk of what?' And he even became indignant at the explanatory questions they put to him: Was he homosexual? No, certainly not. What an extraordinary question! Drug abuser who shared possibly infected needles? Good God, no! I wouldn't dream of such a thing! Whatever next! But in fact, the next question stopped him short: *Do you indulge in casual, unprotected sexual relationships?* Hot denial was again at the tip of his tongue, but he bit it back and an awkward silence ensued, which his interrogator had no difficulty in interpreting. 'How many such contacts have you had in the past six months?' He had listed all three – no, four – but never for a moment did he doubt the source of his affliction: images of Gigi and Tara still haunted his dreams. 'I was raped!' he stammered. 'It was nothing to do with me . . .' They nodded. They had heard it all before.

Písemsky obtained the best treatment his money could buy. After all, he reminded himself when the initial shock had receded, it was by getting hold of the money that he had created this need for it. He was put immediately on a course of AZT: despite the doubts about its efficacy as an inhibitor, he would grasp at even the frailest straw. His life expectancy should be counted, they said, in years rather than months, as would have been the case earlier. Perhaps three years. So who knows, he told himself, maybe before then they'll have discovered a cure.

In the sleepless small hours he was racked with despair, but as each day dawned he resolved to drain from it every drop. If he was living on borrowed time, he would live it to the full. One major change in his plans was, however, forced upon him. There was no longer any question of his ever being accepted as a person fit to be accorded the privilege of Canadian citizenship. But his role in the Cuban tourist development plan guaranteed him a welcome there – though simply being a Russian would no longer have done. So he would retain his old passport: he had been born a Soviet citizen and he would die a Soviet citizen.

Health care in Cuba, the clinic agreed, was remarkably good, given the US blockade. But there were few drugs, and certainly none that would be available to him. He would therefore monitor his progress carefully, in accordance with the instructions they gave him, observe a strict regime and return to the clinic whenever any sort of deterioration was noticed, and in any case at not longer than three-monthly intervals for CD4 cell counts. Stocked with drugs for all eventualities, he returned to Havana, where almost his first act had been to take Pérez's advice to find an apartment as a *pied-à-terre* in the city, in easy reach of the international airport.

Now, he paraphrased a Russian expression, let's see if we can live till Monday.

# BORROWED
# TIME

# 20

It had been a very busy three years. Work on the Trinidad site had begun almost at once and progressed at a great pace, spreading along the coast toward Cienfuegos to the west and the isolated sands to the south-east. The lodges had been cleverly designed to give an outward appearance of romantic castaway shacks, while the interiors were luxuriously appointed with everything that the sun-seeking holiday-maker could wish for. The scope of development had quickly been extended to other locales: around a crocodile farm, as a base for botanical tours, as birdwatching hides. At Písemsky's suggestion, a subsidiary company had been set up to manu-facture solar water-heaters, almost unknown in Cuba and hitherto vastly expensive, and this on its own was a highly profitable as well as beneficial venture.

At Písemsky's initiative, too, the pleasure-dome concept had been developed on the model of a round Mongolian tent, which as a Russian he called a *yúrta*, and he had remi-nisced at some length about the windswept uplands of Mongolia, where in spring the meadows were carpeted with purple gentian, the air invigorated and swept away the cares of the city, and there was hardly a sign of human habitation anywhere in sight. 'The size of Western Europe,' he had explained excitedly to a glassy-eyed Macinaw, 'and a popu-lation of only two and a half million.' Resisting obvious comparisons with Canada, Don had heard him out. Písemsky seemed to be given more and more to reliving scenes from his former life. He quite often forgot the simplest things from the recent past, but would suddenly go off at a tangent and recount at great length episodes from decades earlier.

The central dome at each site was of a scale beyond Macinaw Enterprises' capabilities and was built under sub-contract by Matsukawa, a Japanese concern. It contained several restaurants and bars, shops, hairdressers and beauty salons, and all the basic facilities of a luxury hotel. In the small, subsidiary domes were, in the first instance, a night-club, a casino, a concert hall, a games room, a gymnasium and a sauna. A major feature of the scheme was its flexibility: further modular satellite domes could be added as required, and it was this apparent advantage that led, oddly enough, to the first disagreement between Macinaw and his new directors.

As the work on the first site neared completion and the first intakes of tourists began to arrive, it became apparent that they did indeed comprise people of a different sort from those who patronised the Varadero hotels. Whether they represented any recognisable 'set' or not, Písemsky was unable to tell, but they seemed to have a great deal of money to spend and, as he cynically formulated it, as the bank balances went up, the behavioural standards went down. Despite the path he had chosen to follow since arriving in Cuba, he still had within him an instinctive streak of the puritanism that had governed the actions of his revolutionary forebears. And anyway, he would certainly have retorted, if challenged, there is no comparison between these people and me. They are a totally different case.

Over a few drinks with Don one evening, Písemsky went off on another of his digressions, reminiscing this time about the Black Sea resorts of Sóchi and Yálta, favourite holiday places for Muscovites. Sóchi, he said, was where you went with your wife; Yálta was where you went with someone else's. He was clearly drawing a tentative parallel with Varadero and the new resort of Trinidad. Actually, he continued, most Muscovite couples took separate holidays: after all, he giggled, half the point of going on holiday is to get away from your spouse.

As he had walked through the dimly lit streets of Havana near his new apartment, Písemsky had frequently been accosted by pimps who attempted to inveigle him into the depths of shadowy arcades, where rows of giggling girls flaunted their wares, swaying their hips and gesturing obscenely. He had been offered a 'good time' for as little as one dollar, and though at a personal level he had shuddered and almost literally taken to his heels, he had nevertheless noted that amongst the interested customers were a number who were unmistakably tourists. His reactions were undoubtedly mixed, but foremost was a realisation that tourists were prepared to buy sex much as they bought rum and crocodile skins, and that properly organised, the sale of that commodity could constitute a lucrative business. At the same time, the happy thought occurred to him, by instituting a strictly hygienic regime, he would be able to protect others from suffering his own fate. The idea of a geisha house was therefore put forward, and despite Don Macinaw's protests, and with the tacit agreement of the authorities, a brothel became part of the pleasure-dome complex. Písemsky found no difficulty in justifying this step: after all, he insisted, nobody has to use this facility if he doesn't want to. But if men want women, they'll go and find them, and if we don't provide them, they'll simply go to someone who does. At least we will provide regular medical supervision and guaranteed freedom from disease. It will be just a part of the service, like everything else. To his own amusement he even located a tyrannical *oiran* superviser, Lola, whose related talents had been vouched for by Khúyin.

The name of Khúyin was, however, quite soon to become taboo. The deals with Haiti had been successfully completed, and ironically the arming of the two sides had led to something of a compromise between them, so that UNO had negotiated agreement for Aristide to return to Port au Prince. There had then been a hiatus in the arms dealing, during which the Major's men had been redeployed as very necessary security guards on the building sites and had given every sign of adapting without protest to such a role. Then with very little warning, a Russian freighter had deposited on the Trinidad quay a number of large containers of arms, which Písemsky had quickly contrived to 'bury' amongst the great volume of materials and equipment in the storehouses, alerting the Major to the need for extra vigilance. He had not found it necessary to inform Don: Why give him extra worry? he thought. He has enough on his mind as it is. Macías had managed to have the crates picked up by a Panama-registered ship and conveyed to Mexico, where they had continued by a devious jungle land route to their Guatemalan destination. It was only when they were subsequently unpacked that many of the contents were found to be not only obsolete but defective or quite unserviceable. Indeed, the greatest number of casualties resulting from Khúyin's consignment had been amongst the purchasers. Thereafter, trade in arms had ceased. Macías had disappeared, probably in fear of his life, though unwelcome rumours had occasionally been heard that he was planning a diversification and would one day wish to continue the relationship with his erstwhile partners.

Before that day arrived Don Macinaw had suffered a severe heart attack, precipitated by the intense workload he had borne, together with the taxing amount of travel between Canada and Cuba and, if truth were told, by his own obesity and consumption of alcohol. By this time, the project was running without the necessity of his constant presence, and he had retired to convalesce at his summer house on Lake Huron, in northern Ontario, where he spent his days fishing. Písemsky had several times visited him there on his three-monthly trips to Toronto for treatment at the clinic. At first, Don had congratulated him on 'cracking the weight problem', but as Písemsky had begun visibly to waste away, Don had lapsed into an embarrassed silence on the subject. Eventually, Písemsky discontinued his visits, relying upon increasingly stilted communication by telephone.

Macías had arrived unheralded, his oily smile as broad as ever, and requested a meeting with his former associates to discuss his proposal for a new venture. Briefly, after the

Guatemala débâcle he had taken refuge in Colombia, where his connections in Haiti and Cuba had enabled him to establish contact with a drug-dealing ring. As Haiti became the centre of increasing activities by international political agencies, it was becoming less satisfactory as an entrepôt for the drug trade, and attention was now turning to Cuba as a potential alternative. Macías had been quick to point out the existence in Cuba of a ready-made organisation which would easily absorb such a role. A chance, he said, for a real killing; an unfortunately prophetic statement.

The reactions of his colleagues were mixed. Pérez, who had been enjoying his legitimate status and the esteem accruing from it, would have no part in the scheme, and in fact it was shortly after this that he obtained a new posting to Europe and quit the scene. The Major had quite frankly been getting bored: any new activity would be welcome, but he looked to the others to dictate the play. It fell therefore to Macías and Písemsky to elaborate a plan of action (the latter's initial qualms were soon dispelled as the Mochítsky method was brought into operation: the use of drugs was an aspect of freedom of choice, and if people wanted them they would turn to whoever would supply them, so it might as well be us). With surprising speed a plan for the 'diversified' programme took shape.

The Major, they decided, would go to Moscow (a prospect he greeted with enthusiasm) to meet Khúyin and make him 'an offer he couldn't refuse': new consignments of arms specified by Macías would be shipped to Cuba and redirected by various routes to Colombia, and payment would be made in cocaine, to be transferred from seaplanes to boats of the deep-sea fishing fleet operated by Macinaw Enterprises from the ports of Santiago and Trinidad de Cuba. This too would be arranged by Macías – no problem. Once landed, the cocaine would be transported to the tobacco factory near Baracoa, where it would be processed by a team supervised by Písemsky's grateful Haitian acquaintance, recently revisited, and his student son. Packaged in boxes of Havana cigars, the cocaine would be exported to

Russia to fulfil orders submitted by a Moscow subsidiary of Khúyin's burgeoning commercial empire. These stages would be the responsibility of Písemsky, who was increasingly gripped by a sensation that everything was suddenly coming together with a sort of uncanny inevitability over which he had no control, though this in no way inhibited his assuming credit for the brilliance of the master plan.

As their own share of the profits, both partners opted for raw cocaine. How they disposed of this was their own affair, and in general each of them kept the details of his operations strictly to himself, though both relied on the Major and his task force for overall security.

For the Major personally Písemsky had a private mission – to identify and 'have a chat with' the owner of the telephone number in Baracoa who had facilitated the delivery of 'merchandise' to the US naval base at Guantánamo that he had monitored. Not surprisingly, his approach met with ready cooperation, and soon the way was clear for Písemsky's share of the drugs to be routed via Guantánamo to the Greens in New York, where payment would be wired to his Toronto account. In a matter of months the system was up and running.

There was just one mishap, which in fact gave Písemsky a frisson of malicious glee. Macías's attempt to smuggle his share of the first consignment into Key West was successful, but the second run was intercepted and in an exchange of fire with a US customs patrol one of his men was killed and another seriously wounded before their boat scurried back to Varadero. Alarmed at the potential damage to the tender Cuba–USA relations which were being carefully nurtured, at least unofficially, the Havana authorities made known their displeasure, and again Macías thought it prudent to absent himself for a while, this time in Moscow.

Písemsky, whose mistrust of Macías had in no way diminished despite their newly established collaboration, rejoiced at this unlooked-for bonus. The longer Macías stays away, he thought, the more pleased I shall be. He can't do me any harm by going to Moscow.

# 21

For the first two years Písemsky had struggled with the HIV virus, rigorously adhering to the regime stipulated by the clinic, and although he continued to be afflicted as before, there was little noticeable deterioration, apart perhaps from increased discomfort from swollen glands in his groin and armpits. The building project developed and continued virtually of its own momentum, so that apart from occasional board meetings, where he now shared control with the Japanese, there were few demands on his time or his waning energies.

A feature of this period that attracted the excited attention of many visitors was the appearance on the wall of the Matsukawa company boardroom in Havana of a Modigliani canvas and a Bonnard. *'Saa! Kore wa kirei desu ne!'* Japanese guests would invariably exclaim, their eyes caressing the jutting white breasts and buttocks of *Nude against the light.* 'Beautiful!'

Events in Russia seemed now to be taking place in another world. Earlier, the sight of tanks firing into the White House had evoked in Písemsky a sort of vicious glee, and now he viewed the slaughter of Chechen 'black-arses' in Grózny with sneering disdain: Great Russian democracy in action, Yéltsin style! Involuntarily he recalled one of Gorbachóv's more memorable pronouncements: *Our choice of aims does not allow us to be indiscriminate in our methods of attaining them.* The end does not justify the means.

By the end of the third year, as his weight had fallen away and his physical powers ebbed, Písemsky's haggard face was seen less and less in Trinidad. Instead, he would haunt the parks and squares of Havana, though gradually his eyes became unable to bear the glare of the sun, no matter what protective measures he took, so that he began to spend an ever greater proportion of his time lying listlessly in a darkened room, listening to music, until that, too, became more than he could bear. After the third year he began to make extended visits to Toronto, staying for several weeks in the hospice attached to the clinic. But still he clung to life.

Písemsky was not afraid of dying, he would say with one of his joyless giggles, as long as it did not hurt too much. But however doomed he was, however imminent his departure from this life, he still did not actively want to go. He would still recall, again with a giggle, what he considered the perfect epitaph for any man's tombstone: 'He died reluctantly'.

As the shades gathered about him, Písemsky was becoming now aware of yet another menace growing ever closer. In a copy of *Nezavísimaya Gazéta* left by a Russian tourist, he had read of an armed break-in at the Moscow House of Friendship, where a gang of masked men had been disturbed trying to enter the basement strongroom. Shots had been fired, though no injuries were reported. The police suspected an organised gang of criminals with international connections, increasingly often referred to as mafia.

A communication from the Bayer-Hofmann bank in Zürich, received via Toronto, advised him that a computer hacker had been suspected of breaking into the data bank on international accounts. Programs had since been changed and other security measures adopted, but such incidents were becoming increasingly difficult to avoid.

From New York, Písemsky learned of an attempted robbery at the offices of Mulrooney & Associates, Art Dealers, of Madison Avenue. Files and records had been rifled, though it was thought that nothing had in fact been removed. Mulrooney and his female partner had been badly beaten.

A sad letter from Green the younger, addressed to

Písemsky via Roberto Guevara, told him of the violent death of Dr Vernádsky: *'As we all knew, he was extremely short-sighted, and it is probable that he never even saw the yellow cab that deliberately knocked him down at a Greenwich Village street corner and sped away up town without stopping.'* Green the elder had been very distressed; he and Vernádsky had known each other since childhood in the Odessa ghetto. For some reason he had become convinced that he was himself the intended victim and now spent his days in prayer at the synagogue he had scarcely ever entered in the past several decades. Green the younger had taken over the family business and was planning to move his *'base of operations'* to somewhere *'nearer you'*.

Roberto Guevara had himself not escaped attention. A break-in at the Tomás Terry theatre had resulted in apparently wanton damage to precious costumes and props.

Písemsky saw all this as the leading edge of shadow creeping inexorably in his direction. When, he wondered, would his turn come? But perhaps, he giggled in Mochítsky fashion, I'll cheat the hangman yet!

To Písemsky at this time the mere idea of sexual involvement with a woman was repulsive; he would shudder at the thought. But at the same time he yearned for affection, for the warmth of physical contact with another human being. His need to hold someone close and to be held was a physical ache which troubled him far more profoundly than any of his other afflictions.

He found solace, not with a woman, but with a little boy, whom he heard before he saw him, sobbing uncontrollably, huddled in the shadowy doorway of the shabby building where he had his apartment. Without a word he had taken the boy in his arms and they had clung to each other until, half-leading, half-carrying, Písemsky had taken him to his apartment, bathed him, fed him, and cuddled him to sleep.

The boy was dumb – whether from physical causes or from psychological trauma Písemsky never discovered – but his hearing was normal and he quickly learned to respond to the Russian *mál'chik*, 'boy'. He tapped within Písemsky a well of tenderness that neither Márfa Timoféyevna nor Raísa

213

Lázarevna had ever suspected, and they quickly became inseparable, walking hand in hand through the darkened evening streets, ignoring the lascivious chuckles and obscene comments from the depths of the unlit porticoes, sharing their food and sleeping in close embrace in Písemsky's bed. Though Písemsky fondled and caressed him without inhibition, their relationship was never overtly sexual, nor did Písemsky ever wittingly expose him to infection by the disease that was with increasing momentum sapping his life away. For the brief period that they were together Písemsky was almost happy.

This emotional Indian summer could not, as he knew, be long-lasting, and indeed, the end was soon to come. When his periodic visit to Toronto could no longer be delayed, Písemsky made what he thought was adequate provision for Mál'chik's welfare during his absence, but when he hurried like an anxious father back to his apartment, the boy had gone, leaving Písemsky quite bereft. This was, though he would not admit it even to himself, his last visit to Cuba. The end was surely in sight. But in vain he told himself that it had all been for the best, that there was no future for him with Mál'chik. There was no future for him in any case and, deprived of this last source of comfort, he felt himself at last slipping without control into the abyss of black despair.

Seated at his desk on the morning after his return to Havana, Písemsky took from the bottom drawer a shapeless bundle, carefully swathed in a soft cloth, and gently unwrapping it revealed the revolver that the Major had given him on the Cienfuegos road, and for which he had been unable to envisage any conceivable need. Perhaps he'd find a use for it yet. Even now he was hesitant, but he loaded it gingerly, with just one bullet, and had slipped off the safety catch when the unexpected arrival of a visitor prompted him to thrust the revolver hastily into the top drawer.

The visitor was Macías, whose appearance evoked in Písemsky not only the usual tremor of distaste but also a curious sense of foreboding. Their conversation was constantly interrupted by bursts from automatic drills in the neighbouring blocks (as European and émigré investors anticipated a relaxation of the US embargo, Havana was becoming one vast building site), but despite the noise and his faulty vision, Písemsky was able to comprehend that Macías was both taunting and threatening him. Conducting an inventory of the contents of the House of Friendship in Moscow, preparatory to selling it as a private residence to an importer of sex aids and girlie magazines (no doubt considered a logical extension of cultural exchanges with the West), the authorities had been puzzled by a locked strongroom in the basement. Enquiries had elicited from Túsya Tambóvskaya that it contained crates of precious art treasures intended for exhibitions in Latin America which had never in fact taken place. Mr Mochítsky, she reported, was considering the possibility of exhibiting them in Cuba, but as far as she was aware no arrangements had been made before he had mysteriously disappeared several years ago. In the absence of any instructions from above, she had taken no action, and the crates were presumably still *in situ*... 'After all,' she said innocently, 'they are as safe there as they would be any-where else in Moscow today.' She was probably the most sur-prised of all when it was revealed that the room was in fact empty.

The resulting *scandale* had come to the attention of Khúyin and thence to that of his associate in the Cuban drug ring, Macías. He, in turn, had learned that the ikons had been turning up in North American émigré churches, but that most of the paintings had not been accounted for. Visiting the Matsukawa boardroom on his return to Havana, he had found no difficulty in drawing conclusions concerning the source of Písemsky's personal wealth.

'Where are the rest of the paintings?' he demanded men-acingly.

Písemsky would not be intimidated. 'You cannot frighten me,' he said coldly. 'I shall soon be going where you will not be able to reach me.'

'I know you are finished,' Macías hissed. 'But you'll tell me before you go.'

Seizing Písemsky's emaciated shoulders, Macías shook him like a floppy-limbed *Tomasíta* doll.

'Both your wife and daughter, Zoya, are making names for themselves in President Yéltsin's office,' he said. 'How long d'you think they would last if he knew what you had been doing?'

Despite his astonishment at Macías's reference to Márfa Timoféyevna, Písemsky managed a faint snigger. 'President Yéltsin! D'you think I care what that man does? You can't blackmail me with that...'

But Macías went on: 'And what if Zoya found out you were responsible for her mother's death?'

Písemsky was wounded now. For the first time he faced a fact that he had always refused to acknowledge even to himself, a thought that ever since his enigmatic conversation with the Major in Baracoa he had thrust out of his mind. Who else, after all, could his Mossad 'guardian angel' have been? And why had she suddenly disappeared?

Macías saw that this time he had struck home. He delivered a final blow.

'And what about your little playmate? What shall we do with him?'

When Macías released him, Písemsky slumped as though already lifeless into his chair. Macías leaned over him, their faces almost touching, and Písemsky saw the whites of his eyes.

'I have to go,' he whispered hoarsely, 'but at least I can take you with me.'

As the stuttering rattle of automatic drills rose in a crescendo around them, Písemsky summoned the despairing strength to open the desk drawer, took out the revolver, and shot him.

# 22

By late that evening Písemsky was again within the sanctuary of the Toronto hospice, gulping oxygen as the tubercles consumed what was left of his lungs. The night was filled with fantasies and he cried out in terror, until a nurse took pity and administered a morphine injection that sent him into a coma-like sleep until day broke.

In the morning, he lay for several hours, apparently calm, at peace. Then suddenly he raised himself upright in his bed. 'I will not go gentle!' he exclaimed to a startled nurse.

As she began her morning ministrations he displayed a new tetchiness:

'No! I will not drink it up for *you*,' he exclaimed in reply to a gentle urging. 'I will drink it up for *me*. I may be a sick man, but I am not a congenital idiot. Please don't treat me like one.' But she recognised the signs and took no offence.

A violent gust rattled the windows of his room, and he broke into a manic giggle, recalling – as he did increasingly often – some lines of Browning that he had learned as a student of English at the Moscow institute so long ago:

> *Fear death? – to feel the fog in my throat,*
> *The mist in my face,*
> *When the snows begin, and the blasts denote*
> *I am nearing the place . . .*

Impatient of all attempts at restraint, he struggled into his clothes, muttering unintelligibly to himself, and tottered out of the building and into the street, where he stood swaying unsteadily on his feet, looking distractedly around him, uncertain which way to go.

A few doors from the clinic, he saw a short line of people filing into the Gallery of Modern Art, where a series of posters attached to the iron railings announced the opening of an exhibition of works by Pablo Picasso. With a spasm of horror he saw that one of them reproduced the all too familiar outlines of the first lithograph he had sold, *Bull, Horse and Woman.*

Muttering to himself and attracting looks of distaste from all around, he barged through the queue and entered the gallery. Small knots of people, couples, and a few individuals were standing before various pictures, studying them with puzzled expressions and occasionally raised eyebrows, all in hushed silence. In the centre of the room, however, was a larger group of people craning their necks to see the two lithographs in a buzz of suppressed excitement. Without a word of apology, Písemsky burrowed his way to the front and with a feeble lunge attempted to tear one of the lithographs from the wall with an anguished cry of: 'Disgusting! Filth! It ought to be locked away...' He was restrained by a dozen hands amid cries of alarm, mixed with embarrassed guffaws.

Judy, in the far corner, engrossed in a study of *Artist with Kneeling Model,* frowned at the commotion but did not look up as Písemsky was seized by a burly attendant, who with no regard for his obvious frailty, bundled him roughly out of the doorway into the street, where he clung for support to the railing, trembling and gasping for air.

Gradually recovering his breath, Písemsky saw on the far side of the street the open doors of a Catholic church. Without heed of the danger, he lurched into the stream of traffic, and to the raucous accompaniment of squealing brakes, screams and curses, he miraculously contrived to arrive safely on the other side, where he staggered through the church doors into a tiny side chapel and slumped onto a seat, half sitting, half lying, totally inert. The slanted rays of the morning sun streamed through the stained-glass window of the chapel and like a theatre spotlight illuminated his pitiable body. To the casual observer he might have been quite dead.

But a quiet footstep aroused him, and as he wearily half-opened his eyes and looked up, he saw outlined in the tinted sunbeam the head and shoulders of a bearded old man, his grey hair shining like a halo and his head leaning at a curious angle. The Rublyóv ikon!

With a feeble cry, he thrust out his shrivelled hands to ward it off. 'Go away! Leave me in peace!'

He felt a strong arm about his shoulders and a calm voice speaking urgently to him. 'My son, my son. Do not be afraid. Let me help you.'

'Who are you?' he whispered. 'What do you want?'

'I am Paul,' the voice replied, 'Father Paul,' and as the figure moved out of the light, Písemsky saw that it was a black-robed priest, his face etched with concern.

He giggled weakly, but this gave way to spasmodic gulps and at last, at long, long last the tears began to flow, running unheeded down his cheeks, into the furrows about his mouth and chin, and down to his scrawny neck. Sobbing uncontrollably, he clutched Father Paul's hand and for a while the two men sat silently, side by side. At length, having regained a little composure and with a brave attempt at a normal tone, he said: 'Father, I am not of the faith. I am not a believer. But I must confess, I must confess.'

Together they moved slowly into the confessional, where Písemsky slumped again in silence, until speech at last began to come, at first haltingly, then swelling into a torrent as the whole story of his recent years poured from the depths of his soul in a welter of words. Father Paul sat stony-faced, with only a flicker of pain as Písemsky was seized by a fit of coughing and then, catharsis completed, fell silent. Eventually, he spoke.

'My son, you have sinned grievously,' he said gently, 'against God, against your fellow men, and most of all, against yourself.' He sighed. 'But you have suffered grievously, too, and very soon you must seek peace face to face with your Maker.'

He paused and Písemsky began again to speak. 'Always I found someone else to blame. Always I convinced myself that I had no other choice. But that was not true. I know now that it was not true. I and I alone am responsible for what I have done. I know that now.'

'Then you have found salvation,' Father Paul said simply.

They sat for a while without words, each struggling to comprehend the gravity of the moment. Then Father Paul uttered his final pronouncement.

'Go home, my son. Go now and make your peace with Russia.'

His voice conveyed inexpressible sorrow, pain and compassion. But not, Písemsky was sure of this, not reproach.

# 23

It was all surprisingly easy. A direct flight from Toronto to Moscow, with enough alcohol to keep him relaxed and without pain throughout the journey, rapid baggage reclaim at the new Moscow terminal, and a sleek limousine to the Rossíya hotel. A hot bath, a half-bottle of vodka, and oblivion.

Mochítsky woke at four in the morning and knew that it was pointless trying to sleep more. The vodka and exhaustion after the flight had already granted him longer than most nights afforded, and he was grateful at least for that.

Heaving himself with much grunting from the bed and into an armchair at the window, he hauled on the cords that opened the heavy curtains and gazed with a mixture of dismay and despair, transmuted gradually into trembling anger, at the Coca Cola advertisements and the unfamiliar symbol on the top of the Spássky tower, where once had glowed the dim but constant light of the red star, which with the cracked tones of the Kremlin chimes had symbolised for so many millions the great experiment in building a new world. The great experiment: the light that failed. Built by giants and demolished by dwarfs.

Looking out for a last time over Red Square, Mochítsky murmured a much repeated refrain: '*Krásnaya plóshchad'*,' he whispered, 'Beautiful Square.' The name, in old Russian, meant beautiful, not red. It had nothing to do with Lenin, even when what was left of him was still lying there in its glass cage, like a stuffed owl. 'And beautiful it still is.' He lapsed for a moment into a troubled reverie.

So here he was, back where it had all started. Well, more or less. It was really at Márfa Timoféyevna's dacha that the whole business had begun, with poor old Perdéyev and the unspeakable Khúyin. And now he'd come back to make his peace with Russia. Well, he knew what he must do . . .

At ten in the morning, a gleaming new Russian-built Volvo sped along the broad new motorway signposted *Tula and the South*. Waking from a doze that dulled the ache, Mochítsky looked about him and was lost. He rapped on the bullet-proof glass screen that separated him from the driver and spoke into the microphone.

'I don't want to go on this road,' he growled. 'Take the old road, through Polevóye Seló.'

The driver grumbled. 'I don't know if it's still there. And if it is, it will ruin my tyres.'

A handful of dollars settled the dispute, and after much circling and further grumbling they eventually emerged on the old Tula road. Almost immediately they came to the familiar hill and once again he stopped the car. 'Let me out here, will you.'

The driver looked at him doubtfully. 'Are you sure?'

More dollars changed hands and the driver moved gratefully off without a backward glance.

Painfully, with several false starts and stumbles, Mochítsky began the ascent. His breath came in raking gasps, and he stopped frequently to rally his failing strength. In one such pause he caught, between gasps, the unmistakable tang of woodsmoke. He stood still, savouring it. It must be coming from the dacha. Perhaps Márfa Timoféyevna was cooking for him? He shook his head, with a rueful giggle. I must be out of my mind. What was it that Chátsky had said about returning travellers? 'Even the smoke of the homeland is sweet . . .' Well, they had called him mad and chased him out again. But it was with Chátsky's words that Zoya had retorted when he, in pique, had called her mad... It was all so confusing. He sighed and began again the ascent.

On hands and knees now, he clung to trailing branches and tufts of grass as he hauled himself slowly toward the brow of the hill. Twice more he stopped, the second time for several minutes. No, he could not go on. Then another memorised line swam up from the depths of his subconscious: '*I was ever a fighter, so – one fight more,*' he muttered, '*the best and the last!*'

Gritting his teeth, he dragged himself further up the slope, until a spasm of coughing overcame him and again he lay prone, mopping the blood-flecked sputum from his chin. He was sweating profusely, and the ache in his chest was creeping down his arms. But he struggled again to his feet.

At last he reached the brow, and there, just as he remembered them, were the silver birches, gleaming in the morning sunshine as they had on that first day. He slumped to his knees, then as though in obeisance pitched slowly forward onto his face, and the gasp that escaped him was his last.

On the third day, Zoya found him. She did not recognise him.